"I should never have kissed you that night,"

Grant said. "It just never occurred to me that I ran the risk you'd—"

"I'd what?" Rennie asked. "Become infatuated with you?" She stood, trembling. "That's what you think, isn't it? That I have some adolescent crush on you!"

Grant leaned back in his chair, his blue eyes hard and his face expressionless. "Can you deny it?"

"Yes!" Rennie lied fiercely. She knew that the emotions she felt now for Grant had nothing to do with the romantic fantasising she'd indulged in as a teenager. This was completely different. But she could see there was no hope of convincing him otherwise. "I deny it," she said. "Absolutely."

Grant smiled, a faint, disbelieving smile. "I'm not about to lose my head over a lovely young woman, Rennie—even one over the age of consent and legally adult. Frankly, it could lead to nothing but trouble...."

Dear Reader,

Each month, Silhouette **Special Edition** publishes six novels with you in mind—stories of love and life, tales that you can identify with—romance with that little "something special" added in.

August is a month for dreams . . . for hot, sunny days and warm, sultry nights. And with that in mind, don't miss these six sizzling Silhouette **Special Edition** novels! Curtiss Ann Matlock has given us *Last of the Good Guys*—Jesse Breen's story. You met him in *Annie in the Morning* (SE#695). And the duo BEYOND THE THRESHOLD from Linda Lael Miller continues with the book *Here and Then*—Rue's story.

Rounding out this month are more stories by some of your favorite authors: Laurey Bright, Ada Steward, Pamela Toth and Pat Warren.

In each Silhouette **Special Edition** novel, we're dedicated to bringing you stories that will delight as well as bring a tear to the eye. For me, good romance novels have always contained an element of hope, of optimism that life can be, and often is, very beautiful. I find a great deal of inspiration in that thought.

What do you consider essential in a good romance? I'd really like to hear your opinions on the books that we publish and on the romance genre in general. Please write to me c/o Silhouette Books, 300 East 42nd Street, 6th floor, New York, NY 10017.

I hope that you enjoy this book and all of the stories to come. I'm looking forward to hearing from you!

Sincerely,

Tara Gavin
Senior Editor
Silhouette Books

LAUREY BRIGHT
The
Older Man

Silhouette Special Edition

Published by Silhouette Books New York

America's Publisher of Contemporary Romance

SILHOUETTE BOOKS
300 East 42nd St., New York, N.Y. 10017

THE OLDER MAN

Copyright © 1992 by Daphne Clair de Jong

All rights reserved. Except for use in any review, the reproduction or utilization of this work in whole or in part in any form by any electronic, mechanical or other means, now known or hereafter invented, including xerography, photocopying and recording, or in any information storage or retrieval system, is forbidden without the permission of the publisher, Silhouette Books, 300 E. 42nd St., New York, N.Y. 10017

ISBN: 0-373-09761-1

First Silhouette Books printing August 1992

All the characters in this book have no existence outside the imagination of the author and have no relation whatsoever to anyone bearing the same name or names. They are not even distantly inspired by any individual known or unknown to the author, and all incidents are pure invention.

®: Trademark used under license and registered in the United States Patent and Trademark Office and in other countries.

Printed in the U.S.A.

Books by Laurey Bright

Silhouette Special Edition

Deep Waters #62
When Morning Comes #143
Fetters of the Past #213
A Sudden Sunlight #516
Games of Chance #564
A Guilty Passion #586
The Older Man #761

Silhouette Romance

Tears of Morning #107
Sweet Vengeance #125
Long Way from Home #356
The Rainbow Way #525
Jacinth #568

LAUREY BRIGHT

has held a number of different jobs but has never wanted to be anything but a writer. She lives in New Zealand, where she creates the stories of contemporary people in love that have won her a following all over the world.

Chapter One

Rennie ran her fingers lightly up Ethan Ryland's leg, under cover of the crowded table, only to have her hand firmly removed and clamped in his. Rennie laughed at him, her sea-green eyes calling him a prude, and he smiled back at her chidingly, muttering for her ears alone, "Behave yourself!"

"Just trying to help," she whispered into his ear. Risking a glance at the cool-looking blond woman across the table from them, she found herself fielding a speculative and not exactly approving stare from the man sitting next to Celeste Ryland. Grant Someone, she remembered vaguely, Celeste's escort. Not bad looking for his age, which she guessed at fortyish. Slightly austere, with that aquiline nose and firm chin. His stylishly cut hair was greying at the temples, his blue eyes rather chilly.

She turned as a hand touched her shoulder, bared by the strapless gold dress she wore. She'd been glad that Ethan had offered to bring her tonight—it meant her father hadn't had a chance to see the dress beforehand, since he'd come ahead with her mother. She'd been glad on several counts to join Grant What's his name and his friends at their table instead of searching the crowded ballroom for her parents.

Ethan turned to take a good look at the young man who was asking her to dance.

"It's all right," she assured Ethan. She had known Kevin since schooldays, when he had called her Carrots and she had got into trouble for retaliating by kicking his shins. She had never particularly liked him, but smiled at him as she allowed him to fold her into his arms, because he had picked just the right time to remove her from Ethan's side, and childhood prejudices didn't count, anyway. She saw with satisfaction that Ethan had seized his chance and got Celeste up to dance.

"Who's he?" Kevin growled in her ear. "The old guy you're with?"

"Ethan isn't old," Rennie said. "He's a family friend." He had been a young honorary uncle to her and her brother ever since she could remember. Her parents' rambling old home in the heart of Auckland was open house to anyone who liked to drop in or needed a place to stay. Ethan had always been a favoured guest. And on this visit it had been obvious that he was troubled. A lot of the time he looked grim and almost haunted. They had put it down to his having lost his beloved older stepbrother about a year ago. They'd been delighted if a bit puzzled when he insisted on being invited to the Legal Society Ball, thinking he was making an effort to pull himself out of his depression. But Rennie had seen his face as he gave Grant's beautiful partner a seemingly casual greeting, and within seconds she had realised with stunning comprehension that the woman was Ethan's widowed sister-in-law. And how he felt about her.

Poor Ethan. Rennie set out to help.

And she thought, loosely hooking her arms about Kevin's neck so she could peer over his shoulder, that her strategy was working. It had been hard to tell if Celeste was worried by the boldly flirtatious glances Rennie had been throwing Ethan's way, her intimate whispering into his ear,

or even the teasing caress that he had so smartly nipped in
the bud. But now Rennie could see that Celeste's expression as she looked up at Ethan was tense, her cheeks flushed,
and there was something in her eyes...

Rennie looked away with a flash of compunction. If
Ethan had been miserable, he wasn't the only one. She
shivered a little, and Kevin's arms tightened. She hardly
noticed. She had lost sight of Ethan and his partner. Then
she saw them again, Ethan practically hauling Celeste after
him across the floor. They stopped at the table, and Grant
got to his feet, his brows raised as he said something to Celeste. Then he looked at Ethan and, watching his expression, Rennie muttered, "Don't you dare stop them!"

"What?" Kevin raised his cheek from its resting place
against her bright hair.

"Nothing." She smiled brilliantly at him to make up for
her preoccupation. He had turned again so she was facing
away from the table, and she crossed her fingers behind him.

But it was okay. Ethan paused on the way out, said,
"Excuse us a minute," to Kevin and took her aside. "Sorry,
I'm running out on you," he said. "You'll come home with
your parents?"

"It's okay." Celeste was standing a little way off, unable
to hide a blaze of hope in her face, mixed with trepidation.
"She's in love with you, you know," Rennie added with assurance. "Good luck." She gave him a quick hug and
shoved him toward Celeste before returning to Kevin.

"What's going on?" he asked curiously.

"Nothing to concern you," she said airily. The music
quickened, and she eased herself out of his arms. "That's
more like it! All that slow stuff was beginning to be a bore."

He didn't look as though he agreed, but as she swayed her
hips and shoulders and lifted her arms, moving to the beat,
he followed suit, watching the light play on the slim curves
outlined by the brief sheath of gold satin, and the long legs
encased in shimmering nylon.

Grant, left without a partner, was alone at the table. He
was watching her, leaning back in his chair, his arms folded.

He looked more disapproving than ever, she thought, and wiggled her hips extra energetically, throwing back her hair as the music reached a climax, her eyes half-closed.

Kevin swooped on her, his face slightly sweaty, and fastened an arm about her waist. "Do you want to go back to your seat?" he asked. "I'm with a young crowd over there," he added hopefully.

She didn't fancy returning to the table and that chilly blue stare. "I should find my parents," she said. "I might join you later."

She approached her parents, dying to tell them about Ethan. They'd been worried about him, too. They greeted her warmly, and her father, after the first gulping breath at the sight of her dress, bravely ignored it. But they were as usual the centre of a hilarious circle, and she couldn't broadcast Ethan's private affairs to the entire group. Someone soon swept her off to dance again, and she thought that really Ethan might prefer to tell them himself, if things went right for him. And if things didn't—well, maybe he would rather she said nothing. He hadn't confided in the family during the several weeks he had been staying with them.

She was dancing with Kevin once more when she noticed that he was still sweaty, and a bit pale, too.

"Are you all right?" she asked him, as he seemed to grow heavy against her.

"Sure," he said, straightening up. "It's hot though, how 'bout some fresh air?"

It wasn't until they were outside in a darkened courtyard, with her supporting him, that she realised what was wrong. "How much have you drunk?" she asked him.

"Not that much," he muttered. "'Scuse me."

She should have left him to it, she supposed. But instead she let him be sick and then led him to a tap on the wall and stood by while he rinsed his mouth and splashed water on his face.

"Thanks, Rennie." He was still swaying a little. "You're a great girl, y'know that?"

"Sure," she rejoined crisply. "You better sit down for a while."

She found a wooden bench, and he sank onto it, pulling her down with him. "Thanks," he said again. "Great girl."

She tried to ease herself away but he clung with surprising strength, grappling her closer. "C'mon. Gimme a kiss, eh?"

"No! Kevin, stop it!"

"Aw, Rennie—"

She found herself engaged in a struggle, tried to kick at him but missed, and when she flung back her head to avoid his kiss he began devouring her bare flesh above the strapless bodice. Which, with all the energy she was putting into avoiding him, at the moment didn't feel very secure.

"Kevin!" She was furious with him, and with herself for allowing him to get her into this predicament. And as his hands tightened until they hurt her, she began to be frightened.

The way they were sitting made it impossible for her to kick at him or use her knee. She reminded herself there were about five hundred people only yards away. If she screamed . . .

She made another attempt to push him off, but it was disastrous. He toppled from the bench, clinging to her. She tried to stay upright, heard a seam in her dress rip with the strain as he clutched at it, then went down with him onto the paving, banging her elbow and knee painfully, so that she did give a tiny scream.

A voice said quietly but with force, "What the hell . . . ?" And Kevin's grip at last loosened. Rennie started to scramble up and felt strong hands lifting her to her feet. She turned to find the Grant person at her side, with a look of wrathful contempt on his face.

"Are you all right?" he asked.

"Yes. No." She inspected her elbow, which was stinging, and realised it was bleeding, a couple of drops falling onto her dress. "Damn!"

Kevin was getting unsteadily to his feet. "Mind your own business—" he slurred, and tried an ineffectual swipe at the other man, who parried it easily with one hand and said with sharp authority, "That's enough! You'd better start apologising, don't you think?"

He wasn't a particularly big man, but the implicit threat in his even voice made Kevin step back. "Sorry, Rennie," he muttered resentfully. "Didn't mean to hurt you."

"Then why didn't you *stop*," she said furiously, rather glad that Grant had kept a steadying hand on her uninjured arm, "when I told you to?"

"One little kiss," he whined. "Be a sport, Ren. Di'n' think you'd mind."

Still holding Rennie's arm, Grant said bitingly, "Apparently she does. Go home," he added, "you bloody young fool, and not in a car. Find a taxi."

Kevin seemed about to argue, but a movement of Grant's head sent him off into the darkness, grumbling under his breath.

Grant whipped a white handkerchief out of his pocket and efficiently tied it about Rennie's elbow. As he jerked the knot closed, he said, "And he's not the only fool. If you didn't want him to make love to you, why let him bring you out here?"

"He said he needed some fresh air."

He gave her a withering look. "Even at your age you can't be that naive."

"He looked sick. I didn't realise until we were out here that he was drunk. I suppose that was stupid—"

"You could say that."

"I'd just as soon you didn't."

"I'm sure," Grant agreed dryly.

"Anyway, what's it to do with you? I could have handled it—"

"Oh, yes? You weren't handling it too well when I came along."

Rennie was silenced for a moment. "I didn't want to overreact. He wouldn't really have hurt me."

He looked her over in eloquent silence.

The ground hadn't been too clean. Her super-special dress was dirty as well as bloodstained, and there was a little gape in front where the seam had ripped. She'd scraped her knee, too, she realised, and ruined a stocking.

She said, "I've known him since we were kids."

"What does that have to do with it?" Grant enquired.

Nothing, she supposed.

Then Grant added, "Especially in view of the signals you'd been giving him. A bit pointless, wasn't it, since Ethan wasn't here to see any more?"

"What?" Working it out, she couldn't believe the implication he was making.

"I suppose your feelings were hurt," he went on, "and your ego needed a boost. But that sort of behaviour will only get you into trouble sooner or later. Be careful who you encourage in future—and how."

Rennie took a breath. "Do you go around dispensing free advice to everyone you meet, or am I just privileged?"

"It's good advice," he said. "I don't suppose you want to go back to the ballroom looking like that. How did Ethan suggest you get home?"

She gathered that he disapproved of Ethan, too.

"My parents are here," she said stiffly.

"Are they expecting you to go home with them?"

"I hadn't got round to asking them."

"Shall I find them for you?"

"I don't want to spoil their evening," she said coldly. "I'll get a taxi."

"I'll take you."

"Thank you, but please don't bother—"

"No bother. If it's any consolation, my evening's already spoiled. We can leave a message for your parents." He pulled a notebook from his pocket. "Sit down a minute."

She discovered that sitting down was what she most wanted to do. The incident had shocked her more than she liked to admit. But she wasn't going to simply do everything this bossy man told her to. "Don't do that," she said, as he started to scribble a note. They'd think it strange and worry.

She tried again to suggest getting a taxi, but Grant said as he closed the book and returned it to his pocket, "Someone needs to keep an eye on you. If you don't want your parents to know what you've been getting yourself into, I suggest you accept my offer and shut up."

"How do I know I'm not getting myself into something else?" she demanded. "Going home with a strange man?"

He said scathingly, "Do you really think you're in any danger?"

She didn't, of course. Apart from the fact that she vaguely supposed him to belong to her father's generation, and that Celeste Ryland had trusted him to escort her, Rennie knew from the conversation at the table that he was a partner in a law firm. And he'd hardly have reached that level of his profession if he was in the habit of attacking young women.

"Come on," he said, reaching for her arm again. "My car's parked on the other side of the building. We can go this way."

As they drove he hardly spoke, and Rennie, smarting from the disparaging opinions he had expressed, didn't want to talk, either. But when they reached her house he said, "Do you have a key?"

She shook her head. "My brother will be home."

"Sure you'll be okay?"

"Yes. Thank you," she added with some difficulty. She didn't want to feel beholden to this man, but he had, in his way, been kind. "I'll get your handkerchief washed and return it—oh, I've forgotten your name."

"Grant Morrison," he said. "And I can afford to lose the handkerchief. You needn't bother. Just try not to invite such situations in future."

That did it. She knew she was being ungrateful, but she couldn't stop herself. She snapped, "You know, that attitude wouldn't get you anywhere in court these days! It's not done any more to blame the victim."

He was silent for a moment. "Point taken. Every woman should be able to go anywhere day or night, and wear what she likes, and say whatever she wants, and still say no to an offer of sex. But we don't live in an ideal world, men aren't all angels, in fact some of them are downright animals, and any woman with a grain of sense knows that she has to use a bit of discretion to protect herself. Whatever your rights, and however hurt your feelings were tonight, you weren't acting with an ounce of discretion, Rennie, and you know it."

Ignoring her angry gasp, he went on ruthlessly, "Ethan is old enough to handle a teenager with a crush and not lose his head. But when you turned your considerable battery of charm on that stupid, drunken kid, you ran the risk of getting more than you bargained for."

She thought with great longing of the time she had kicked Kevin in the shins. Seething, she fought for some adult self-control, and managed to say coldly, "You're quite wrong, but it's obviously no use arguing, even if I felt any need to justify myself to you. People in middle age tend to get fixed opinions that are very difficult to shift. And they're often pompous with it." She noticed a slight quiver in his expression and felt a shaft of satisfaction. "Thank you for bringing me home," she said graciously. "Good night."

Pompous! Grant thought, irritably watching her march up the path on her incredibly long legs. She was almost as tall as he was, in her high heels. Middle-aged? The cheeky little... Not too middle-aged to appreciate those legs, or the swing of her hips, which he could swear she was exaggerating for his benefit. Serve her right if he followed her up the path and...

Oh, come on, he said to himself, regaining a sense of perspective. From the viewpoint of her eighteen or nineteen years, he must seem middle-aged. Face it, you'll soon be pushing forty. You've got kids closer to her age than yours. You're old enough to be *her* father! Just. Although he hadn't actually, at that age...

Old enough all the same. He slammed the door as he got into the car, and drove off feeling if not pompous, decidedly middle-aged.

Chapter Two

Rennie put on a long-sleeved knit top and a pair of jeans before joining her family and Ethan for breakfast. Seventeen-year-old Shane was pouring cornflakes into his plate while her mother cut bread for toast, and her father, who always cooked breakfast on Sundays, was transferring sausages and bacon from a pan to a dish on the table.

Ethan looked up from a cup of coffee as she sat down. "Sorry about deserting you last night, Rennie."

"That's okay," she assured him again, adding innocently, "How's Celeste?" He looked much more like himself this morning. She thought the query was safe.

He grinned. "Fine, and so am I. As a matter of fact, now that you're all here, I'd like to make an announcement. Celeste and I are going to be married—just as soon as we can arrange it."

Noticing the sharp look her father had cast at her, Rennie hoped that in the excitement of Ethan's news, he'd forget to ask how she had come home. But as she helped to

stack the dishes, he said, "I thought you had left early with
Ethan last night. Who brought you home?"

"A friend of Ethan's." She clattered a pile of plates together and picked them up.

Ethan, who was taking some dishes to the sink, turned to
look at her. "Who?" he asked blankly.

She gave him a reproachful look. "Grant Morrison."

He looked slightly puzzled. "Morrison? A bit—mature
for you, isn't he, Rennie? I thought you'd be coming home
with your parents."

Her father said, "I told your mother that dress was too
old for you."

"It wasn't like that," Rennie protested. "He just offered
me a lift. And there's nothing wrong with that dress, Dad.
You just don't realise I've grown up."

"Mmm. Maybe. But do be careful who you accept a ride
with, won't you?"

"Yes, Dad." She resisted rolling her eyes as she walked
past him with the pile of plates.

"It's okay, Frank," Ethan said. "He's Celeste's solicitor. My brother knew him quite well."

Marian Langwell said, "Your brother was much older
than you, wasn't he, Ethan?"

"Yes. But Morrison wouldn't be Alec's age."

"He's about forty," Rennie offered, busily scraping
plates. "And anyway, he's not interested in me. He was being kind, that's all."

Ethan said absently, "Mid-thirties, more likely. Alec was
friendly with Grant's older brother. When Grant was at
university he joined one of Alec's expeditions to New
Guinea during the long holidays."

Rennie looked up. "But he's a lawyer, not an anthropol-
ogist!"

Ethan shrugged. "Not all the students Alec took along
were planning anthropology majors. He liked to take people he could rely on."

"Oh, I'm sure Grant Morrison's very reliable."

Ethan's brows rose. "Rub you up the wrong way?" Then with a quick frown he said quietly, "Did something happen between you, Rennie?"

"He brought me home, that's all," she said, and turned away from him to stack the dishwasher.

She didn't see Grant Morrison again until Ethan's wedding. There were not many people in the small church, a dozen or so all told, and afterwards they were invited to Ethan's aunt's house for a meal. The aunt was a large, booming woman with only partial hearing, and since she hated to miss any of the conversation, most of it was conducted with raised voices.

Except for Shane and two small girls who had been Celeste's bridal attendants, Rennie and Grant were the only guests not part of a couple. Rennie supposed that was why Aunt Ellie had decided to seat them next to each other. She gave him a stiff nod as he held her chair for her, and noticed the amusement in his smile as he took his place beside her.

"Still haven't forgiven me, Rennie?" he murmured, under cover of Aunt Ellie's instructions to the rest of the company.

"I've no idea what you mean," she lied.

He picked up an open wine bottle and poured some into the glass in front of her before helping himself. "You do." He carefully put the bottle down again. "I know your pride's hurt, but how would you have felt if I'd just turned around and left you to it?"

Rennie gazed at the bubbles rising in the glass. He couldn't have done that, of course. And if he had, she'd have had reason to be angry. She said, "You needn't have read me a lecture afterwards. I already knew I'd—misjudged the situation."

"And got a bad fright. All right, I apologise for the lecture. Having carried out my rescue act, I suppose I felt entitled. I just wanted to be sure it wouldn't happen to you again."

"You needn't worry. I still think he wouldn't have deliberately hurt me."

Grant's mouth tightened. "I should hope not. How's the arm?"

"Fine. It was just a graze." She lifted her elbow to show him, and he touched the pink mark with a finger, smiling at her.

It was a nice smile, she thought with surprise, softening his features and making him look younger. The greying hair made him seem at first glance more than his years, she supposed. "You should smile more often," she told him.

"What?" His brows rose.

"It makes you look ... nicer," she said. "Less—" She hesitated, and he said encouragingly, with a thread of laughter, "Less—?"

"Forbidding."

"Forbidding? Is that how you see me?"

She was saved from having to reply by Aunt Ellie's penetrating voice announcing that now the reverend would say grace. Afterward Rennie busied herself passing dishes to her neighbours and filling her own plate, and noted with relief that the woman at Grant's other side was occupying his attention.

When they had finished eating, Aunt Ellie proposed a toast to the bride and groom, and Ethan stood and thanked them all. The plates were cleared and the table folded down and pushed aside, while the bride and groom circulated and chatted to their friends. Rennie gave Ethan a hug, kissed Celeste on her cheek and said, "Congratulations to both of you. Sorry about calling up the green-eyed monster. And don't bother to thank me, Ethan," she added, batting her eyelashes outrageously to remind him what he owed her. "Just be happy together!"

Ethan gave her a small slap on the bottom. "Behave yourself, young Rennie," he said.

Celeste smiled at her with a hint of bewilderment. Then someone else arrived to give their good wishes, and Rennie stepped back and moved away.

"What's your name?" One of the bridal attendants was standing at Rennie's side, gazing up at her with curiosity. Her blond flyaway hair was tied in a ponytail and her eyes in a round baby face with a determined little chin were a clear, direct blue.

"Rennie. Renalda, really, but Rennie for short." She smiled down at the child. "What's yours?"

"Ellen. You can read me a story if you like."

"Sure. If we can find something to read from."

"I found some." Ellen took her hand and led her to a bookcase in a corner of the room. "Find one with pictures," she ordered.

Most of the books were novels but Rennie found an illustrated book of New Zealand birds and Ellen led her to a chair. As she sat down, Rennie saw Grant leaning against the far wall with an empty glass in his hand and a faintly bitter regret on his face. Following his gaze, she realised that he was watching Celeste and Ethan. They stood with hands entwined, talking to Rennie's parents but unable to resist casting frequent glances at each other, giving the impression that for a moment or two they had lost the thread of the conversation altogether.

Ellen ensconced herself on Rennie's lap, and commanded, "Story!"

Guessing that a list of habitats and colourations hardly constituted a story, Rennie began to weave a tale about a blue-plumaged pukeko stalking on long red legs through the swamp, bush and mountain in search of adventure, meeting with various other birds on the way who either helped or hindered her quest.

Rennie noted that Grant had moved closer, and was openly listening. Making up nonsense for Ellen was one thing. Having an adult audience of one highly critical lawyer was quite another. She floundered to a hasty finish and closed the book, saying firmly, "And they lived happily ever after. And I'm afraid that's all for now, Ellen."

As the child scrambled off her knee the book fell to the floor. Before either of them could retrieve it, Grant stepped forward and picked it up.

"I didn't bother Celeste, Daddy," Ellen announced virtuously.

Rennie glanced up in surprise.

"I never thought to tell her not to bother anyone else," he said dryly. "I didn't think she'd try it with someone she didn't know."

"I don't mind at all," Rennie assured him.

He studied the cover of the book in his hands. "I had no idea *Birds of New Zealand* was so exciting," he said as he handed it to Rennie. "I was riveted."

"I'll bet."

"I'm thirsty," Ellen announced.

"Well, if you ask nicely, I might get you a drink," Grant offered.

"Please can I have a drink?" Ellen said obediently.

"What would you like?" he asked. "Orange or lemonade? And you, Rennie?"

By the time they had returned the book to the shelf he had found a glass of orange juice and one of white wine.

Finishing her drink in ten seconds flat, Ellen went off hand in hand with the other young attendant, and Rennie was left standing by the bookcase with Grant.

"Did you ever think of being a teacher?" he asked her.

"Law runs in the family. I never thought of doing anything else, really. Why are you looking like that?"

"Going into the family business? I'd have thought a strong-minded young woman like you might want to strike out on her own."

"I'm not going to work for my dad. I'll be looking for another firm, when I'm qualified. Strong-minded?" she queried. "I was quite sure you thought I was a dimwit. In fact, I seem to remember you calling me a fool."

"One doesn't necessarily preclude the other."

Rennie flashed him a look, and he said, laughing suddenly, "Okay. Everyone's entitled to do something foolish once in a while."

"Even you?"

"Want your pound of flesh, do you? Even I. But if you don't mind I won't go into details." He looked across the room at Celeste and Ethan again.

"She's beautiful," Rennie said.

"Yes, she is. I hope she'll be happy." He didn't sound too confident. That odd expression compounded of bitterness and regret crossed his face again.

Rennie looked at him, then at Ethan. Ethan was right for Celeste, anyone could see it. "He'll look after her," she assured Grant. "He's a good man."

"He made her very unhappy for a long time," Grant said, with a hint of censure.

"He was unhappy, too," Rennie bridled. "It wasn't all his fault." She didn't really know that much about it, but she was fond of Ethan and criticism of her loved ones was apt to make her defensive.

"You're biased," Grant said, "aren't you?" The light eyes had sharpened but there was a hint of sympathy in them.

"Maybe I am," Rennie admitted. "But Ethan wouldn't deliberately hurt anyone he loved."

"You've a lot to learn about love," Grant told her. His mouth had a cynical twist.

"You seem to have a jaundiced view of it."

Grant shrugged. "Maybe divorced people are not qualified to make pronouncements on true love."

"You're divorced?"

"Three years ago."

"Then you're biased, too."

"Haven't I just admitted it? Come on, I'll get you some more wine."

Changing the subject, she thought. Maybe his marriage was still a sore point, or he was embarrassed at finding himself commenting on it to a virtual stranger. She guessed he was the kind of person who wouldn't often discuss his private life.

When he had brought her the wine, she asked, "Is the other little girl yours, too?"

"No, my other child is a boy, but he declined to take part. He's at the age where he thinks weddings are soppy. Ellen has a better sense of occasion."

Rennie's father joined them and soon had Grant talking shop. Rennie mostly listened, but now and then ventured an opinion of her own. Once or twice she thought Grant was slightly impressed.

At midnight, long after Ellen and the other little girl had been temporarily tucked up side by side in a huge bed, their hostess announced that it was time the bride and groom were leaving, and herded the guests out onto the footpath to wave goodbye. There were more kisses all round, and some confetti scattered, and cheers heartily led by Shane.

Ethan took with good grace the tin cans and toilet paper streamers that Shane had somehow managed to attach to his car. As it noisily turned the corner, Grant's voice said quietly in Rennie's ear, "It's over. You did well. Now you can relax."

She turned to look at him. Of course, she remembered, he thought she had a teenage crush on Ethan. About to disabuse him of that misconception, she took a breath, and then he bent his head closer and his hand touched her shoulder. "You'll get over it," he said. "I know it's hard to believe at your age. But I promise you, the hurt won't last forever."

Rennie shut her teeth. Really, he was too much. Anyone would have thought she was thirteen instead of going on twenty.

In a small voice, she said, "Thank you, Grant. How do you know?"

"Experience."

The others were trailing into the house, ready to collect belongings and take their leave.

"Come on," he said, placing a hand on her waist to urge her inside. "It'll all look better in the morning."

Rennie sighed. "If you say so."

"Believe me."

Her parents were saying goodnight to Ethan's aunt. Rennie stopped in the doorway, turning what she hoped was a soulful look on Grant. "You're very comforting," she breathed. "I'd . . . like to talk to you about it sometime."

He looked faintly taken aback. "Maybe you should talk to your mother," he suggested.

"Oh, no! She wouldn't understand!" Rennie assured him untruthfully. "Or my father. But I do feel I need to talk to someone . . . older."

She could have sworn that he winced inwardly, although not a quiver appeared on his face. As he hesitated, his eyes narrowing, she added hastily, lifting her chin, "But never mind. I know you must be very busy—" she allowed a faint tremor to enter her voice, "—only I've never felt like this before, you see," she added, her bright head drooping. "I don't know how I'm going to bear it."

Grant was silent, but peeking at him briefly she thought he was at least a little uncomfortable.

"Don't worry about me. I'll be all right," she said, with an air of forlorn bravery, stepping away from him.

Her mother turned from saying good-night to Aunt Ellie, and called to her. Grant was still standing by the door when they left, and she directed a wavery smile at him, not quite meeting his eyes. He turned to watch them, and even at a distance he looked tense and undecided, as though wondering if there was something he ought to do.

Serve him right, she thought, as she climbed into the car alongside her brother. She hoped his conscience was pricking him badly. He was ready enough to jump to smugly arrogant conclusions about her and dispense lordly advice, but when she directly asked for his help he had backed down awfully smartly.

Chapter Three

Rennie walked briskly, the wind tugging at the green silk scarf wound into her hair and whipping her nylon jacket as she dug her hands into the pockets. She was beginning to wish she had taken the bus home instead of deciding to walk. The wind hadn't been this strong or this cold when she left the university, and she'd wanted to blow away the cobwebs after a full day of lectures and tutorials.

As she stepped onto the bridge over the motorway, her boots ringing on the concrete slabs, a group of youngsters pushed by her, and she moved to the side of the narrow walkway, next to the parapet. Cars streamed along the carriageway beside her, their engines growling. When a thundering truck roared past, shaking the bridge, she turned her head and felt something tug at her hair before the long strands were blowing into her face and she realised the scarf had come off.

A metal standard fixed to the parapet held a defaced and broken board that had once said something about fines for throwing or dropping objects from the bridge. The scarf had blown against the board and become snagged on the jagged timber. As she reached for it, the silk square was plucked away by the wind and floated down, not falling onto the motorway where the cars rushed along unheeding below, but catching on a rusty protruding bolt outside the parapet, about level with the path.

It was a nice scarf and she didn't want to lose it. Hopefully, Rennie leaned over the parapet. She reached down, found the scarf just out of range of her groping fingers, and straightened, contemplating the problem.

The green scrap fluttered, and she held her breath, wondering how long it would stay in that precarious position. If it floated down to the roadway, it could be a danger to the rush-hour traffic. Something appearing like that from nowhere, perhaps flattening itself against a windscreen—suppose it caused an accident? She'd better do her best to retrieve it, short of climbing over. The concrete parapet wasn't solid; there were interstices large enough to slide her hand into sideways...

She got a hand through as far as her forearm, but the space was too narrow and too high. She couldn't grasp the fabric. She straightened again, looking over. Still there, undulating in the wind. Impatiently she brushed the unruly hair from her eyes. She glanced at the cars flowing along the bridge behind her. If she stopped someone, asked for a coat hanger, a piece of wire or something? But that would create a bottleneck on the bridge, also a hazard to traffic.

She looked about for something to stand on. No such luck. If she could slip her foot into the interstice, it might give her the extra few inches she needed. But her leather boot wouldn't fit. She pulled it off, and managed to get a toehold. Good, it was about six inches up. She held the top of the parapet with one hand, and levered herself upward, and began to lean forward, her fingers outstretched.

And then all hell broke loose. There was a screech of brakes behind her followed by a loud crumping sound, a chorus of horn blowing, and several people yelling. One of them was yelling her name, but she had hardly registered that when she was suddenly yanked backwards.

Her stockinged foot slid painfully from its perch, and she lost her balance, falling against a solid male chest. Her hair was blowing wildly, and she was breathless with shock. There was a bruising grip on her arm and an awful lot of noise. She heard someone say, "What's going on?" And someone else shouting, "Look at my car! Didja have to stop like that? No signal or anything—"

And then a familiar voice said loudly, *"She was going to jump, you fool!* There wasn't *time* to signal."

She shook the hair out of her eyes and stared up in stupefaction at Grant Morrison's white, scowling face. "No..." she said, but her voice was drowned by the aggrieved car owner, soon joined by a couple of others, one of them contending that he had been following too close, anyway, and another taking his side.

Grant cut them all short. "I'll pay for the damage," he said. "Here's my card. Send me the bill." He was still holding on to Rennie's arm, and when she tried to ease away, he increased his grip until it hurt.

"We're holding up the traffic," he said. "Get in my car."

"I can't," she protested.

His teeth gritted, he said, *"Get—in!"*

Rennie gaped at him. In all her life, no one had ever spoken to her in that tone. She had seldom seen anyone look so furious.

She had a sudden, stupid desire to cry. "I can't! My scarf is over there, and it might cause another accident if it blows down on the roadway, and I've only got one boot!"

A few people had gathered about, some asking questions that Grant ignored and Rennie was too shocked to answer. He pushed her toward his car and opened the door. "Get in," he repeated, and she did.

He slammed the door behind her, giving her a look that conveyed starkly, *Stay there, or else!* He strode over to the parapet, stooping across it easily and whisking the scarf up in his fingers, then he picked up her boot and, when he had returned to the driver's seat, handed them to her with elaborate courtesy.

The other driver had backed his car off with a slight scraping of metal. Grant put his into gear and moved on carefully, his face set like a stone mask.

Rennie found she was shaking as she replaced her boot. The scarf she folded and pushed into her jacket pocket. "How," she asked, "did you come to be there?"

"I sometimes come home this way. Luckily for you."

"Not really," she said carefully. "It wasn't what you—"

"You may not think so right now," he interrupted, "but you'll live to thank me, believe me."

"For getting my scarf? Thank you."

He misinterpreted the irony in her voice. "We both know that isn't what I meant." Not even looking at her, he said, "Have you tried anything like that before?"

"No, I haven't! What I was—"

"He's not worth it," Grant said. "No man is. For heaven's sake," he said tightly, "don't you realise this is just a phase you're going through? You're an intelligent girl. And a beautiful one. Your family's successful, and seems happy—you've had all the advantages. You have so much to look forward to. What you were about to do was not only spineless and pathetic, it was criminally wasteful."

She twisted in her seat to look at him. "I'm sorry if I gave you a fright. And about your car, and the other one. But you didn't have to rescue me, you know. You do seem to have a Sir Galahad complex, Mr. Morrison. If you'd just minded your own business—"

He turned on her for an instant and said one word that made her mouth fall open. Then he swung the car into a corner and drove along a narrow, sloping side street lined with verandahed colonial houses and overhanging plane trees, before coming to a jarring stop.

"Listen to me," he said as he turned to face her, his eyes alight with temper. "You ungrateful little...idiot! You don't have a monopoly on heartbreak, you know. Most of us have

had our share. Celeste, for instance. Her first husband drove
his car over a cliff.''

Rennie gasped. "I didn't know that! Poor Celeste!''

"Yes, poor Celeste. I expect she still wonders if she could
have prevented it, if it was her fault. Is that what you wanted
to do to Ethan? Make him spend his life being sorry he
didn't fall in love with you?''

"That isn't what I—''

"Then what did you want? It's a very stupid and final
way to get attention, Rennie. A childish, immature ruse to
make people sorry they weren't nicer to you. The thing is,
you won't be around to see them being sorry. So it won't do
you much good, will it?''

"Oh, do stop *yelling* at me!'' Rennie said, although he
hadn't been yelling exactly. "If you'd just *listen* for a
change—you're not very good at that, are you?'' Reminded of the last time they had met, she added indignantly, "I did ask if I could talk to you, remember, but you
didn't want to know. So why all the sudden concern now?''
If she had been genuinely suicidal, she thought resentfully,
his brush-off might have been just what sent her over the
edge.

To her surprise, his whole manner changed. He flushed,
she saw his hand tighten on the wheel, and he looked away
for a minute. "You're right,'' he said. "I'm sorry, Rennie.
I didn't take you seriously enough. I guess I've forgotten
what it's like to be as young as you are.''

He was back on that tack again, she thought, harping on
her youth and inexperience. Still, after an apology like that
he deserved to be let off the hook, she supposed. She had
better explain, and from the beginning.

But then he put a hand on her hair, pushing the tangled
mane from her face, and smiled at her. And she felt his fingers brush her cheek, and totally forgot what she was about
to say.

How extraordinary! she thought, blinking at him. She
saw something in his eyes that she was not too young to
recognise, and felt a quick pleasure.

Then he dropped his hand and moved back a little. "If you want to talk," he said, "I'm available any time. But I haven't done too well so far, have I? Perhaps you should see a counsellor... a professional of some sort."

Rennie swallowed an acute sense of disappointment. He was very carefully not looking at her. He had felt that same flare of awareness that she had, but had decided not to do anything about it. She said huskily, "You're passing the buck. If you don't want to see me any more, why don't you just say so? To my face."

He knew what she meant, but when he turned to her his eyes were quite cool, the flame of desire deliberately doused. "I've said I'm available," he told her after a moment. "The offer stands, if you want to take it up."

She wanted him to touch her again, to see if that frisson of pure pleasure would return. Her heart was still thumping with the sheer surprise of it. But he wouldn't, and she dare not take the initiative herself. She moistened her bottom lip with her tongue. "I want to," she said. "When?"

He seemed to hesitate. "Tomorrow," he said. "We could have dinner together. Somewhere quiet, where we can talk."

"I'll pay my share," she offered.

"Don't be silly. You're a student and I'm a fairly successful solicitor. Do you think I'm going to take you out and let you pay for your own dinner?"

"Are you taking me out?" she challenged him.

Again he hesitated. "We're going out. So that we can talk. That's what you want, isn't it?"

She wanted to ask what he wanted. But he obviously wasn't to be drawn. Don't push it, she told herself. That was her besetting sin, her family had often told her. Rushing in where angels feared, and all that. Something told her that in spite of his propensity for jumping to unwarranted conclusions where she was concerned, Grant was not a man to be rushed. She smiled at him, all innocence. "Yes," she said. "Thank you, Mr. Morrison." She couldn't resist the small revenge.

"Grant," he said curtly. "You don't have to call me mister."

She refused to let him pick her up from home. He didn't object very strenuously to meeting her in town. In fact he looked, she thought, slightly relieved. Rennie told her mother she had a late lecture and might stay in town for supper. If Marian assumed the addition "with friends" Rennie absolved herself of any obligation to disillusion her.

Rennie did have a late lecture that evening, but she skipped it. There really wasn't any reason not to tell her parents she was having dinner with Grant Morrison, but she remembered her father's unease when Ethan had commented on Grant's age. And she could hardly tell them that she was supposedly using him as a shoulder to cry on over her non-existent unrequited love.

He picked her up outside the friend's flat where she had changed from her jeans and sweatshirt into a dark red silk velvet skirt and loose, heavy cream lace top, and replaced her boots with medium-heeled court shoes. She disliked high heels except for very special occasions because they restricted her free-swinging walk. She was watching for the car, and ran out to it with a black velvet jacket slung over her shoulder and a bag containing her daytime clothes in her hand.

"Can I put this in the back?" she asked him. "I had to change."

He took it from her and put it on the rear seat. "You look very nice," he said perfunctorily, as if talking to a child who had asked him to admire her pretty dress, and opened the door for her.

"It wasn't a hint," Rennie muttered resentfully as he closed it after her. She watched him get into his seat, her eyes steady and considering.

He gave her an enquiring smile, and said with a tinge of heartiness, "Well, do you have any preferences as to where you'd like to go? As it's a week night, I didn't bother booking."

Oh, so that's the way of it, is it? Rennie thought. Well, if you're going to humour the little girl, you can humour her good and proper. Tentatively, she mentioned what she knew perfectly well was one of the most expensive restaurants in Auckland. "I've never been there. I've heard it's good," she said, "but a bit dear. Perhaps we'd better go somewhere else?"

"No, no." He hadn't noticeably blenched. "If that's what you fancy, that's where we'll go."

She restrained an impulse to bounce on the seat, clap her hands and exclaim, "Oh, goody!" Even a man as obtuse as Grant appeared to be might smell a rat if she overdid things to that extent.

The restaurant was on the top floor of a hotel, overlooking a spectacular view of the Waitemata Harbour. A container ship was making its way slowly to the nearby wharves, smaller fishing boats and a few pleasure launches and sailboats dotted the water, and on the North Shore, across the green expanse, lights pricked on here and there at the approach of darkness. Rangitoto, the island volcano, raised its gentle slopes in the distance.

Grant secured them a table in a quiet corner. It might have been because he imagined she would want to unburden herself in relative privacy, Rennie acknowledged fairly, but she couldn't help wondering if he was embarrassed to be seen with her. He acted like an uncle treating a favourite niece to a night out. And to give him credit he didn't flicker an eyelid when she ordered rock lobster with lemon butter, the most expensive dish on the menu. He just said, "The same for me," and handed the menu back to the waiter.

Rennie toyed with her glass, which the waiter had filled with sparkling wine before bringing the menus. She had pretended to know nothing about wine, and Grant had ordered a Martinborough Chardonnay—a New Zealand white that was a gold medal winner.

"You like seafood?" he asked her as they waited.

"Love it," Rennie answered. "You don't mind that I ordered the rock lobster?" She injected a faint note of anxiety into the question.

"I'm having it, too," he reminded her. "I think our seafood must be the best in the world."

"Have you travelled much?"

"A bit. England, America, Australia, of course. And a few side trips on the way to and from."

"Ethan said you'd been on one of his brother's expeditions to New Guinea."

"Years ago, in the days of my youth."

"I've been to Sydney a couple of times, but that's all. Tell me about your trips."

"What do you want to know?"

He kept her entertained right through the main course, answering questions and, quickly identifying her areas of interest, expanding on his descriptions of different ways of life and the more out-of-the-way places he had visited.

When the sweets arrived on a trolley she chose a mocha cake while he asked for a cheese board. Cutting into a creamy round of locally produced brie, he said, "I'm talking too much. Your turn."

"I haven't so much to talk about," she said. "School, university. That's all I've done."

"Your family," he said. "I could see at the wedding that you're a close-knit lot. You get on well with your brother, don't you?"

"Mostly, yes. We used to have the odd spat when we were younger. But Shane's reasonably intelligent, and we talk quite a bit. He's not a bad kid."

She caught the amusement in his expression, but he didn't comment. She sighed. It wasn't hard to read his thoughts.

"Your mother seems a pretty accessible lady," he said. "But you haven't confided in her?"

It was on the tip of her tongue to tell him she could confide anything in her mother. "Oh," she mumbled, taking refuge in another bite of her cake, "she's pretty busy you know." She picked up her wine-glass and swallowed a mouthful. "She's a legal executive in Dad's law practice, and president of Volunteer Drivers for the Disabled, and she's on lots of committees. And the house is usually full of people. She and Dad are always inviting someone—well, so do Shane and I. They've always encouraged us to bring our friends home. But it's hard to get a chance to talk in private, if you know what I mean. Do you think we could have coffee now? This cake is delicious, but I'd love some coffee with it."

That last hasty sip had made her realise that she had drunk quite a lot of wine, including the champagne. Coffee seemed a good idea, not only to distract Grant while she tried to decide what to tell him when the inevitable time for confidences arrived, but also to steady her surroundings.

When the coffee was put in front of them, Grant said, "Well, you wanted to talk."

Panic set in. Rennie looked down, her chin resting on one hand while the other fiddled with a spoon. "Er, it's not that easy," she floundered. "In cold blood, so to speak." Hastily she picked up her coffee.

"It's what we're here for."

She ought to tell him he was barking up the wrong tree. Here he was, waiting for her to speak, the perfect opportunity. He had just given her a superb dinner that was going to make a considerable hole in his pocket. It was ridiculous to feel disappointed that he was doing it from avuncular kindheartedness and a sense of conscience. Her own conscience told her that she ought to confess her deception now, before she got herself in any deeper. It was unfair to take advantage of the man because he was sorry for her.

She gazed about the room for inspiration, and saw nearby a couple holding hands across the table, smiling at each other. Unexpectedly, she felt sadness take hold of her, and she looked at Grant, who was studying her, his eyes filled with compassion.

She blinked, shaking her head.

His hand swiftly covered hers on the table, and he said, "Rennie—"

The waiter appeared at his elbow. "Everything all right, sir?"

Grant withdrew his hand immediately, and sat back. "Fine, thank you. Would you bring the bill, please. Unless you want anything else, Rennie?"

Rennie declined. She was chagrined and angry at the way he had released her hand. It was nothing for him to be ashamed of, for heaven's sake! And she had liked the feel of his warm palm against her skin, his fingers beginning to curl about hers. His hands were long and strong, and looked sensitive. . . .

She shook her head again. Too much wine, for sure. She said, "You want to go?"

"Only if you do," he answered. "It strikes me this isn't the best place to talk, after all. Particularly if it's going to upset you."

He didn't want to be seen sitting at a table with a weeping young woman. Rennie almost laughed then. That *would* make him feel uncomfortable. Discomfort, she diagnosed, didn't sit easily with Grant Morrison. He liked to be in control.

When they left the restaurant she was still vaguely simmering. On impulse she said, "Let's walk." The night air and some exercise might dispel her admittedly unreasonable sense of anger and frustration, and give her the courage to tell him the truth, a task that seemed more impossible by the minute.

They were not very far from the waterfront, and by tacit consent they headed in that direction, past the railway station and along Tamaki Drive, where the dark waters of the Waitemata lapped at the stones along the foreshore and reflected the lights of the city. The night was cool but clear and dry, and what wind there had been during the day had died now.

"Am I going too fast?" Grant asked her once.

"No." Rennie shook her head. "I like a decent pace."

He smiled down at her and tucked her hand into the crook of his arm. "Good. So do I."

Eventually they stopped and leaned over a railing, listening to the water chuckling and slapping amongst the stones, and watching the coloured ripples made by the lights. Rennie raised a hand to push back her hair, and Grant shifted his arm to put it round her, his hand cupping her shoulder.

She turned her head to him, found him gazing out at the water, and waited until he looked down at her, waited for the flare of awareness in his eyes. And it came. She held her breath. His hand tightened, and then he dropped it, leaning back on the railing apparently casually. "Ready now?" he said.

Rennie was experiencing a sharp sense of disappointment. "Ready?" she repeated. "For what?"

"To talk about Ethan," he said. "Tell me about it."

Oh, damn! she thought wildly. Couldn't he see that the last thing she wanted was to talk about another man? If he was honest, it was surely the last thing that he wanted at this moment. But maybe she was reading things into his actions from her own imagination. Certainly that brief awareness she had evoked was no longer there. He looked cool, remote, politely interested.

Okay, she thought, her temper taking over. You want me to talk about Ethan. I'll talk about Ethan.

"I've always loved him," she said huskily. "You know, he's been around since I was a kid. He was nice to me, he used to bring presents sometimes. I still treasure a shell that he gave me soon after he first went to live on that island— Sheerwind. It sounded such a romantic place. He promised one day I could go and stay there." That part was easy because it was true. "And when I was fourteen," she improvised, remembering the crush she'd had on the bus driver who drove her route on most school days and trying to recall that emotion, "I thought he was the most handsome man I'd ever seen. Sometimes just catching his eye in the— mirror would make me happy for days."

"Go on," Grant encouraged.

"Well, each time he came to stay, the feelings got stronger. I just . . . lived for his visits," she added, glancing at Grant to see if all this was having any effect. If so, it wasn't visible. "When he was away I felt...bereft. Only half-alive. I can't describe," she said honestly, "how it was."

"But he never gave any sign of reciprocating this...devotion?" Grant asked dryly.

Rennie shook her head. "Except that I knew he was fond of me. I dreamed that one day he'd see I'd grown up and ask me to marry him. Instead..." She let her voice trail off.

"He married Celeste."

"I though he'd wait for me," she said mournfully. Much more of this and I'll throw up, she thought. She sighed, not noticing Grant's sharp glance at her. "But—" she added an artistic little catch to her voice, "—it wasn't to be."

Peeking at his face, she saw that he seemed quite impassive. Even faintly bored. How could he? she wondered indignantly. Here I am to all intents and purposes baring my shattered heart to him, and he looks no more interested—less—than if he were listening to cricket scores or sharemarket prices.

She grasped the railing in front of her, scowling at the shimmering darkness of the water. "I suppose this is pretty dull for you," she said, "listening to me maundering on."

"No, of course not," he answered politely. "I want to hear all about it."

Liar, she thought. She racked her brains and went on inventing incidents and feelings, throwing herself into the part of besotted teenager, until invention failed. I'm good, she thought, surprised at the conviction she thought she managed to convey. Even Grant seemed moved when she finally wound to a halt. He put his arms about her and brought her close. "My poor child," he murmured into her hair.

Triumph mingled with guilt. What now? Pull away, point and shout "April Fool!"? Not yet, anyway, it was nice being held by him, with his hand soothing her hair, even if he did think he was comforting a child...

She snuggled closer, her head against his shoulder. His lips brushed her temple, and his hands were on her back, smoothing the velvet of her jacket.

Then those hands moved down to her skirt, and up again, under the jacket, and Rennie was electrified. Now his fingers were on her bare skin beneath the lace blouse, running up the groove of her spine, and his other hand gently tugged at her hair, raising her mouth to his.

The kiss had nothing to do with comforting a child. His mouth was warm and insistent and very sure, his technique extremely adult, and after her first startled reaction, which he totally ignored, she enjoyed it very much. When his hand shifted, lightly skimming her ribs, and came to rest with a thumb just under her bra, moving lazily over the hammering of her heart, she felt as though flames had erupted about her. Then, with his thumb still in the same place, he hooked one of those long fingers into the side of her bra and began caressing the soft skin.

Excitement spiralled within her. She felt her mouth open further under his, her breathing quicken. More. She wanted more. She wanted . . .

That wonderful warm hand moved again, the finger sliding along the taut curve of fabric to the fastening at the back. And then a car passed by with flaring headlights, and she wrenched herself away from him, gasping, "What are you doing?"

"Don't you like it?" he asked. "I thought you did."

"Well, I . . . I didn't expect it, from you!" she said, totally confused. If she was honest, she had wanted him to admit in some way that she attracted him, but the kiss had been much more devastating than she had foreseen. "I've just been telling you that I'm in love with another man!" That it wasn't true was surely neither here nor there.

"Ah, yes," he said. "Well, I thought it would be . . . interesting to see if you could respond to someone else, in spite of your deep feelings for Ethan."

Interesting! She struggled to keep her voice under control. "Oh," she said. "Why?"

"Well," he drawled, capturing her hand and holding it in a deceptively casual although, she discovered, inescapable grasp, "as you seem to be attracted to older men, I thought it might be enjoyable—for both of us—and help you get Ethan out of your system, if I offered myself in his place."

Regrettably, Rennie found her voice rising to something resembling a squeak. "Offered yourself? Are you p-*proposing?*"

He looked at her thoughtfully. "Well, no, actually. Not proposing marriage, if that's what you mean. Something less permanent. After all," he added coaxingly, "I'm not much older than Ethan. And I think we've just proved that you don't find me exactly repulsive. So...what about it? We could have a lot of fun. And cure you of your puppy love at the same time."

An affair. He wanted to have an affair with her.

"Shall we try again?" he asked, and swept her back into his arms, his mouth claiming hers once more, parting her lips, his hands sliding down to hold her against him.

She wasn't prepared for the explosion of pure rage that shook her. She shoved him away with all the force at her command, and swung a hand at his face, catching him a glancing blow on the chin as he whipped his head aside. "You *bastard!*" she panted.

She clenched her fists and lifted them, but he grabbed her wrists and held them away. And laughed. Laughed at her, infuriating her more than ever. She tried kicking out at him, and he twisted her wrists aside so that she couldn't reach him. He was still laughing.

"All right, Rennie," he said. "Tit for tat, and that makes us even. I didn't mean it, any more than you meant any of that romantic fairy tale you've just been spinning me about your great, wonderful, undying love for Ethan."

Chapter Four

Rennie stood still. "You knew! You—you sod! How could you—?"

"Rather easily, once I realised I was being taken for a ride," Grant rejoined coolly. He cautiously let go her wrists, waited for a moment and then added, "You laid it on a bit too much at the end. Carried away by your own imagination." His lips twitched.

Rubbing at one of her wrists, Rennie said, "I'd decided you weren't going to notice."

"Really." He put his hands in his pockets and looked at her consideringly. "Have I been that thick?"

"Yes. *And* you wouldn't listen."

He cocked his head enquiringly.

"I told you I wasn't pining for Ethan. You didn't believe me. And if you hadn't been so busy manhandling me yesterday on the bridge and tearing strips off me afterwards, you'd have heard me telling you I had no intention of jumping. All I wanted was to get my scarf."

"Your *scarf?*"

"I was just trying to retrieve it, that's all. It blew off in the wind. You got it back for me," she reminded him.

"You mean it blew over there *before* you started climbing the parapet? Is that true?" he asked blankly.

"How did you think it got over there?"

After a few seconds of thought, he said on a note of disbelief, "I've made a monumental fool of myself!"

"Well, yes—you have rather," Rennie confirmed. She tried to look sorry for him, but her lips curved in spite of herself, and a bubble of laughter escaped.

He looked at her wrathfully, and grasped her shoulders. "Don't you laugh at me!" But then his mouth began to curl upward, too, and she collapsed against him, still laughing.

"Well, you got your own back very nicely," he admitted at last, holding her away from him as he grinned down at her.

She asked him, "When did you realise?"

"I was sure after the wedding that you'd been having me on. Then when I saw you apparently about to jump from the bridge, I was convinced I'd done you a gross injustice. That was enough of a fright for me, you know," he reproached her.

"I meant to tell you then but you didn't give me a chance."

"Didn't I? I suppose that's fair comment. I was in shock."

"And tonight? You didn't know all along, did you?"

"I had my suspicions now and then. You didn't act like someone who'd tried to kill herself the day before. I wasn't sure though, until you began on that harrowing tale of teenage trauma. Hamming it up something awful, Rennie. You couldn't have expected me to swallow that!"

"Considering what you'd already swallowed—" she said heartlessly.

Grant stepped back from her and held up a hand. "Okay, okay. I admit it. I should have known you weren't such a wet fish."

"Well, thank you!" she said, slightly mollified. "I guess we can call it quits, now. You've had your revenge." She held out her hand.

Grant took it in his. "Quits it is." He looked down at her quizzically, still holding her hand. "I must say, I didn't expect you to be quite so offended by my suggestion. I've never seen such a picture of outraged virtue. Most unusual in this day and age."

"It was the way you did it," she said. "Leering at me! You meant me to be offended, didn't you?"

"Guilty, I'm afraid." He smiled ruefully. "I hardly expected to be physically attacked, though."

"I'm not going to apologise," Rennie told him roundly.

"No, I think we're past that, don't you? Now that we've cleared the air, we'd better be getting back to the car and I'll drive you home."

He took her hand as though it was the most natural thing in the world, and they walked side by side in companionable silence. As they left the waterside, Rennie said, "I'll pay for my share of the dinner. It was mean of me to make you take me there."

"You're a good sport, Rennie." He glanced down at her. "But that's quite unnecessary. Believe me, it was worth it. I haven't had such an enjoyable evening in years."

It was nice of him to say so, even if it wasn't strictly true. Stopping herself from naively asking if it was, she said truthfully, "Neither have I." It was astonishing, but she couldn't remember the last time she had felt so stimulated and alive.

"That's very sweet of you, Rennie," he said. Obviously he didn't believe a word of it.

"I mean it!" she protested. And then, sure that he wouldn't suggest it himself, she added, "Maybe we should do this again. Not so expensively of course, and without the—"

"Play-acting? Don't you think the event would lack some of the flavour of tonight? In a metaphorical sense."

"For you?" They had reached his car, and she turned to face him, preventing him from unlocking the door for her.

"For you, I meant," he answered.

"I don't know until we try it out, do I?" she suggested, and gave him her most winning smile.

He stood swinging the key in his hand, then gently moved her out of the way and unlocked the door. He turned to her and touched her arm. "Come on," he said. "I'm taking you home."

"Well?" she queried as he drew the car up outside her door.

He didn't pretend to misunderstand. With slow deliberation he switched the engine off and turned to face her. "Rennie," he said. "It wouldn't be a good idea to start—seeing each other."

"Why not? I know you only kissed me to make me fall for that phoney line of yours, but I wasn't the only one who enjoyed it."

"Most men enjoy kissing. Especially someone as attractive and responsive as you are. As you say, I'm afraid I had an ulterior motive. It doesn't mean I'm planning to repeat the experience."

Rennie flushed at his bluntness. "Are you giving me the brush-off?"

"You're a delightful young woman, and I like you a lot. I'm also divorced and about twice your age—"

"What does that have to do with it?"

"Some people might say, quite a lot. Your parents, for instance."

"My parents have brought me up to make my own decisions, and they're very broad-minded."

"Lots of parents are broad-minded until it comes to their own offspring."

Rennie thought that might be true of her father. "Anyway, I'm over eighteen, so they don't really have any say in the matter."

"And you'd be happy going against what they felt was in your best interests?"

Of course she wouldn't. She would always value their advice, no matter how old she was. But she had to make her own decisions in the long run. She said crossly, "I wish you'd stop trying to be a Dutch uncle, and go with your feelings for once."

"If I did that—"

"Yes?" she said hopefully.

"Never mind." He sounded rather grim. "Believe me, you'd be shocked rigid."

She gave a gurgle of laughter. "Do you really think so?"

"Yes, my provocative little virgin, I do."

Looking into his eyes, Rennie caught her breath. "H-how do you know I'm a virgin?" she asked, refusing to move her gaze from his.

"You are," he said, daring her to lie. "Aren't you?"

Rennie shrugged. "It's no disgrace."

"No, it isn't. And don't believe anyone who tells you any different."

Rennie folded her hands in her lap and looked resigned. "Are you about to give me another lecture?"

"No. I'm about to tip you out of this car and say goodnight."

"Why?" she demanded as he reached across and opened the door for her. "You said you liked me. You can at least give me a good reason."

"I just did."

"Because you're twice my age? What does that matter? No one thinks anything of it any more. Well, hardly..."

"All right," Grant said, his face close to hers. "Because I'm not in the habit of seducing teenagers. Clear enough for you? Now, shoo!" He gave her a peck on the lips and a meaningful little shove.

Rennie sighed, climbed out onto the pavement and said, "I'm not a cat!" She heard him laughing before he closed the door and drove away.

* * *

For a few days she half hoped he would relent and contact her. But it seemed he wasn't going to change his mind. Regretfully, she tried to put the episode behind her. When she found herself daydreaming about his firm mouth searching hers and his hands touching her skin, when she recalled the delicious tingling of her body, the hot melting in her bones, she told herself that she had never felt like this before merely because she had never been kissed by a man of his experience. It had meant nothing to him but a brief, pleasant incident. He had probably shared intimate moments with dozens of other women.

Including his wife. She wondered what his ex-wife was like, and why the marriage had gone wrong.

Then her father said casually at the dinner table one night, "Oh, I ran into Grant Morrison today, Rennie. Celeste's friend. He was asking after you."

"Was he?" She looked up eagerly, her cheeks flushing, and Shane cast her a curious, interested glance.

"Mmm." Her father was poking at the casserole on his plate.

"What did he say?" Rennie asked.

"What's this green stuff?" Frank asked his wife suspiciously. He turned a blank expression to Rennie. "Say?"

"It's zucchini," Marian told him.

Frank grunted. "He said, 'How's Rennie?' Is that a fancy name for marrow?"

Rennie demanded, "Is that all?" as her mother answered, "Baby marrows."

"Just as tasteless. All what?"

"They're good for you," Marian said. "Full of vitamins."

"Is that all he *said?*"

"What else should he say?" Frank asked his daughter, pushing the zucchini aside. "He hardly knows you, after all. Does he?"

"No, no," Rennie agreed hastily. "I'm just surprised he remembered me at all, really."

She caught her brother's eyes. Shane's expression was frankly disbelieving, and mischievous. He opened his mouth, and closed it quickly when she gave him a murderous glare.

Marian said a few days later, "Ethan phoned. He and Celeste have returned from their honeymoon, and they've asked us all to come round to Celeste's house for drinks on Saturday night, before they take off for Sheerwind."

"Just us?" Rennie asked, looking up from the book she was reading.

"I've no idea," her mother said. "He didn't say."

"Does it matter?" Shane asked.

Rennie shrugged. "I'd like to know if it's a party or not. So I know what to wear," she added.

"Something pretty," her mother advised vaguely. "I don't think it's meant to be formal, though."

She wore a floral print dress in autumn colours. It hugged her breasts and nipped her waist before falling to a full skirt, and left her shoulders bare although it had soft, gathered sleeves. She pinned her hair carefully up, used a bit more makeup than usual on her creamy skin, and put on a pair of high-heeled shoes that she seldom wore but which emphasised her narrow feet and slim ankles. When she came into the hall as they were preparing to leave, Shane whistled and asked, "Who are you trying to impress?"

"Not you!" she retorted, and swept by him to the door.

"You look very nice," her father told her, and she instantly wanted to run back inside and change into something else, but it was too late.

They were not the only ones invited, she discovered. By eight-thirty almost everyone who had attended the wedding was there. The house was an old one that Celeste had lived in before her marriage to Ethan, and her workroom had been cleared for the party, the tables she used for her fabric painting covered with white cloths and holding an array of

food, glasses and drinks from which the guests were invited
to help themselves.

Rennie drank two glasses of white wine and talked to
Ethan's aunt, and tried not to allow her eyes to stray toward the door every five minutes.

"Enjoying yourself?" Ethan asked as she returned to the
'bar' to refill her glass.

"Lovely, thanks," she answered. "You're looking well.
Celeste is, too. I'm very glad for you, Ethan."

"So am I. I nearly blew it, you know. What are you
drinking?" He took her glass.

"I was drinking wine, but I'll have an orange juice now,
thanks. You're going back to Sheerwind soon?"

"Yes, we miss the island. We're keeping this house on,
though. Celeste still has a share in the shop where she sells
her fabrics and clothing. This will be a handy base when either of us needs to visit Auckland on business. We plan to
divide our time between here and Sheerwind. You must visit
us there."

"I'd love to."

"Good. Here's your orange juice." He was handing it to
her when Grant walked into the room, and somehow the
juice slopped onto her hand.

"Sorry!" Ethan grabbed a paper napkin and began
mopping up the spill.

"It wasn't your fault," she assured him. She concentrated her attention on the small mishap, putting down the
glass to wipe her hand with the fresh napkin Ethan handed
to her. By the time Grant had walked over to the table she
was able to meet him with a careless smile, and her hand
when she retrieved her glass was quite steady.

She saw the slight reserve with which the two men greeted
each other. "You've seen Celeste?" Ethan asked as he
poured the other man a drink.

"Yes. She seems very...contented."

"She is." Ethan's glance was straight.

Grant nodded. "I'm glad. Congratulations again."

"Thanks. Well, if you two are happy, I think I'll go and join my wife."

"You're late," Rennie told Grant, and then flushed. She hadn't meant it to sound like an accusation.

"I got held up." He took a good swallow of his drink, as though he felt the need of it. "Is there anywhere to sit?"

"There are chairs in the other room, but I think they're all occupied. Are you tired?"

"Tired," he said, "is a wholly inadequate word."

"What have you been doing?"

"Trailing around the zoo all day with two kids. I thought I was reasonably fit, but—" he shook his head "—today I'm feeling my years."

"Do you have custody?"

"No, they live with their mother and I have them every second weekend. And I'm rapidly running out of ideas of where to take them."

"How old is Ellen's brother?"

"Toby's eight."

"And Ellen's about four?"

"That's right. There aren't many suitable films, and in any case their mother doesn't like the idea of them sitting in a stuffy picture theatre too often. But it's still too cool for the beach, we've done the Underwater World and the Safari Park and the transport museum, and I think even they are getting bored with the zoo. And frankly, if I ever see another hippopotamus or cage full of monkeys, *I'm* likely to end up behind bars."

More people came up to refresh their drinks, and Rennie and Grant automatically moved away, crowded into a corner. Grant leaned a shoulder against the wall and said, "And how have you been?"

"Okay. Dad said you asked after me."

"Yes."

"You could have called me, if you wanted to know."

"You're very good for my ego."

She made a face at him. "You're absolutely rotten for mine."

Grant laughed, and took some more of his drink. "Don't tempt me."

"Could I?" She was flirting quite deliberately, enjoying herself.

He smiled. "Easily, as if you didn't know. Don't push your luck, little one."

There was an edge to his voice, a tension in his body that communicated itself to Rennie. She said, "What's the matter?"

"Matter?" He frowned at her, wearily.

"What's wrong?" she asked bluntly. "You're not just tired. You're . . . angry."

He gave a small laugh. "How perspicacious of you. I had a row with Jean—my ex-wife—after I took the kids home to her. Very civilised, very quiet, because we don't want to upset the children, we're careful about that. But a row all the same."

"What about?"

He said, "I gave the kids hamburgers and chips, at their request. They took longer to get through the meal than I'd expected. I guess she was worried. She doesn't approve of junk food anyway, but she might have overlooked that if we hadn't been so late. However, I'm not about to burden you with my problems. Forget it. Come on, let's go into the other room and join the party properly."

Both rooms were equally full now, but the record player was in the lounge, and she wondered if he preferred the noisier setting because it would inhibit intimate conversation.

Her mother looked up when they entered the room, and smiled as they stopped by her.

"You remember Grant, don't you, Mum?"

Marian smiled at him. "Of course. From the wedding. My husband said he had a very interesting talk with you."

"Mum," Rennie said, "Grant has two children to entertain every second weekend. He says he's running out of places to take them. They could visit us, couldn't they? They'd love the old tree house and the swing. And my doll's house." She turned to Grant. "My granddad made it for me. It's a replica of a Victorian cottage. I still have it in my room."

"Yes, of course," Marian agreed. "Bring them any time. We often have children to visit, and they usually enjoy themselves."

"Thank you. That's very kind."

Rennie smiled at her mother, wanting to thank her, too. Marian gave her a searching look, and directed an interested one at Grant. "Any time," she repeated.

From then on the party seemed to look up for Rennie. Grant stayed by her side for most of the evening, although they were hardly exclusive. They laughed a lot, and talked, and once or twice she caught his gaze resting on her with a warmth that made her pulse beat faster. She gave him a dazzling smile, and his answering one was a little wry, but it didn't douse the light in his eyes.

When she left with her family, Rennie was careful not to insist that he bring the children to visit. She sat in the back of the car with Shane, her fingers firmly crossed, looking out the window. She jumped when Shane said suddenly, "He seems a decent bloke."

"Who?"

"You know who. But he's a lot older than you, isn't he? I hope you know what you're doing, Ren."

Maybe I don't, she thought. Not yet. Not exactly. But I know I want to find out more about this man—what he thinks, how he feels. I know I'm attracted to him, excited by him. And not only physically. Just talking to him gives me a buzz, a lift. And the fact that he knows more about life than I do, that he's experienced more, that's part of it. Perhaps that's why he seems more real to me than the younger men I've been out with.

Chapter Five

Two weeks later, Grant phoned on Sunday morning and asked Marian if he could take up her invitation to visit with the children. "After lunch, he said," Marian told Rennie.

"Why not for lunch? Did you ask him?"

"Darling, of course I asked him. He said he'd take them out for lunch and call in afterwards."

"He's being polite," Rennie said. "It doesn't sound as though he really wants to come at all."

Marian regarded her daughter thoughtfully. "He might just feel a bit diffident about descending on a strange household with two children." She paused. "Of course, it's possible the children are horrors, and that's why he's reluctant to inflict them on us for any length of time."

"Ellen isn't," Rennie said. She couldn't imagine any child of Grant's being a horror.

Toby was a sandy-haired little boy who seemed quietly self-possessed, saying hello politely and then taking stock of his surroundings while he stood with his hands behind his back.

"Daddy said you'd show us your doll's house," Ellen told Rennie.

"Yes. Would you like to see it now?"

"Yes."

Grant murmured, "Please."

"Yes, please," Ellen amended. "Toby, too."

"Of course, Toby too. Come on, I'll show you." She took the little girl's hand, and directed a questioning glance at Grant.

He shook his head. "I'll wait here." Rennie's father had offered him a drink when they arrived, and he was sitting on one of the cane chairs in the glass-walled conservatory that caught the available sun at the back of the house. As she left him with her parents, she felt as though the adults had sent the children off to play. But maybe he wanted a respite from his offspring. A pity, she thought as she showed Ellen and Toby how to open the hinged front of the doll's house and display the handmade furniture and tiny dolls inside. They seemed nice children, and he didn't have that much time with them.

"Are we allowed to touch?" Ellen asked.

"Of course." Kneeling by the child, Rennie took out one of the dolls and handed it to her.

"You'll be careful, won't you, Ellen?" Toby said.

Ellen nodded vigorously. "Is this the mummy doll?" she asked Rennie.

"That's right. And Toby can play with the daddy doll, if he likes." She handed him the one that was dressed in trousers and shirt, and in a few minutes the two of them were conducting a conversation, and moving the dolls from room to room.

Rennie sat on the bed and watched them, oddly reluctant to return to the conservatory. Toby and Ellen found two smaller dolls in another part of the doll's house and were now including them in the game, giving them high, squeaky voices. There seemed to be a pretend argument in progress, until the mother doll was brought in to quell it. Rennie was amused at the accurate rendition of adult inflection that Ellen managed to convey. Toby, bringing the father doll out of the Victorian parlour, deepened his voice and added a stern warning, sending the "children" upstairs to bed.

Rennie looked out of the window. The spring day was cool and breezy, although the sun was shining and most of the blossoms on the old plum tree in the back garden had fallen. When she and Shane were younger they used to climb it, going after the little dark red plums that grew in the topmost branches, even when the ground was littered with fallen fruit. Somehow those they had to climb for had tasted better.

She wanted to show Toby and Ellen the garden, too, with the swing and tree house. But they were absorbed in their game and she didn't like to disturb them. She stood up, thinking she would slip out. Toby was walking the father doll into the children's bedroom. "Good night," Toby made him say in his deepest voice. "You are very naughty children, and I don't want to live here any more."

Ellen's wail was so realistic that Rennie for a moment thought it was genuine, but she saw that it was supposed to be coming from the smaller dolls in the beds. Toby, changing character, joined in too. Then, reverting, he made the father doll kiss the children and stop their crying. "If you're very, very good," he said, "I'll come back."

Rennie stood riveted as Toby walked the doll out of the house and put it down on the carpet some distance away. Ellen picked up the mother doll and, taking it to the bedroom, began sniffing. "Daddy's gone, Daddy's gone away. You naughty, naughty children! Now stop talking and go to sleep! Daddy's not coming back, not ever, ever, ever!"

Rennie's throat was aching. She stayed very still, as Ellen moved the doll back to the kitchen and stood it at the sink. Toby swung shut the hinged front, picked up the male doll again and brought it up to the closed door of the house. "Knock, knock, knock," he said, just as a real knock sounded on the open bedroom door, and Rennie jumped.

"Sorry," Grant said, looking at her askance. "Your mother's offering juice and biscuits for the children in the kitchen, and a cup of coffee for you if you want it."

Ellen scrambled up and ran to catch his hand and drag him into the room. "Look, Daddy! It's got a real kitchen with all the pots and things, and a little tiny cradle for the baby, and a fireplace with a fire in it!"

Grant stooped and peered in as she pointed. "Yes, I see."

He spent a few more minutes admiring the various features his daughter pointed out, then straightened and said to Rennie, "It's good of you to let them play with it. I thought you were just going to allow them a quick look."

"It's meant to be played with. It's very sturdy."

"We were very careful, Daddy," Ellen assured him.

"Yes, moppet, I'm sure you were." He put his hand on her hair. "Now, do you want a biscuit and a drink before we leave?"

"You can't go yet!" Rennie exclaimed in disappointment. "I want them to see the tree house. And they haven't even had a swing."

"Swing, Daddy!" Ellen said enthusiastically.

"Aren't you tired of them?" Grant asked Rennie.

"Certainly not! I'm just getting to know them."

Grant shrugged. "Okay. But we mustn't outstay our welcome."

"You won't. Come on, you two." Automatically she held out her hands, and the children quite naturally took one each. "How would you like to have your afternoon tea in the tree house? My brother and I used to do that sometimes."

They took to the idea with enthusiasm and Rennie carried a tray out so that Grant could hand it to them when he had helped Ellen follow her brother up the ladder leading to the hut, weathered but still strong, which nestled in the wide fork of an old pohutukawa. One of the branches held the swing that she had spent hours on as a child. The garden was an old-fashioned half acre, and the few trees had had time to mature since the house was built almost eighty years before.

"It must have been a good place to grow up," Grant commented as she waved to the children and turned to go back to the house.

"It was. Mum sometimes makes noises about moving to a more modern house, easier to keep clean and with less garden. But I think she's rather fond of this one. Although she says she's just too lazy to do anything about it."

Grant laughed. "Lazy? I shouldn't think so. Your mother appears to me to be a bundle of energy. Your family is what's generally known as high achievers. I'm told you're an A student. And Shane is probably going to be dux of his school?"

"There isn't much doubt of that. He's always come top in most of his classes. Shane's the really clever one. I have to work at it. Who's been boasting? Dad?"

"The subject just happened to come up."

They were nearing the house when she stopped and turned to him. "Grant, there's something I think I should tell you."

His face closed. He looked towards the open door. "Are you sure?"

"Yes. It's important. You see, when the children were playing with—"

But she was interrupted by a shout of "Hey, Ren! Who's cooking tonight?" Followed by a casual, "Oh, hi, Grant." And Shane came bounding up the path from the road, with two other teenage boys trailing behind him.

"I am," she told him, before introducing Shane's friends to Grant.

"Tim and Sandy are staying for dinner, okay? We'll help you if you like," Shane offered.

"Just so long as you do the dishes," Rennie answered.

Somehow she and Grant got swept into the house with the boys, and she had no further chance to talk to him before he collected the children and took his leave.

She walked with him to the car, the children on either side of them. He ushered them into the back seat and supervised while they buckled their safety belts.

As he turned to say goodbye to her, she plucked at his sleeve and pulled him towards the gateway. "Did you know," she asked baldly, "that Toby and Ellen think it's their fault you left their mother?"

He looked a little impatient. "Amateur psychology, Rennie? You've only just met them. They didn't *tell* you this, did they?"

"Not in so many words, but—"

He shrugged. "Well, then—"

"Oh, please listen," she begged. "It's none of my business, I guess, but you should *know*." She told him about the game they had played with the dolls, and he shook his head, still only half convinced.

"Jean and I explained that it's nothing to do with them. It's one of the few things we still agree on. That the children must be protected from our—differences."

"Well, they seem to think it is."

He rubbed at his neck. "Then I don't know what to do about it." He touched her arm and said rather stiffly, "But thanks, Rennie. I appreciate your concern."

Watching the car drive away, she hoped he did. She had the impression that he was embarrassed and wanted to get away from her as quickly as possible. It couldn't have been pleasant to have an outsider telling him how his children felt about his seeming desertion of them. And an outsider was just what she was.

Exams loomed, and Rennie pushed aside everything else to concentrate on preparing for them. At least it gave her something to occupy her mind.

It was two days after Rennie's last exam that her mother told her, "Rennie, I heard some disturbing news today. Grant Morrison's wife—ex-wife—died suddenly."

Rennie felt an odd sensation in the pit of her stomach. "Died? When?"

"Yesterday, I believe. The funeral notice is probably in today's paper. Those poor children. And Grant—even though they were divorced, it will have been a shock for him."

"Yes." Rennie felt shocked herself. She had never known the woman, but Grant . . . "What can we do for him?"

"Not much, probably." Marian cast her a penetrating glance. "You're not close to him, are you, Rennie?"

Rennie shook her head sadly. She couldn't claim that.

"Then we can offer our sympathy, and tell him we'd like to help if he needs anything. But he probably has family, closer friends. They're the ones he needs now."

"Yes. I—don't even know how to get in touch with him. I suppose he's in the phone book, but should we ring?" He might feel it was an intrusion.

"We could send a note care of the law firm he's with. They'd pass it on."

"If he needs someone to baby-sit the children, I'll be free from now on. That might help," Rennie said. "I could offer."

"Yes, do that. And if he'd like them to come here for a few days, we can make room."

"Thanks, Mum. I'll write a note now. And I'll deliver it myself, first thing tomorrow."

The firm must have passed the letter on the same day, because in the evening Rennie answered the phone to Grant's voice. "Rennie?" he said. "Thank you for your note. It was very kind of you and your family. I'm grateful."

"Grant—I don't know what I can say. Are you all right? And the children?"

"I'm all right. And Toby and Ellen don't realise properly what's happened, yet. I suppose I don't either. When a thing like this comes so suddenly, it's hard to take it in."

"She hadn't been ill?"

"They think a brain embolism. It was very quick. She probably didn't know anything about it. She was shopping with Ellen. Ellen was frightened, of course, but the people in the store were very good, and the police did their best to keep her calm. Fortunately they were able to get hold of me reasonably quickly. I picked up Ellen from the police station and Toby from school and took them home.''

"Home? To your place or—"

"No, I'm staying at the house now. I thought it best that I move in with them, rather than disrupting their lives still further."

"Yes, of course."

"Rennie—did you mean what you said about helping?"

"*Yes*. Yes, of course I did!"

"Two of the neighbours have offered to baby-sit or have the kids over, but they have their own families to look after, and Ellen, at least, seems reluctant to leave the house."

"I'll come over."

"Tomorrow? I'll take some time off, but I need to spend a couple of hours at the office handing over half-finished work, and then there are arrangements to be made for the funeral.... The children took a fancy to you, and I know you'd be good with them. It'll just be for a few days."

She said, "I'm glad you asked. Give me the address."

The house was a large, modern brick bungalow with a small lawn in front where an abandoned tricycle and a sandpit in one corner proclaimed the presence of children. When Grant opened the door to her he looked paler than usual, and his cheekbones seemed more prominent. He hadn't shaved, and he wore a shirt that was only partly buttoned. She wanted to put her arms about him but felt strangely shy.

"Thanks for coming." He held the door open for her, and she stepped into a wide hallway.

"Am I too early?"

"No." He touched the stubble on his chin. "Sorry, I was hoping to make myself decent before the kids needed their breakfast, but they couldn't wait. They're in the kitchen."

"I'll go and say hello, shall I?"

He came with her. Toby and Ellen, seated at a cluttered table in a sunny window corner of the yellow and white kitchen, accepted her presence with obvious pleasure. There was cereal and sugar spilled on the table and a puddle of milk on the floor. Ellen greeted her with a tight hug about her thighs, clutching at her skirt.

"Ellen, wipe your hands—" Grant suggested, too late. He cast an apologetic glance at Rennie.

"It's washable," she assured him. Ignoring the sticky smears on the blue cotton, she bent to give Ellen a quick hug. Looking up at him over the child's fair head, she said, "You go and get tidied up if you like."

When he came back, shaved and with a tie on and his hair smoothly combed, she was supervising Ellen's buttering of a piece of toast and arbitrating over whose turn it was to have the picture card in the cereal box.

"Have you had breakfast?" she asked Grant.

"Don't worry about me. Get yourself anything you like, though."

"I had something at home. We'll be fine, if you want to leave us."

"Daddy?" Toby said. "Do I have to go to school today?"

"Not today, son. Maybe you could help Rennie look after your little sister. I have to go out for a while."

"To work?"

"Yes, but not all day. I'll be back soon after lunch, okay?"

He turned to Rennie. "If you can stay that long?"

"No problem. Take as much time as you need." She noticed Ellen was looking dubious, and said, "Ellen, how about we make your daddy a cake for his tea? Do you know how to make chocolate cake?"

Ellen shook her head.

"Mummy says chocolate's bad for you," Toby said.

There was a small silence. "Well, there are other kinds of cake," Rennie said. "How about carrot cake? Maybe your mummy wouldn't mind us making that, if you have some carrots. Do you know where there are some recipe books?''

"In the cupboard," Toby told her. "We're not allowed to touch them."

Ellen said, "Are you coming back for tea, Daddy?"

"Definitely. Before that. And I'll look forward to a nice big piece of cake. So don't you let Toby eat it all before I get here, okay?"

Toby chuckled, and Grant ruffled his hair, casting Rennie a grateful look over his head before he kissed both the children goodbye.

When he returned in the afternoon, Ellen was having a nap and Rennie and Toby were crawling round on the lounge floor. A wayward and apparently random construction of wooden building blocks and plastic railway lines covered most of the carpet.

Toby saw Grant first, giving him a tentative smile.

"Looks like you've been having fun," his father said.

"We'll put it all away before bedtime," Toby promised.

Rennie scrambled to her feet and said, "Did you get everything done?"

"Not everything." He saw her looking at the suitcase in his hand and said, "I called at my flat and collected some more clothes. I'll go and unpack them."

When he came out of the bedroom she had the kettle on. "Tea or coffee?" she asked him. "If Jean kept anything stronger, I can't find it. Perhaps you'd know—"

"No, there wouldn't be," he said. "Coffee's fine. But you shouldn't be waiting on me."

"You look as though you need it. Sit down. Black?" she confirmed.

He nodded, stirring in a spoonful of sugar from the bowl she placed on the table, shifting a couple of colouring books and some crayons out of the way. "Are you going to join me?"

"In a minute." She picked up one of the crayons that had rolled onto the floor and dropped it on the table with the others. "I won't give you carrot cake, because Ellen would want to be here when it's cut. But have you eaten? You didn't have breakfast, did you?"

"Didn't I? No, I suppose not. I had a couple of sandwiches at lunch time. Someone ordered them for me. Everyone's very kind."

"I could make you something—"

"No. Sit here with me. Please."

She poured coffee for herself and sat opposite him. "If there's anything I can do—"

He smiled at her. "You're doing it. Who made the children's beds?"

Rennie grinned back at him. "They helped. Toby's quite good at his, and Ellen was—enthusiastic."

"I didn't mean to leave them for you, but I seemed to run out of time. I can't tell you how grateful I am for this."

"You needn't be. I want to do it."

"There wasn't anyone else I could think of. My father's dead, and my mother's heart isn't good. When I take the children to visit her we can't stay very long, she gets too tired."

"What about the rest of your family?"

"My brother lives in Australia. There were only the two of us. And Jean's family are all in the South Island, though they'll be here for the funeral, of course. One of my partner's wives volunteered, but the children have never met her. At least you're someone they know. They've talked about you a lot, and the day they spent at your place. Wanted me to take them there again—"

"Why didn't you?"

He was silent for a moment. "Perhaps I would have."

"Do. When this is all over."

"Maybe. Thanks. You'll be wanting to get home."

"There's no hurry. Have your coffee before it gets cold."

He smiled faintly and lifted the cup.

"When will the funeral be?" Rennie asked him.

"Day after tomorrow. To give Jean's family time to get here."

"Did she come from a large family?"

"Two sisters and a brother. Her mother died years ago, her father's living with one of the sisters now. She wasn't particularly close to them. They've seen the children maybe four times since Toby was born."

"Are the children going to the funeral?"

"Some people have told me I should take them. Said they need to accept that their mother's dead, and attending the service helps. I don't know. What do you think?"

Rennie shook her head. "I'm no expert. And I don't know Toby and Ellen that well. I think...what's right for one child may not be right for another. You're their father."

He ran a hand into his hair. "Yes, but I hardly know them either. A few hours every second weekend. I'm just beginning to realise how little time I actually spent with them. Well, it's all got to change now. They're my responsibility."

"Daddy!"

They hadn't heard her, but Ellen had woken from her nap, and was barefoot in the doorway. She ran across the floor and flung herself into her father's lap, nearly spilling his coffee before he managed to put it down. "Daddy!" She wound her arms about his neck, holding on tight.

"Hello, moppet," he said. Then his arms went about her, and he hugged her to him, dropping his cheek against her hair, his eyes tightly closed.

Watching, Rennie felt tears sting her eyes. She got up and took her cup to the sink so that he shouldn't see.

Chapter Six

Rennie spent part of the next day with the children, but Grant sent her home soon after lunch.

Next morning he phoned, early. "I'll take the children with me to the funeral. Toby wants to come. Ellen, poor little scrap, doesn't understand what's happening, although I tried to explain. Says she wants Mummy to come home. Tomorrow's the weekend, and I'll stay home for the first couple of days next week to get some permanent arrangement sorted out. Thanks for your help, Rennie."

She felt a little let down as she replaced the receiver. He didn't need her any more. She didn't feel she should attend the funeral, but she couldn't help wondering how he and Toby were going to feel, and her heart went out to the little boy. And Ellen, who wanted her mother back home and didn't understand what death meant.

When her parents had left for work and Shane for school, she washed her hair and sat in the sun drying it, did a bit of desultory housework and tried to read a book. The telephone shrilled and she flew to answer it, with a premonition that it was Grant.

"Rennie?" he said. "Look, I'm awfully sorry to do this. Can you possibly come here after all? Ellen's hysterical. She won't let me take her out of the house. If you have other plans—"

"No. I'll be right over. I'll get a taxi."

By the time she got there, and was let in by a solemn-faced Toby, Grant had calmed Ellen, who was sitting on his knee. There were traces of tears on her flushed cheeks, and she had a thumb in her mouth.

"Hello, Ellen," Rennie said quietly, sitting down on the sofa beside them.

Ellen turned her head to her father's shoulder, giving a little hiccup. Grant gave Rennie a look of harassed apology. "Ellen, say hello to Rennie," he ordered.

"No, it's all right. Maybe she'll talk to me later, when she feels better."

Toby said, "She's not supposed to suck her thumb."

"Just for today," Rennie said. "Sometimes people need something for comfort."

Toby blinked rapidly. "I don't suck my thumb."

"No, you're older, aren't you? But you know, even grown-ups need comfort when they're sad. A hug or a cuddle is nice."

Toby looked slightly suspicious. "I don't want a hug," he stated firmly.

"That's okay."

"Sometimes I do," he conceded. "But not today."

"That's fine. I want them sometimes too."

Ellen lifted her head and turned to look at Rennie. Then she wriggled round and flung her arms about Rennie's neck.

"Thank you, Ellen," Rennie said. "That's a lovely hug."

When Grant murmured, "Toby and I have to go," Ellen became tearful again, but after repeated assurances that he would be back in time for tea, in the end reluctantly released him.

Rennie managed to keep her fairly well occupied and reasonably happy, although now and then her mouth would droop and her eyes take on a puzzled and saddened expression, but she asked no questions. Rennie dispensed hugs and stories, and invented games, and hoped that she was doing the right things.

In a corner of the lounge a table had been set up with cups and saucers, and some biscuits and cakes covered by a cloth. Obviously Grant was expecting people to come back after the funeral.

When he arrived, three or four other cars drew up behind his. Ellen ran to the door to meet him as he opened it, wound her arms about his legs and clung. Toby, looking pale and red-eyed, stood stolidly at his father's side, and Rennie smiled at him and moved forward to take his hand and draw him into the house as Grant picked the little girl up.

"I'll put on the kettle if you like," she told Grant.

"Thanks."

"Want to come and help, Toby?" she asked.

He nodded.

A couple of women came into the kitchen almost immediately. Rennie gathered that they were neighbours. They efficiently poured tea and coffee, and Toby was pressed into service handing round plates of biscuits. "Better to keep him busy, poor mite," one of the women said practically. Rennie was relieved to see the colour coming back into his cheeks.

Another woman asked Rennie, as she placed a sugar bowl on a tray, "Have you had much experience with children?"

"I've done a lot of baby-sitting," Rennie said. "Ellen and Toby are very good."

"Yes, Jean did a fine job. Never raised her voice. And yet the house always looked spotless—well, relatively, anyway. Made me feel like a total slob, and a harridan."

Rennie smiled. "You were friends?"

"I suppose," the woman said rather doubtfully. "We got on, and she was always willing to help if I got sick or anything. There aren't many of us stay-at-home mums left, and we have to stick together. I admired her. It can't have been easy after her husband left her."

"Wasn't it a mutual decision?" Rennie asked involuntarily.

The woman shrugged. "It was before we came to live here. She never said much, but I got the impression that he was a bit of a cold fish. Well, I suppose she was disillusioned. He seems nice enough. Oh," she added guiltily. "I shouldn't be gossiping about him to you."

Rennie stayed in the kitchen as much possible, not wanting to intrude on the grief of people who had known Jean. But she had to emerge eventually, and Grant, still holding Ellen in his arms, introduced her to a number of people before she unobtrusively edged her way out of the room and returned to the kitchen with some cups to wash.

When the visitors had all left, Grant came in holding Ellen's hand. "Thanks a lot, Rennie," he said. "I'll run you home in the car."

He couldn't leave the children, he would have to bring them as well. Ellen looked sleepy, Toby had already been subjected to a stressful day, and Grant himself was showing signs of strain about his eyes and mouth.

"No," she said. "I can find my own way home. But I don't need to go yet, if there's something more I can do."

He smiled wearily. "That's kind, but we've imposed enough. You needn't stay any longer."

"Why can't Rennie stay, Daddy?" Toby came into the room, his feet dragging a little.

"Because she has to go home sometime, Toby. We mustn't keep her too long."

"Can't she stay for tea?" Ellen asked.

Grant looked at her, and she said swiftly, "Yes, of course I can. I'll help you feed the children and put them to bed."

When that was accomplished, and the children had dropped almost immediately off to sleep, Grant and Rennie had coffee in the kitchen.

"I'll call you a taxi," Grant said. "You must let me pay your fare for this morning, too."

It wouldn't be any use arguing, she knew. "There's no hurry."

"Do your people know where you are?" Grant asked her suddenly.

"Yes, of course. I left a message."

"Good. I don't know what I'd have done without you. The last few days have been a nightmare. On top of everything else, getting those two settled for the night has taken me hours. Making sure they wash behind their ears and clean their teeth, and finding the right pyjamas. And the first night I scoured the house for Ellen's rabbit while she screamed till she was blue—" He shook his head wearily. "Jean had a point when she used to tell me I didn't know what it was like."

"I'm glad I could help."

He said, looking at her with tired eyes, "Yes. I think you are. There are good people in the world."

"You sound as though it surprises you."

He shrugged. "Sometimes one forgets."

"More coffee?" she asked as he emptied his cup.

He stared at it for a moment. "No, thanks. It's been a strange sort of day."

"Do you want to talk about it?"

He shook his head and got up. "I can't ask you to listen while I unload all my guilts and hang-ups." He took his cup to the sink and stood with his back to her, staring out the window at the slowly dying sunlight on the garden.

"You can if you want," Rennie said, pushing back her own chair and going to stand beside him. "If it would help."

Almost as if talking to himself, he said, "Jean had a—relationship with a man. I never knew him, though I'd gathered there was someone. He was there today. No one had told him. He read about it in the paper. That's a hell of a way to find out."

"Yes. But it's not your fault. Did he—imply that it was?"

"No, nothing like that. He didn't even say that they'd been close. Toby recognised him as 'Mummy's special friend.' But I'd guessed already. I knew by the look on his face. That's how *I* should have felt. She *was* my wife. Once."

"Did you mind?" Rennie asked softly. "That he was there?"

"No. He had a right. More than I did, perhaps. But he had no—status. It was awkward for him. He didn't want to come back here. Understandably."

"It must have been difficult for both of you."

"I wasn't married to Jean any more. We hadn't been close since before Ellen was born. But today I felt very close to her. As though I could—talk to her. Tell her—"

Rennie waited a moment. He was standing with his hands clenched, staring out at the sunset.

"Tell her what?"

"How sorry I was," he said. "That things had gone wrong for us. That I'd failed her, not made the sort of life for her that she pictured when she married me. That all the bright promise had gone to ashes in the end."

"I'm sure she knows."

He turned to face her. "Do you believe in life after death?"

"Don't you?"

"I don't know."

"Did Jean?"

"I don't think we ever discussed it. There were a lot of things we never discussed. Maybe that was the trouble."

"Maybe. What did you say to the children about that?"

"That when people die they can't be with us any more, that I don't know where they go, though some people say they go to heaven, which is a very beautiful place where everyone's happy and there's no pain and no sickness. And that wherever she is, I'm sure she's thinking about them and still loves them." He paused. "It felt very inadequate."

"Honesty can't be inadequate, surely," Rennie said. "They're bound to grieve, but they have you."

"Yes, and I'm all they have, for what it's worth." He said abruptly, "I'm scared."

Automatically, Rennie moved closer to him and slid her arms about him. His own arms came up and held her, a long sigh escaping from him. "After the divorce," he said, his voice muffled, "I tried to maintain contact. But I felt myself growing further and further away from them. Jean was sensitive about what she saw as interference with her child-rearing methods. Which was understandable. She had the day-to-day care. If we had different ideas, I had to concede the decision to her, because obviously it was important that we be consistent in our treatment of the children, otherwise they'd only get confused."

Rennie nodded. "It can't have been easy for you, though. You must have felt they didn't belong to you any more."

"Yes. Increasingly, as time went on. They saw more of the neighbours than they did of me. And now I'm their only parent."

"You'll do fine," she assured him. "You're great with them. Of course they'll miss their mother, but you'll make it up to them."

"Rennie," he said, rubbing his cheek against her hair. "I shouldn't be burdening you like this. You're too young."

"Rubbish. I'm glad you felt you could talk to me." In the last few days he had treated her like an equal, even asking for her advice.

"It was right, what you said to Toby about hugs. It's just what I need, to be held close to someone."

"I'm glad," she said again.

"It's been a long time..." He stopped, and she felt a change in him, his arms holding her tightly, his breathing controlled, but there was a new tension in the air.

She looked up then, and caught something in his eyes that she would not have seen in Toby's. She stared back gravely, her lips slightly parted, her heart beginning a slow, heavy pounding.

After a while he sighed again, loosened his hold and said, "I'll call that taxi for you."

As he dropped his arms from her she said, "You don't have to."

"It's the least I can do—I won't send you home in a bus."

"I meant," Rennie said, "you don't have to send me home. I could stay—if you like."

He went very still, looking into her clear, steady gaze. His hand touched her shoulder, moved gently up the side of her neck, and then he laid it against her cheek. "Rennie," he said. "You're very generous, but it wouldn't do. On a number of counts. But thank you." He bent and kissed the top of her head. "I'll get that cab."

Rennie phoned at the end of the following week, in the evening when she hoped Grant would be home. "I don't want to intrude," she said, "but I wondered how you and the children were doing."

"You're not intruding. And we're doing quite well. Toby's shed a few tears and asked some searching questions that I've done my best to answer. They're both a bit quiet, but the woman who's caring for them in the daytime seems confident they'll soon be back to normal."

"Do they like her?"

"I think so. She produced some very good references and has had children of her own, who've left home now. My two have to get used to her, of course. But they're fairly adaptable kids."

"I'd like to come and see them sometimes, if I may."

"Of course. I'll tell Mrs. Beddoe you may drop in. You haven't got yourself a holiday job?"

"Not yet. I've been looking, but they're not easy to get."

"If I hear of anything that might suit, I'll let you know."

"Thank you. If I visit, may I take the children out for a little while? Perhaps to an ice cream parlour or something. Unless you don't approve."

"I don't think an occasional treat will hurt them. You may have to talk Toby into it, though. He's inclined to be a bit rigid about things that he thinks his mother wouldn't have allowed them to do."

"Was Jean very strict?"

"Not unreasonably. A little more than I was, and of course since the divorce she was the one who made the rules and had to enforce them. She was a good mother. I think it's just Toby's way of keeping her presence in his life. Understandable, but a bit wearing."

But when Rennie called at the house and, after meeting the capable-looking woman who introduced herself as Mrs. Beddoe, asked the children if they would care to go on a bus trip to a play-park and have some ice cream with her, it was Ellen who said, "No. I don't want to go."

"Perhaps there's somewhere else you'd like to go?" Rennie suggested. "What about the Domain? Have you ever been there? There's lots of room to play, and we could feed the ducks on the pond."

"No," Ellen said unequivocally.

Mrs. Beddoe said, "Some of the children round about have asked her to come and play, the mothers have rung up to invite her, but she doesn't want to. I thought I might take them to the zoo the other day, but no. She'd rather stay home."

"We've been to the zoo," Toby said. "Lots of times."

Maybe Grant wasn't the only one who had been getting bored with the zoo. "Is there anywhere you'd like to go?" Rennie asked Ellen.

The child shook her head, and put her thumb in her mouth.

"Don't do that, Ellen," her brother admonished, and grabbed her hand, pulling it away.

Ellen began to sob quietly, tears pouring down her cheeks.

"Mr. Bossyboots," Mrs. Beddoe said, shaking her head. "Leave your sister alone, Toby." She knelt down by Ellen, put an arm about her and began drying her eyes with a handkerchief. "Big girls don't cry unless they're hurt, and they don't suck their thumbs."

"She's not allowed!" Toby said, red-faced.

"Not a big girl!" Ellen announced. "I'm only a *little* girl!" She sniffed, gave a final sob, and stared defiantly at them all.

Mrs. Beddoe laughed and patted her, getting up. "Little girls need afternoon naps. Maybe you need one now?"

Ellen looked uncertain. "No," she announced, and reached out to Rennie, taking firm hold of a handful of butter-yellow skirt. "I want to stay with Rennie." She pushed her head against Rennie's hip and looked at the other woman as though she was being threatened.

"They'll be all right with me," Rennie said, exchanging smiles with Mrs. Beddoe, "if there's anything you want to do."

"I wouldn't mind slipping out to the shops for a few things," the woman confessed. "Some of the cupboards are a bit bare, and Mr. Morrison said get anything I thought was needed. I wanted to go earlier but Ellen made such a fuss, and you said when you rang you'd be taking them out, so I thought I'd leave it till this afternoon."

When Mrs. Beddoe arrived back in her small car, the three of them were sitting on the front steps in the sun, and Rennie was reading to them from *The Paper Bag Princess*. They got up to help Mrs. Beddoe carry the groceries into the kitchen, and the two children willingly unpacked the bags while she and Rennie put the goods away.

"And for being so good, you deserve a chocolate biscuit each," Mrs. Beddoe said, removing two biscuits from their packet.

Rennie waited, and sure enough, "Chocolate's bad for you. Mummy said so," Toby declared.

Mrs. Beddoe hesitated only a moment. "I'm sure Mummy was quite right," she said. "Too much chocolate is certainly bad for anyone. And some people are allergic, which means even a little bit is bad for them. Did Mummy say you must *never* have chocolate?"

Toby thought, his eyes longingly on the biscuits in her hand. "Not never," he admitted cautiously. "When she had her birthday, her special friend gave her a box full of chocolates, and she said he shouldn't, but she ate one straight away, and she let us have some of them. But only one at a time. She said it was all right because it was a present.''

"Well, this is a present from me," Mrs. Beddoe said. "And you can only have one," she added firmly as she handed them over. "You mustn't spoil your tea. Go and eat them outside, so we don't have to sweep up the crumbs.

"Whew!" she said comically to Rennie as the children trailed out the door.

Rennie laughed. "You handled that awfully well."

"You get used to handling them—children. It comes with practice. Are you doing teacher training?"

Rennie shook her head. "No, but I like children."

"That's obvious. And these two like you. One of my daughters was a teacher. She has a little boy, and wants two more children, but she intends to go back to work once the youngest starts school."

"I must go," Rennie said, glancing at the clock. Grant had made it so obvious that he expected her visit to take place when he wasn't here, she didn't want him to find her hanging about as though waiting for him when he got home.

"Where do you live?" Mrs. Beddoe asked her.

"Meadowbank."

"Whereabouts?"

Rennie explained more fully, and she said, "Oh, I pass by there on my way home. I could drop you off if you like. Mr. Morrison will be home soon. I'll just get their tea ready for him to serve up."

It was a perfect excuse. Rennie allowed herself to be persuaded, and when Grant walked in half an hour later she was grating cheese while Mrs. Beddoe put the finishing touch to a salad and the children set the table, Ellen putting out the knives and forks and Toby the plates, carefully straightening the cutlery as he did so.

Grant seemed pleased to see her, Rennie thought with relief. Then he was picking up Ellen and greeting Toby, and asking Mrs. Beddoe how their day had been.

"And Rennie came to visit," Ellen told him, interrupting the reassuring answer Mrs. Beddoe was giving. "And she played in the sand with us, and read us stories and helped Mrs. Beddoe put the groceries away."

"Did she, indeed. And did you go out with Rennie?"

"No." Ellen wriggled, her face closing, and he put her down.

"Ellen didn't want to," Toby said.

"I see." Grant's glance went from her to the two women.

Rennie said, "Perhaps Ellen and Toby would like to visit me again sometime soon?" Looking at Ellen, she said, "You could play in the tree house again."

Toby said, "Yes, please. The tree house, Ellen!"

Ellen was silent.

"Would you like that, Ellen?" her father asked.

Ellen's thumb went into her mouth.

Grant crouched down to her level. "Wouldn't you like to go and see Rennie?"

Without removing her thumb, Ellen shook her head.

Grant looked up at the two women. "It seems we've got a problem," he said softly.

Mrs. Beddoe nodded. "Don't push it," she advised. "It's probably best to take things slowly. I have to be off, Mr. Morrison. I'm giving Rennie a lift. There's shepherd's pie for your tea. You can brown the cheese under the grill if you like, but keep an eye on it or it'll burn."

On the way home Rennie said, "Grant probably won't ask, but—Mrs. Beddoe, without going behind his back exactly, will you let me know if there's anything I can do?"

"Inviting the children to visit you was a good idea. They've obviously had a good time at your place before, and Toby wants to go. He might even bully Ellen into it. A nice lad, but he's a little manager, isn't he, and seems to feel responsible for his sister."

"More so since they lost their mother, I think."

"Quite likely. Everyone reacts differently to grief, even children. And Mr. Morrison—"

"What about him?"

"I don't know him well, of course. But it seems to me he's a man who would push his own feelings aside instead of dealing with them, while he takes care of everyone else's problems. He seems to be coping almost too well with his wife's death. In my experience that's sometimes not a good sign."

"They were divorced," Rennie said.

"Yes, he told me. He was frank about the family's circumstances, because of the children. Said I needed to know. Still, she was their mother. And when two people have been married—divorce can't change what they've already shared. Some people, of course, end up hating each other. That's tragic."

"He didn't hate her," Rennie said. He had spoken with respect and regret of his ex-wife.

"No," Mrs. Beddoe ageed thoughtfully. "He doesn't seem to be a vindictive man. When he talks about her he sounds quite dispassionate. 'Their mother,' he calls her to me. Shows no emotion about her at all. But he must have felt something for her."

Chapter Seven

Grant phoned again one Sunday and asked Marian if he could bring the children over.

"Of course," she told him. "Rennie told me about the problem with Ellen. I'm glad she's decided to come."

When they arrived, Toby barely asked for permission before making straight for the tree house, calling over his shoulder, "Come on, Ellen."

But Ellen wouldn't leave her father until he offered to take her into the garden. Once persuaded to climb into the hut and join her brother, she kept peeking out to make sure that Grant was still within calling distance.

Rennie joined him where he sat on a garden seat built around the trunk of an old English oak.

He smiled at her. "It's progress of a sort," he said. "This is the first time I've been able to get Ellen to leave the house. Even at home she's constantly checking where I am. And Toby. I guess she isn't sure any more that anyone's going to be around forever."

"Mrs. Beddoe said she'll get over it."

"I was lucky to find that woman. I'd hoped to get some-one to live in, but the only applicants who were willing had children of their own. I felt that at this stage my two needed somebody's undivided attention."

"Daddy?" Ellen's anxious face looked out of the tree house doorway, and Grant gave her a reassuring wave.

"Looks like I'm stuck here for a while," he said to Ren-nie. "I hope your parents don't think me terribly rude."

"Of course not. They understand."

"If you want to go in..."

"No, I'm fine here." It was a pleasantly warm day, and there was a bee buzzing among the daisies on the lawn, and a few tiny blue-grey moths teetered on blades of grass. Time Shane did some mowing. "I could bring you a drink if you'd like one."

Grant shook his head. "I'm all right."

Hesitantly she asked, "Do you remember what I told you, about the time they were playing with my doll's house?"

He looked up tiredly. "Yes. I mentioned it to Jean. I thought maybe she might have inadvertently let some of her resentment against me show—"

"What did she say?"

"She was angry at the suggestion. And angry that some-one else had picked up that the children were bothered. Just as I was," he admitted, giving her a faint, apologetic smile. "But when we'd settled our emotions, we talked to the chil-dren, together. I hope it got through. I don't really know."

"I wouldn't have brought it up again, but—"

"I know. Jean's death could make it all worse. They have their father back, at the cost of losing their mother."

"How are *you* coping?" she dared to ask him. "Emo-tionally?"

He looked down at her with a hint of amusement. "You're not studying psychology, are you?"

She met his eyes defiantly. "I'm expressing a friendly in-terest, not writing a thesis. You do have emotions, don't you?"

His eyebrows lifted. A faint spark lit his eyes, then was deliberately doused. "I don't have any room to indulge them. The children and my job are my concern right now. That's all I have time for."

"Do you have any close friends you can talk to?"

Grant moved restlessly. "Look, I'm not into baring my soul to anyone, Rennie. I know you mean well, but I'm accustomed to shouldering my own burdens, thanks. I don't need to share them out among my long-suffering friends, who have troubles of their own."

"Well, if you need an extra shoulder—"

He touched hers lightly with one hand. "This one? Thanks, but it would be grossly unfair. And unnecessary. How's the job hunting?"

"No good. Too many students after too few temporary jobs."

"Your father doesn't have a space in his office?"

"He's already given me some of the field experience I need for my course credits. But I don't want to rely on him. I'd like to be able to find a place myself, maybe even do something a bit different for a change, rather than law. Widen my experience. Meantime Mum says it's nice to come home every night to a meal cooked by someone else, anyway."

"I can appreciate that. I like having Mrs. Beddoe do the cooking and cleaning. That's one burden I don't mind offloading."

After the children were persuaded to come inside for drinks, and Toby was engrossed in a book of aeroplanes which Rennie's father had found among the books in the lounge, Rennie asked Ellen casually if she would like to see the doll's house again. When Grant made to rise, she gave him a covert warning with her eyes, and he stayed where he was as she held out her hand to Ellen.

The little girl took it, gave Grant an uncertain glance, and then went with Rennie.

"You can play with it if you like," Rennie told her, but Ellen shook her head, clinging to Rennie's hand, and just gazed at the doll's house, her thumb in her mouth.

"That's okay," Rennie said after a minute or so. "Would you like me to read you a story?"

Ellen nodded, and Rennie showed her the small collection of specially loved childhood books she could not bring herself to part with. Ellen chose a thick illustrated volume of fairy tales, and snuggled comfortably up to Rennie on the bed through two stories before she became restless and Rennie said, "Shall we go and find your daddy?"

Ellen nodded, wriggling off the bed and trotting to the door. When they appeared again in the other room, Grant looked up enquiringly and Rennie gave him a reassuring smile as Ellen clambered onto his knee.

"I want to go home now," she announced.

Grant gave Marian an apologetic look and said, "Okay, moppet. Say thank you to Mrs. Langwell. You ready, Toby?"

He added his own thanks, and as Rennie walked to the car with him, the two children going on ahead, he said, "It went better than I expected. You did wonderfully well with Ellen."

"I'm sure she'll come right if she's not forced. It must have helped that they'd been here before, so it wasn't totally unfamiliar territory. And she knew you were nearby."

"It's a big step. Thanks." He brushed his lips against her cheek before stepping forward to unlock the car.

On Wednesday evening Rennie went to a film with a group of friends. She came home to find a note on the telephone pad in Shane's scrawled hand. "Call Grant Morrison."

She had stayed in town for a late supper, and it was after eleven. Shane's room was in darkness, and when she peeked in he was a humped, still shape in the bed. If she shook him awake he wouldn't be pleased, and probably couldn't tell her any more. She would have to wait until morning.

She phoned Grant's number at eight o'clock.

"Thank heaven!" he exclaimed. "Rennie, are you still looking for a job?"

"Yes. You've heard of something?"

"You might say that. Mrs. Beddoe's daughter in Christchurch has had an accident—she's in hospital with broken bones and some internal injuries. It isn't clear yet how bad. Naturally Mrs. Beddoe wants to get down there as soon as possible, but she's anxious about Toby and Ellen. We both think it could be disastrous for Ellen to bring in another stranger when she's hardly had time to get used to Mrs. Beddoe. She suggested you might step in. I wonder—"

"Yes," Rennie said. "Yes, of course. I can start today if you like. Now, in fact."

"You're sure?"

"Absolutely. I'll be there in about half an hour."

"Make it an hour," Grant told her. "I can hold the fort until then. I'll drive Toby to school and take the morning off to show you the ropes and ease Ellen into the new situation."

Ellen accepted with apparent equanimity that Rennie was going to take Mrs. Beddoe's place, and even let her father go to work with a minimum of fuss, although afterwards she wouldn't let go of Rennie, and insisted on being read story after story until Rennie was hoarse.

Rennie suggested a walk, but Ellen shook her head decisively. Games and a sleep were similarly vetoed. Finally Ellen took her thumb from her mouth and said, "Make a cake."

They were in the middle of it, both of them liberally sprinkled with flour, Ellen's hands happily covered in sticky dough, when she said suddenly, "Daddy said Mummy died because she was sick."

Rennie carefully continued scraping the wooden spoon in her hand with a knife. "Daddy's right," she said.

"He said she didn't want to go away."

"I'm sure she wanted to stay with you and Toby," Rennie told her firmly. "But sometimes, no matter how much we want to, we can't stay with the people we love."

"Daddy said he loves us very much."

"Yes, darling, he does. He always loved you, even when he wasn't living with you."

"He said he's going to live with us for always, now." Ellen lifted her hands and spread the pudgy fingers. "My hands is all gooey, Rennie."

"That's all right. We'll put some flour on them and it will come off easily."

Rennie spun the process of baking out as long as she could, and afterwards Ellen consented to having an afternoon nap. She was still asleep when Toby came home from school. Rennie gave him juice and a cracker with cheese, and listened to him read from a school reading book.

"What are we having for tea?" he asked her.

"Steak," she told him. She had found some in the freezer.

"Can we have gravy?"

"Do you like gravy?"

Toby nodded. "Mrs. Beddoe makes lots of gravy. She puts stuff in it."

"What sort of stuff?"

"I'll show you." He led the way into the kitchen and pointed. "Up there."

Rennie opened the high cupboard he had indicated. It was full of sauces, pickles and flavourings.

"I'll lift you up," she suggested, "and you show me which one."

He knelt on the counter under the cupboard and peered at the shelves. "This one!" he said at last, and made a grab for a bottle of soya sauce. As he pulled it out, it knocked against an adjacent bottle of tomato sauce, which fell to the bench and smashed, splashing its contents over Toby, Rennie, the counter and finally the floor, where it spread around the broken pieces of the bottle.

"Don't move, Toby!" Rennie said sharply, as the boy seemed about to overbalance. She lifted him and swung him away from the mess and onto the floor, taking the soya sauce bottle gently from his hand.

He had gone pale, and his eyes widened and filled with tears. "I didn't mean to!" he said. "I didn't mean to be naughty! I didn't!"

"You weren't naughty!" Rennie assured him. "It was an accident, that's all. I wasn't angry with you, I just didn't want you to cut yourself." She pulled a paper towel from the roll on the wall and began wiping some of the tomato sauce off his clothes.

Toby sniffed. "It was an accident," he repeated, evidently not very convinced.

"Yes, it was. Everyone has accidents sometimes. You didn't do anything wrong."

"I'm sorry," he whispered. "You've got tomato sauce on you, too."

"I know. I bet I look funny!" she added lightly. "You do. Your father will think we're a couple of sausages."

But he wasn't to be laughed out of it. "Will he be angry?" he asked fearfully.

"No, of course he won't. It wasn't your fault, Toby. And it'll wash off. Don't worry about it."

By the time Grant came home she had Toby's clothes soaking in the laundry, and had sponged the worst of the stains off her own T-shirt and jeans. But Grant's eyebrows rose as she greeted him. "What happened to you?"

Before she could answer, Ellen flew past her and Grant bent to lift the child into his arms. As Ellen buried her face in his shoulder, he looked at Rennie again. "Is someone hurt?" he asked sharply. "Where's Toby?"

"It's all right," she said. "It's not blood, it's tomato sauce. Toby's in his room, getting into some clean clothes."

"Clean clothes? He had clean clothes this morning. Is he covered in tomato sauce, too, by any chance?"

"By some chance," Rennie admitted. "Don't growl at him, will you? It was an accident."

"I certainly hope so," Grant said mildly. "What makes you think I'd growl at him?"

"I don't. But he seemed very anxious, as though he expected someone would."

"I'll go and talk to him. Oh, do you want to leave now? It's well after five."

Ellen, who had been silently hugging her father, suddenly twisted in his arms. "No!"

Rennie looked at her panic-stricken face and went to her swiftly. "It's all right, Ellen, I'll come back tomorrow."

"*No!* Don't go 'way, Rennie! Don't go 'way!"

None of Rennie's or her father's reassurances could console her, and she became more and more frantic, until Grant, prising her arms away from Rennie's neck, told Rennie, "Just go. She'll settle down eventually."

Ellen was screaming, now, her cheeks red and tear-streaked. Grant's face was taut with strain. "Stop it, Ellen!" he said sternly, his arms close about her as she flailed against him. "That's enough, sweetheart. Come on, now."

Toby had come out of his room and was standing in the doorway, watching. Reluctantly, Rennie started towards the door with her bag.

Toby looked at her. "Is Ellen being naughty?" he asked nervously.

"No, Toby." Rennie went down on her knees. "She's just upset because I have to go home."

"Why do you have to?" he asked. His gaze was almost accusing, and Rennie felt like a deserter.

"I'll be back tomorrow," she said again. "I'll be here every day."

"That's what Mrs. Beddoe said."

And Mrs. Beddoe, of course, had instead flown to her daughter's side. Quite rightly and naturally, but how could Toby and Ellen be expected to understand?

She gave Toby a hug and stood up to leave. Ellen's screams had increased in volume, and Grant was just holding her tightly, alternately shushing her and murmuring into her ear, his own expression tortured.

"I don't have to go," Rennie heard herself saying to Grant. "You've got a spare room, haven't you?"

She saw the quick hope in his face, that he extinguished immediately. "We can't expect that from you. Go on home."

"No." She crossed the room again and before she even got there Ellen had flung herself into her arms. She sat down with the child on the nearest armchair and began stroking her hair.

"She'll have to learn eventually," Grant said, rubbing a hand through his own hair, "that she can't get everyone to do what she wants by screaming about it."

Rennie shook her head. "It's more than that." She glanced down at Ellen, who had stopped screaming but was sobbing heavily, and wetting Rennie's already abused T-shirt with her tears. "We can't talk about it now. But I'll phone home and ask Shane to bring over my toothbrush and pyjamas. And a change of clothes," she added ruefully.

Toby came over to the chair and stared at his sister, then at Rennie. "Are you going to stay?" he asked.

"Yes," Rennie answered, as Grant said, "No."

Rennie and Toby both looked at him, and Ellen burrowed closer to Rennie, one hand gripping the sleeve of her T-shirt.

"I think I am," Rennie said calmly, still looking at Grant.

"There's no need—we can't—" Grant started. Then he shrugged. "What are your parents going to say?"

Rennie smiled. "That I'm doing the only thing possible. They certainly won't think that you've seduced me, if that's what you're worried about."

Relief warred with doubt in his face. "I shouldn't let you," he said. "But thank you."

After the children had been settled for the night, Rennie made up the bed in the spare room, refusing Grant's offer of help. When she came back into the lounge, Shane was there, swinging an overnight bag in one hand, and talking to Grant.

"I didn't hear you come in," she said, taking the bag from him. "Thanks for bringing my things."

"No problem."

Grant said, "Can I offer you a drink or something?"

Shane shook his head. "Not while I've got the car, thanks. Mum would have my guts for garters."

"Not necessarily alcoholic," Grant said. "Coffee, maybe, with some of your sister's cake?"

"Rennie's been making cakes?"

"Ellen and I," Rennie told him. "She wanted to make one for her father."

"I can recommend it," Grant told him. "And you'd be helping me out. If my daughter insists on baking too regularly, I'm likely to develop a serious weight problem. I have to eat her cakes so as not to hurt her feelings, but I'm sure she won't mind if I offer some to Rennie's brother."

In the end the three of them sat over coffee and cake and talked for a couple of hours. Grant seemed more relaxed than Rennie remembered seeing him, and he spoke to Shane as an equal, although her brother was so much younger. When he had gone, and she came back to the kitchen to find Grant rinsing cups and putting them on the draining board, he said, "A nice lad, your brother."

"He liked you, too," she answered, automatically taking a tea-towel from the rail and beginning to dry.

"We can leave them to drain if you like."

"It'll only take a minute, and I can put them away. I was thinking—"

"Yes?"

"You said you'd have preferred someone living in. I could, you know. Then Ellen needn't be afraid that I won't come back the next day. I'll be right here."

Grant said doubtfully. "Maybe pandering to her isn't the right thing—"

"It isn't pandering. She lost her mother, and then Mrs. Beddoe." She didn't add that her father's leaving hadn't helped. Grant knew it already. "She doesn't trust anyone to stay around any more. The world's a scary place for her. She needs absolute security for a while, surely? Someone who's always there. And you can't be. You have to work."

"I've been wondering if I should give it up. Stay home and be a father."

"And live on the Domestic Purposes Benefit? Your standard of living would drop drastically, wouldn't it? The children's, too. More alterations to their lives. There's no need for that. As long as I'm here—"

"And how long will that be? The children will come to depend on you more than they do now, and then your holidays will be over and you'll go back to university."

"Leave that aside for the moment. I won't let you down. Mrs. Beddoe may be back by then. And in three months Ellen might be her normal self. I'll do my best to see she doesn't remain dependent on me."

Chapter Eight

"Did you talk to Toby?" Rennie asked, putting away the last cup.

"Yes. I hope I said the right things."

She told him about her conversation with Ellen. "I hope I said the right things, too."

"Sounds fine to me. You're young to be so wise."

"It's just common sense," Rennie answered crisply. She wished he wouldn't keep reminding her of her youth.

He rinsed out the sink and dried his hands, straightening the towel on its rail afterwards. Watching, she said, "You're very domesticated, aren't you?"

Grant glanced up. "I've had to learn, living on my own, since I don't enjoy inhabiting a pigsty."

"Did Jean do it all before the divorce?" She caught herself up immediately. "Sorry, I shouldn't have said that."

"It's okay." He looked wry. "Jean was a perfectionist in everything. She made me feel incompetent. No," he amended quickly. "That's unfair. I *was* incompetent. My parents believed that the man was supposed to be the breadwinner, that housework and babies were women's work. So I'd never been taught any skills in that area. My bungling efforts to help understandably irritated her. It was easier to do everything herself than try to teach me how. She was extremely efficient.''

Rennie remembered the neighbour who had talked of her own feelings of inadequacy compared with Jean. She looked about the kitchen. There were still traces of flour on the floor under the table where she'd missed sweeping them up after the baking session. In a corner near the stove she saw a piece of jigsaw puzzle, and on the bench was a little heap of paper, a board book and some crayons that she had moved hastily from the table when she'd given Toby and Ellen an afternoon snack and Ellen had spilled some milk.

Recalling the neatly folded clothing and undies in the children's drawers, the labelled shelves for their toys and books, she didn't suppose she came anywhere near Jean's standards of housekeeping.

"Was she a career homemaker?"

"She made herself into one," Grant replied. "She was studying law when we met. The plan was that she would complete her degree after we married, and then we'd start a family. It didn't quite happen that way."

"Toby?"

"Yes, Toby came along unexpectedly, and Jean left university to be a full-time mother."

"Her decision, or a joint one?" Rennie asked softly, struck by a terseness in his tone.

He hesitated. "Hers, in the end. But there had been a lot of acrimonious discussion beforehand. I told her we could get baby-sitters or use a crèche so she could finish her studies. But apart from the complications of taking a difficult degree under such conditions, which she pointed out—and she was quite right—Jean didn't believe in letting other people bring up her kids. At first she regarded the pregnancy as a tragedy. She even talked of abortion. That led to a major row that lasted for weeks. I still don't know if I talked her out of it or she changed her mind when she felt the baby moving.''

"And now you wonder if you were wrong,'' Rennie suggested.

"It wasn't as though her health was at stake,'' he said. "And it was my baby, too. I promised I'd support her all the way if she wanted to study part-time, or go back to university when Toby went to school. But then, I wasn't the one having to carry the child, and put my career goals on hold.''

"Five years,'' Rennie said. "And what about Ellen?''

"Yes, Ellen. When Jean suggested we should have another child I was staggered. Of course she loved Toby when he was born. And she reckoned that if we were going to have a family—i.e. the regulation 2.5 children—we might as well have them close together, rather than disrupt her life a second time.''

Answering Rennie's unspoken thought that a four-year gap wasn't so close, he added, "She miscarried that second pregnancy.''

Rennie made a soft exclamation.

"She was four months on,'' Grant said, his eyes darkening as he looked at Rennie without seeing her, immersed in past tragedy. "There was no hope of saving the baby. And Jean was shattered. I don't think she'd ever failed at anything before. I thought she should take a rest, recover her strength. Jean wanted to try again immediately. And nothing happened. But she was determined. It became something of an obsession. We lived on a knife edge until Ellen was born. I couldn't believe we'd produced this perfect little girl.''

"And Jean didn't complete her degree?''

"She started doing some correspondence courses towards it after our separation. Said she had more time. I suppose that was true. But while we were together—no, she was busy being the best damn mother in the neighbourhood.'' His mouth twisted wryly. "Jean never did anything by halves.''

Grant paused, the look in his eyes as they momentarily focused on her making Rennie slightly uncomfortable. "All the trauma didn't bring us closer, it had driven us further apart. It wasn't Jean's fault. She did her best to knit us into a family, but her heart wasn't in it. And by that time, neither was mine."

He straightened from where he had been lounging against the counter, his face closing. "I'm turning into a bore, rabbiting on about my past life."

"I'm not bored—" Rennie protested, but she knew there was no chance of hearing any more that evening. He had already said more than he'd meant to, and was probably regretting taking her so far into his confidence.

"You should go home for the weekend, Rennie," Grant said on Friday night.

"Do you think Ellen is ready for that?" Rennie asked.

"We can't keep you tied to us seven days a week!"

"I don't mind. You needn't pay me for the weekend if it's a problem."

"That's not the problem," Grant said rather shortly. "Of course I'll pay you. What have your parents got to say about all this?"

"Nothing."

"They've hardly had a chance yet, have they?" Grant had not been home when her mother brought a suitcase full of clothes for Rennie and obliquely hinted that she shouldn't allow herself to grow too fond of either the children or their father.

"I'm already fond of them," Rennie had confessed frankly. "And I can't leave them in the lurch, can I?"

Marian sat down on the bed. "No. I wouldn't want you to. But I don't want you getting hurt, either."

Rennie said, "You can't protect me forever. And I'm old enough to take that risk."

Marian was silent for a moment. "Yes. I suppose you are. But Rennie, do think before you—well, before you do anything. You're such an impetuous soul."

"What's Dad been saying?"

Marian laughed. "This isn't only Dad talking. It's me, too." She stood up. "I have to go back to work. Let us know if you need anything else. And darling, take care."

"My mother's not worried," she told Grant. "And my father—well, he worries about everything."

"Not without reason where you're concerned, I should think."

She made a face. "You make me sound like some kind of juvenile delinquent."

He laughed. "Sometimes I wonder."

She tried to be angry, but instead she heard herself say, "That's the first time I've heard you laugh properly since—"

"There hasn't been much to laugh about lately."

"No. Ellen is getting more confident, though. Today she played outside for half an hour with the little girl from over the road, and never even looked for me."

"That's good."

"Yes. But we'll have to take it slowly. I don't think I should try to leave her just yet."

"Well...if you're happy to work Victorian hours... though heaven knows what any trade union would have to say."

"I won't tell them if you don't," Rennie promised.

In the event, she went home for a short while, but with Grant and the children along. Ellen, coaxed to say where she would like to go for an outing, stated a firm preference for "Rennie's place", and although Grant tried to change her mind, she was immovable.

"It's okay," Rennie assured him. "You did want me to go home, after all."

"Not dragging us all behind you like Little Bo Peep with her sheep," he protested. "I thought you'd like to get away from the Morrisons for a while."

"Well, I wouldn't. And I keep telling you my family *likes* having visitors. Besides, Ellen feels safe there."

"Yes, I suppose she does. But there must be other places."

"Give her time," Rennie said.

Toby ran for the tree house after greeting Rennie's parents. Ellen followed, but without letting go of Grant's hand until they reached the ladder and he helped her up it.

Marian brought out a tray for the children, and said to them casually, "You two will be all right while the grown-ups have a drink inside, won't you? You know where to find us if you need us."

Rennie held her breath. Toby said, "Yeah. Thank you, Mrs. Langwell. Say thank you, Ellen!"

"Thank you, Mrs. Langwell."

Marian came back to Rennie and Grant. "Okay?" she murmured.

Grant nodded, and took Rennie's arm. The two children remained in the tree house, their voices happy and unworried.

Later they came inside and with Rennie's permission Ellen dragged her brother off to play again with the doll's house.

Exchanging a glance with Grant, Rennie waited a few minutes before casually following them. Grant silently got up and came along. By tacit consent they stopped just short of the bedroom door, listening.

Evidently Ellen was enacting the part of the baby doll, giving a high, convincing wail. Then she became the mother, soothing, "There there, don't you cry, baby. Mummy loves you."

"Daddy loves you, too," Toby's deepened voice said.

"And Rennie," Ellen added. "Everybody loves you!"

Rennie and Grant exchanged a smiling glance and tiptoed back to the other room.

Listening to Ellen chattering away in the back seat on the way home, Grant turned to Rennie and smiled.

She smiled back triumphantly. "I told you," she said quietly. "She'll be fine, soon."

"I almost dare to believe you. There's some magic about your home. Perhaps because it's so obviously a happy one."

"Don't you come from a happy home?" she asked before she thought.

She wondered if he wasn't going to answer. Then he said, "Not particularly. And I didn't manage to make one for my children, either. Or my wife," he added in a low voice.

"I'm sure it wasn't your fault!"

His glance at her held an exasperated cynicism. "Your faith in me is touchingly naïve, Rennie, but totally misplaced. You know nothing about the complications of an adult relationship."

Rennie flushed and turned away, clamping her lips together.

After a moment, he put out his hand and clasped hers. "I shouldn't snarl at you. It's damned ungracious, considering all you're doing for me."

Childishly, she snatched her hand away. "I'm doing it for the children."

He put his hand back on the wheel. "Yes, of course," he agreed. "And I'm—"

"If you tell me once more that you're *grateful,*" she flashed, "I'll probably scream!"

"Then I won't. Ellen couldn't stand the competition."

Rennie smiled reluctantly. "It's a job," she said. "You are paying me, after all."

"Yes," he agreed. "Maybe we should both remember that."

Did that mean he thought she'd been presumptuous? Rennie sat stiffly, trying not to feel hurt, until Grant slid the car into the garage, turned to the children and said, "Right, you can undo your safety belts now."

He came round to open the door for Rennie, but she was already scrambling out, ignoring the hand he offered to help her. Grant stepped back without comment, but the look he slanted at her was a trifle ironic. Rennie pretended not to notice.

Later that evening he said, "I feel like a small celebratory drink, in honour of Ellen's first outing. How about you?"

Wondering if it was a peace offering, she answered, "If you think I'm old enough. Thank you."

Ignoring the taunt, he said, "There isn't a great deal of choice. Still white or sparkling? Or whisky, if you like."

"Let's open the bubbly," she suggested. "Unless you prefer whisky?"

He shook his head. "The occasion deserves something special. Stay there. I'll get it."

He came back with two wine-glasses and the opened bottle, a wisp of vapour escaping from its top. "I haven't any champagne flutes here," he said. "These will have to do."

He poured the wine and passed one to her. "Here's to Ellen's first step into freedom from fear," he said, joining her on the sofa where she sat with her feet tucked under her.

"To Ellen," Rennie said solemnly, and touched her glass to his before sipping at it.

"Thank goodness Toby's all right."

Rennie looked up quickly, then down again at her glass. But Grant had seen her glance.

"What?" he said softly, resignedly.

He had enough worries on his plate, Rennie decided. She shook her head. "Nothing. Toby's fine."

"But . . . ?" Grant persisted.

"He's fine," Rennie reiterated. "He isn't quoting his mother nearly so often. That's a good sign isn't it? We don't want him to forget her, exactly, but he's accepting that she isn't around to—correct him any more."

"Jean didn't beat them, you know. She didn't believe in hitting kids, as a matter of fact. That was something we did agree on."

He had never mentioned anything that they thoroughly disagreed on, Rennie realised.

She nodded soberly. "Toby's a very good boy."

"Yes, thank heaven."

"Was he always?" she asked carefully.

"Of course not. He's got the normal amount of mischief in him. He isn't a little angel."

"He has been lately," Rennie said tentatively. "He never does anything wrong deliberately, and if he does so accidentally he gets very worried about it."

Grant sighed, looking harassed. "Are you trying to tell me something?"

"I'm not a child psychologist," Rennie said. "But I just wondered if while we've been sorting out Ellen's problems, which are obvious, Toby's quietly struggling with his own. I think it might be a good idea if you took some time to explain to him very clearly that his mother's death wasn't their fault either."

Grant looked appalled. "He can't think that!"

"I don't know," Rennie said. "He's quiet and polite, and doesn't give much away. He's like you in lots of ways."

Grant looked faintly quizzical, but didn't say anything. He drained his cup and stood up restlessly, shoving a hand through his hair, took a couple of steps towards the window, then turned and leaned against the wall. "I thought you considered me rather rude."

Rennie looked up. "Not rude. Insulting in a polite kind of way."

"I never intended to be insulting."

"Well, heaven preserve me when you do intend it, then!" Rennie said.

He laughed. "Should I apologise?"

"That isn't necessary." She couldn't help smiling at him. He had taken off his tie, and the top of his shirt was open, his sleeves rolled up, since he had helped the children with their baths. She was suddenly conscious that he was a very attractive man, and to hide her expression she buried her nose in her glass and drank deeply. "You can pour me some more wine instead," she said, holding out the half-empty glass.

"Slow down," he advised, even as he obeyed. "At this rate I'll be carrying you to bed."

Her eyes flew to his, and she saw him realise what he had said. He removed the bottle just before the glass overflowed. "Strike that from the record," he added as he straightened. "An unfortunate turn of phrase."

Rennie watched him position the bottle on the table, then go to sit down again on the sofa. "Or a Freudian slip," she said recklessly.

"Very possibly." His tone was equable, his expression quite urbane. Perhaps she was imagining the tension she could feel emanating from him. He finished the wine in his glass, put it down and said, "Well, I brought some work home. I'm going to commandeer the kitchen table."

She watched him as he left the room without a backward glance, and a little later glimpsed him going into the kitchen with a briefcase in his hand. Thoughtfully she poured the rest of the wine into her glass, and finished it slowly. The kitchen light was still on when she decided to go to bed.

Coming out of the bathroom, pulling on a pink terry cloth robe, she met him in the narrow passageway. She'd had a hot shower and her face was free of makeup, her feet bare.

Clutching her sponge bag, she stopped in front of him. He surveyed her from the slipping topknot of red hair to her toes, and his mouth quirked.

"Don't say it!" she warned him, guessing at his thoughts.

He raised his brows. "You know what I was going to say?"

"Something along the lines of: 'You look about twelve years old!'" Rennie hazarded.

"Well . . ." he drawled.

"I'm not!" she told him quite fiercely. "And don't you forget it!"

Suddenly austere, the teasing light disappearing from his eyes, he said, "I'm not likely to. Good night, Rennie."

He stepped aside rather pointedly, and she marched past him, closed her bedroom door ostentatiously and threw the sponge bag onto the bed, muttering an extremely rude word under her breath.

At breakfast Toby asked if he might bring a friend home after school.

Grant shrugged in answer to Rennie's enquiring glance. "It's up to you."

"If your friend's mother doesn't mind," she said immediately, "it's fine with me. Should I phone her?" she queried Grant.

"Mummy always did," Toby told her. "I know where the number is."

The friend turned out to be a lively little boy, and as it was raining she couldn't turn the two of them outdoors. The children's room was soon transformed into the flight deck of a space ship, the beds pushed together and piled with an assortment of cushions, stools and upended boxes from which the toys had been emptied onto the floor. Ellen showed her displeasure by howling loudly when an accidental shove sent her sprawling on the carpet, and complaining indignantly to Rennie that the boys wouldn't let her join in their game.

Rennie offered stories, and Ellen sat a row of dolls and stuffed toys along the sofa to listen in. When she got bored with books, Rennie fetched the crayons and showed her how to make a paper bag monster mask with large pointed teeth and red-rimmed eyes. Ellen donned it and demanded Rennie's help to make a "den" in the lounge, pulling the sofa cushions off to make walls, and draping a blanket over the whole. After a while, tired of frightening the dolls and toys, she trotted off to frighten the boys, her little hands clawed and her voice raised in a high-pitched attempt at a roar.

Enchanted, both of them demanded the wherewithal for masks of their own. Then Ellen insisted on making one for Rennie, too. Determinedly fighting off the boys' advice and attempts to help, she completed another mask in shades of violent purple and yellow. Rennie obligingly donned it, and the three children backed off with squeals of mock terror.

Snarling convincingly, Rennie followed, pursuing them all over the house.

After a while she allowed them to turn the tables, confining her to Ellen's den in the lounge.

"You're a naughty monster!" Ellen shouted at the top of her voice while the two boys patrolled in front of the sofa on all fours, looking as fearsome as they could. "You stay there now and be quiet!"

Rennie poked her masked head out from under the blanket with a couple of indignant snarls. Ellen backed away, shrieking, while the two boys increased the volume of their menacing roars and rushed towards her. Rennie reared up and gave an impressive howl, just as Grant appeared in the doorway.

"What the hell is going on?" His voice cut through the racket like a cold knife.

For an instant Rennie was glad of the mask, because it hid the sudden flush on her cheeks. She scrambled to her feet, pulling the paper bag off and pushing her tumbled hair away from her face. The two boys stood suddenly quiet, side by side. And Ellen hurled herself at her father, shouting, "I'm a monster, and I'm going to eat you up!"

Grant's eyes left Rennie's and lighted on his daughter, rushing towards him and clawing at his trouser leg. "Is that so?" he said calmly.

"Yes!" Ellen cried, and sank her teeth into his thigh.

"Ow!" Grant grabbed at her shoulders, pushing her away. "You little—"

Rennie said sharply, "Don't!"

"—monster," Grant finished, calmly getting down on his haunches to confront his daughter. "That hurt, Ellen!"

"Sorry, Daddy. I didn't mean it."

She put her arms out, and he hugged her. "I know sweetheart, you were just playing." He straightened, looking at Rennie. "Got a bit carried away, did you?"

"We didn't expect you until—" Rennie said.

He raised his brows, and she looked at her watch. "Oh, I didn't realise—I've done nothing about dinner."

"Having too much fun?" he enquired in a silky tone. He ran a glance over her, a deliberate reminder that only last night she had asked him to remember she wasn't twelve years old.

The doorbell rang, and Rennie said, "That'll be Timmy's mum."

Grant let her in, and Rennie gave the woman a brief greeting, accepted her and Timmy's polite thanks and fled to the kitchen as Grant saw them out.

"I'm sorry," she said when he came into the room while she was hastily pouring rice into boiling water. "I'll have something ready soon."

"No hurry. Toby's hungry, he tells me, but I suggested they tidy up the place before eating. It'll take a while, I should say," he added dryly.

Remembering that he'd expressed a preference for not living in a pigsty, she flushed again. "I know it looks messy, but there's no dirt and no damage."

"I wouldn't say that," he argued, and as she turned with indignant trepidation, wondering what had got broken, he ruefully rubbed at his thigh. "My daughter has razor sharp teeth."

"She got a bit over-excited," Rennie admitted. "I'm sorry."

"*You* didn't bite me," he pointed out. "You don't need to keep apologising, Rennie."

She turned away from him to take some meat from the freezer compartment of the refrigerator. "Do you like Chinese?" she asked distractedly.

"What?"

"Do you like Chinese food?" she asked. "Not the real thing, but you know, rice and pan fried. It's healthy." She was sure Jean had always planned the evening meal in the morning and had it perfectly cooked on the table at the same time every evening. She looked about for the cutting board, then remembered that Ellen had used it for her play dough.

"That's fine," Grant said. "Anything. What's the matter, Rennie?"

Crossly, she said, "Nothing. If you'd just get out of the kitchen and leave me alone I could get this meal cooked!"

There was a small silence, while she realised what she'd said, and looked up to see an oddly rigid expression on his face. "I'm sorry!" she gulped. "It's your house and I had no right to—"

He walked over to her, took her by the shoulders and gave her a gentle shake. "Rennie, do stop apologising! Is this all because you're a bit late getting a meal ready? It's not like you to be flustered over a little thing like that!"

"You're not annoyed?"

"No! What is it about me," he asked somewhat plaintively, "that makes all of you imagine I'm some kind of ogre?"

"We don't!" she assured him, forgetting to be annoyed at being lumped in again with the children. "Only I know you hate to live in a mess, you told me, and I thought it would be cleared up by the time you got home, and I should have started cooking sooner, but—"

"Rennie, stop!" He reinforced the command with a sudden quick kiss on her mouth that halted her in mid-sentence, her lips parted in surprise.

"It's all right," he said. "It was all good clean fun, the kids were obviously having a whale of a time and so were you. It was just a bit of a shock at first to walk in to Ellen screaming in apparent terror, amid some fairly sinister animal sounds. I didn't know at first what was happening."

"Oh, Grant!" She put her hands on his chest, slid them up to his shoulders. "I didn't realise!"

She felt his hands tighten, and tilted her head, her eyes questioning. "Grant?" she breathed, and with a little beat of gladness in her heart, moved closer to him, hooking her hands about his neck, lifting her face.

But he suddenly pushed her away, so that she came jarringly up against the counter. His face had closed. "I told you," he said, "it's okay. It only took five seconds to figure out it was all a game, albeit a fairly bloodthirsty one."

He moved away from her, not looking at her any more. "I hope the kids won't have nightmares tonight."

Rennie clutched at the counter behind her, sick with disappointment. "I'm sure they won't. It's good for them to be a bit rowdy now and then."

"I'm not arguing with that," he said. "I think you're doing a great job with Toby and Ellen. Actually, I came to see if I could help. But if you really want me to get out—" He raised his brows, a glimmer of a smile on his mouth—

She didn't. She wanted him to come back and take her in his arms again, but she knew he wouldn't. For a minute there he had been sorely tempted, and the knowledge made her blood sing. But he didn't want that kind of involvement with her, she knew, for all sorts of reasons, not the least of which was that he thought her too young.

She remembered him telling her that Jean had always made him feel incompetent in the house, and said casually, "Thanks. You can wash some broccoli and carrots and slice them, if you like." And resolved that no matter how badly he did it, she wouldn't criticise.

He didn't actually do it badly at all, but quite competently and quickly once Rennie found the chopping board and removed sticky yellow play dough from it. When he had finished she had the hot oil ready and was tossing meat strips into it.

"Over here," she said, stirring the meat and gently shaking the pan.

He came to stand by her, and tipped the vegetables deftly in, his shoulder brushing hers before he moved away. Rennie didn't look up, merely reaching over the stove to turn down the heat a little. She wondered if he was tingling all over the way she was. And was certain that if so he wasn't going to do anything about it.

He had himself well in hand now. Best not to rush things. But time, she thought happily as she hummed a tune and stirred soy sauce into the sizzling vegetables, was on her side. Time and propinquity, and Grant's own feelings which he was so determined not to admit.

Toby came in to report indignantly that Ellen wasn't helping, and Grant went off to remonstrate. When he returned Rennie had the dinner ready to dish up and was setting the table in the dining room.

"I'm impressed," he said. "It smells delicious."

It tasted just as good, he told her when they had eaten. Ellen was inclined to be suspicious of the rice, but Toby ate his stoically and asked for more, and after that requested pudding. "We tidied everything up," he reminded Rennie righteously. "And I'm *very* hungry!"

Having been informed several times that Mummy didn't believe puddings were good for growing children except on special occasions, preferring them to have fresh fruit instead, Rennie glanced at Grant for guidance.

He shrugged. "I'm quite partial to a bit of pudding myself," he said, "but Rennie hasn't had time to prepare any tonight."

Toby's face fell. Rennie said quickly, "There's a tin of peaches and some custard powder in the pantry. We could have that."

"Yes," Toby said unequivocally. Rennie smiled and got up to fetch it. She hoped that Jean wouldn't have disapproved too strongly.

Chapter Nine

Determined that there would be no repetition of the chaotic scene into which Grant had walked the previous evening, the next day Rennie began planning dinner straight after breakfast. Inspecting the depleted stock of meat in the freezer, she decided on casseroled beef olives with cauliflower au gratin and creamed potatoes.

The beef didn't thaw as quickly as she hoped, and Ellen had woken from her nap before she could separate the slices and spread seasoning on them. Having Ellen's enthusiastic help meant that some of the rolled up "olives" were a little odd in shape, but the casserole went into the oven with plenty of time to simmer nicely until dinner. Recklessly, Rennie decided to make a proper pudding, and found the ingredients for a sweet with eggs, milk and rice flavoured with golden syrup. Even Jean, she thought, wouldn't have objected to all that protein. And the little bit of syrup couldn't hurt.

Toby was home from school in time to help beat the eggs and grind some nutmeg to sprinkle on top of the pudding.

He wanted to play space ships again, prepared stoically to accept Ellen substituting for his friend Timmy, but Rennie tried to dissuade him. "Wouldn't you rather play outside?" she suggested.

"No." Toby stared at her.

She wanted to tidy up the house—and herself—before Grant came home. "Maybe you could make a space ship out under the tree?" she coaxed hopefully. There was one tree in the yard, a twisted willow, not shaped for climbing or swings, but a tree nevertheless.

"How?" Toby asked.

"Well—"

In the end she accompanied him out to the garage and helped to find some cardboard boxes, a disused rubbish bin and assorted metal objects. A kitchen stool was added to the structure for the pilot's seat, and then a chair for Ellen as the co-pilot.

Rennie returned to the kitchen, and an ominous smell. The rice pudding had run over the top of its dish and was spreading across the oven floor.

From then on it was all downhill. She tried ineffectually to wipe the oven and burnt her hand in the process. The syrup made the spill sticky.

The kitchen rapidly filled with smoke and the heavy, rich aroma of burned sugar. Rennie opened the door to let some of it out, and a few minutes later the children came racing inside, heedless of the mud on their feet leaving grubby marks all the way from the back door to their bedroom.

Busy trying to scrape some of the burnt pudding off the oven with an egg-slice, Rennie didn't notice that when they went out again they were carrying the pillows from their beds. Judging from their voices and laughter, they were having a good time. When she looked out and saw them having a pillow fight, she let it go. Probably they shouldn't have their pillows outside, but they were enjoying themselves.

It wasn't until they had brought them back in that she realised the rough-housing had burst one of the pillows, and added to the mud already trekked in was a trail of tiny foam chips.

And then it rained.

When Grant came in the space ship was a disintegrating heap of cardboard boxes, the house smelled lingeringly of smoke, and he nearly tripped on the vacuum cleaner in the hallway, where Rennie had abandoned it to check on the casserole before remembering that she had not yet peeled the potatoes.

Toby and Ellen were in the bath, playing whales and covering floor and walls with spouts of water. Grant peeped in and retreated, not willing to suffer the same fate himself. He found Rennie in the kitchen, mournfully surveying a casserole dish she had evidently just taken from the oven. In the bottom of the dish several odd-looking darkly browned objects reposed on a thick bed of something he couldn't identify. A stool was standing for some reason in the middle of the floor, and as he moved it he noted that it was wet, as was the chair which stood just inside the back door.

Rennie was wet, too, her bright hair dishevelled and beaded with raindrops, the shoulders of her shirt dark with damp.

She looked up at him and said, as though the ultimate disaster had befallen, "Oh, no!"

Grant's brows rose. "Not exactly flattering, Rennie. Shall I go out and come in again—or just go out and not come in at all?"

"Oh, don't be silly!" she said crossly, just as a pot on the stove boiled over with a loud hiss, hot water cascading down its sides. Rennie said something totally unladylike and banged the casserole down on the bench, then snatched the pot off the ring.

"Need some help?" Grant asked.

"No!" she said fiercely, adding a belated, "Thank you." She turned down the stove and replaced the pot. "They lost their stuffing," she said, glaring at the casserole.

"What are they?" Grant surveyed the dish warily.

"They're supposed to be beef olives."

"They smell good," Grant offered.

Rennie's scowl if anything became blacker. "You don't have to be kind!"

Grant looked at her with some sympathy. "Had a bad day?"

"Not particularly," she admitted, still scowling, "until the last hour or so." She had meant to greet him looking smoothly shining, wearing a dress and with her hair combed and perhaps put up in a knot. The house would be spotless and the children ready for dinner and bed, clean and sweet and amenable. And she would serve them a perfect meal, then they'd all clear up the dishes and she or Grant would read a story for Toby and Ellen before, perhaps, settling down to an evening together.

Now he was looking round him as if he'd blundered into an unexpected minefield, and she didn't blame him. She knew she looked a mess, the house equally so, and her special dinner was ruined. She'd been listening with one ear to the sounds from the bathroom—it was obvious from the noise level that no one was drowned—and she knew that a fair bit of splashing had gone on, so that was probably equally a disaster area.

Underlining that thought, Ellen came bounding into the kitchen, pinkly naked with a towel held ineffectually at her middle, almost stepping on it as she ran towards Grant, crying, "Daddy! Dry me!"

"Okay, sweetheart!" He bent to her, wrapping her in the towel before bearing her off to the bathroom again.

Rennie pushed damp hair from her eyes and set her chin. Might as well get on with it.

While she salvaged what she could, Grant got the children into their pyjamas and wiped the bathroom. She heard the hum of the vacuum and knew she ought to be grateful that someone at least was being efficient. Instead, she felt more angry and humiliated than ever.

The children ate the mushy remains of the casserole without comment and, after glancing at Rennie's face, Grant evidently decided the wisest course was to do the same. The cauliflower was passable, but she'd not had time to make the sauce. And the potatoes had gone lumpy. She'd been so anxious to get the meal over with, she'd skimped on the cooking time.

The pudding looked odd, all black at the edges and sunken in the centre, but Toby asked for a second helping. Rennie managed a grateful smile for him as she handed him the plate.

"I'll put them to bed," Grant offered when the meal was over and the plates carried to the kitchen. "And do the dishes later. You rest, Rennie."

"I don't need to rest," she told him shortly. "I'll do the dishes."

She began clattering the empty plates into the sink. Grant gave her a thoughtful look and left her to it.

She got them all done and was on her knees scrubbing at the still-warm oven with a steel wool pad when he came in and said, "Ah, that's where the smell came from."

"I'll get it off," she promised, rubbing vigorously.

"Leave it—" he suggested.

"No, it will only set harder once the oven cools." She brushed back her hair impatiently with a blackened, soapy hand.

He bent and took her wrist, pulling her to her feet. "Leave it to me," he said firmly. "I'll finish it."

Rennie's chin set. "You don't have to—it was my fault. I must have set the temperature too high. I did want it to be nice, and have everything on time, and the children ready, a decent house for you to come back to—but the pudding went over first, and the children were having a pillow fight and I didn't notice until it was too late, Ellen's was dripping foam all over so I had to sew it up to stop the mess getting worse and so she can sleep on it tonight, and then it rained, and I'd started to clean up but I'd forgotten the potatoes and—don't you dare laugh at me!" she finished wrathfully, and threw the soapy pad in her hand at him.

It bounced harmlessly off his shoulder, and to his credit he was trying not to laugh, but she could see it in his eyes and in the faint twitch at the corner of his mouth. She stood glaring at him, her eyes bright with temper and her cheeks hot.

"I'm not laughing," he lied. "I can see it isn't funny for you—"

"No, it isn't in the least funny!" She managed to hold on to the anger for a few more seconds, but she felt a reluctant smile tug at the corner of her own mouth. "I suppose it is, really," she admitted.

"A bit," Grant agreed. He reached out a hand and brushed his thumb firmly over her cheek. "Standing on your dignity doesn't work when you've got black smudges all over your face, I'm afraid."

"Oh-ooh!" Rennie wailed in a combination of anguish and despair. So she looked a fright as well.

And then Grant laughed in earnest, holding out his arms to her, and she went into them as naturally as breathing, having a resigned little laugh of her own against his warm shoulder, while he nuzzled at her hair.

When the laughter died they stood quietly, their arms loosely about each other, and Rennie was content. She closed her eyes, hoping to make the moment last.

Grant moved and she held her breath for an instant. His hand was under her chin, lifting it. She kept her eyes closed, afraid of breaking the spell.

Grant said, his voice hardly more than a whisper, "Rennie?"

Reluctantly she opened her eyes. He was staring at her with dark intensity, and she stared back, unafraid.

"I shouldn't do this," he murmured, "but..."

She lifted her face a fraction nearer to his and closed her eyes again. And felt her lips part under the brush of his mouth across them, featherlight, tentative, promising.

She made a tiny sound and put her arms right around him, her fingers spread against his warm, hard back. Heard him say her name again, almost as though it hurt him, before his mouth was opening over hers, gentle but inexorable. And then less gentle, with an underlying violence as though he had decided to take what she was offering but was angry about it.

When he broke the kiss, suddenly pushing her away although he retained a tight hold on her arms, Rennie blinked at him in some dismay. His breathing was harsh, and the strange anger was in his eyes. "I'm sorry," he said, as if the words were dragged from him. "I should never have done that."

"Why not?" she demanded. "I wanted you to!" She knew very well she had blatantly asked for it, and not for anything would she admit that she had been slightly frightened by the result.

He shook his head as if to clear it. "You ought to curb that headlong honesty of yours," he said. "It could get you into trouble."

"What do you expect me to do?" she asked. "Go all coy and pretend I'm afraid of being ravished? Some luck!"

"Rennie!" he protested on a reluctant choke of laughter.

"Well," Rennie said, hiding her disappointment and confusion under flippancy, "if I'm not going to get ravished tonight—" She bent to pick up the discarded soap pad.

"Not tonight, not any night," Grant said firmly.

Regaining her confidence, she dared to say, "You wanna bet?"

"I mean it, Rennie," he said firmly. "It just won't do. And you can take that stubborn look off your face, I'm not going to argue the toss with you."

She made a face at him instead, and he laughed. Rennie was glad to hear it, but she looked thoughtfully at the wet pad in her hand and back at him.

Decisively, Grant shook his head. "Don't try it again. You won't get away with it a second time."

Interested, she cocked her head to one side, regarding him.

"Uh-uh!" he warned. "Childish, Rennie. I might just retaliate in kind and put you over my knee."

"Is that a promise?" Rennie asked, wide-eyed.

Grant shook his head, unable to stop a smile. "You are an impossible brat!" And he walked out of the room.

A few days later Grant came home from work and went into the kitchen, where Rennie was standing at the stove, lifting the lid off a boiling pot and listening to Toby read.

"Hi, son," he said, ruffling Toby's hair. "Hello, Rennie." He looked about. "Where's Ellen?"

Rennie lowered the heat beneath the potatoes, and turned to face him. Trying to sound casual, she said, "Playing with Sally, over the road."

"At her place?"

"They've been over there—" she glanced at her watch "—oh, about an hour and a half. Sally's mother was going to bring her back about now, unless she asked to come home sooner."

Grant stood very still. "That's great," he said carefully. "Isn't it?"

"Isn't it?" Rennie couldn't contain her excitement any longer. She almost flew across the kitchen, and put her arms about him in a hug. "She's going to be just fine!"

Grant's arms came round her to return the hug as she smiled up at him.

There was a knock on the door, and Rennie, her eyes shining, stepped back. "That'll be them now."

After the children had been put to bed, and Grant had kissed them good-night, he came into the lounge to find Rennie sitting in a chair with her legs curled under her while she read a magazine, one finger absently twirling a lock of red hair that had escaped from her ponytail.

"You look scarcely older than Ellen," he said. "How can you work such miracles?"

"I didn't. Time did. I told you that was all she needed."

"The certainty of youth!"

"Oh, stop it. You're not that ancient, yourself. I was right, anyway. And you needn't think I don't know why you're always reminding me of the difference in our ages."

Which wasn't quite fair, because he hadn't, lately. Only he had also treated her with a formality bordering on indifference, and tonight, buoyed up by Ellen's giant step forward, she felt rash enough to challenge him.

For a moment she thought he was going to retaliate. His eyes narrowed, and a brief glitter lit them. But he only said mildly, "I don't mean to offend you, Rennie. We all owe you far too much for that."

Rennie shook her head. "Give yourself some credit too, Grant. Having you back in her life on a permanent basis was probably the biggest factor." It must have meant changing his whole lifestyle, but he had done it unhesitatingly. She wondered if there had been another woman in his life, as there had been another man for Jean. And she remembered with a little chill how he had looked at Celeste and Ethan on their wedding day. Celeste had been with Grant the evening Rennie had first met him. And had been borne off by Ethan in the middle of the ball.

My evening's already spoiled, he had told her, offering to take her home. His evening—his life? She studied him, wondering. He had given little away, and she had been too shocked and shaken by Kevin's unexpected attack and Grant's accusations to read beneath the surface.

"What are you thinking?" he asked her, faint amusement in his interrogative glance.

"Do you hate being here?" she asked baldly. "In this house?"

It must be difficult, even painful, for him to be back in the house he had shared with Jean. Surrounded by reminders of her. He was even sleeping in her room. Their room, it must have been once. She wondered if he had chosen it automatically when he moved in to look after the children, or had deliberately left the spare room for his proposed live-in home help.

"Not specially," he answered carefully. "It sometimes feels strange. There are—reminders of happier times. And less happy ones." His gaze strayed about the room. "That pottery vase was a wedding present from a mutual friend of

Jean's and mine who was killed in a car crash soon after-wards. We both treasured it. The picture up there—'' he nodded at a seascape on the wall ''—we chose together. The first thing we bought for our home. We knew it should have been pots and pans, or furniture. But we both fell in love with that.''

''You had a lot in common,'' Rennie said softly, a pain-ful sensation in her chest.

''We thought so, for a time,'' Grant said dismissively. ''Obviously not enough, though.''

''That's sad.''

''Yes.'' He took his gaze off the painting and said, ''I must get the rest of my stuff out of the flat and bring it over.''

''I didn't realise you still had another place.''

''I'll have to get rid of it. Just haven't got around to bringing everything over here. In the back of my mind, I suppose I still hoped to find some place I could start again with the children. But it's obvious I can't move them for a while yet.''

Silently she agreed.

He said, ''Don't you want the TV on?''

Rennie shook her head. ''I was going to play some tapes, but—''

''Go ahead. I don't know if there's anything to your taste here—''

''Some I brought from home,'' she explained. ''You might not like them.''

''Pop music?'' He smiled, and when she nodded, he said, ''I never listen to it, so I wouldn't know, would I?''

She owned some classical and opera music, too, but Grant was well provided with them. She knew he wouldn't mind her listening to his. She stood up and said lightly, ''I'll ed-ucate you, if you like.''

He listened with her for over an hour. ''That's good,'' he said appreciatively, and reached for the tape's case with the list of songs on it. ''I've never heard of this group. But then, I haven't listened to pop much since my teenage years.''

"There is life after the Beatles," Rennie reminded him.

"Actually the Beatles were a bit before my time," he told her rather coolly.

"Oops! Sorry." He'd said he was twice her age but of course he wasn't, really.

"I belong to the Age of Aquarius."

"Flower power?" She cocked her head. "You in beads and a hairband?"

Grant laughed. "That was the sixties and I was only a kid. But I did have long hair when I was at university. I wore flared jeans and anti-nuclear T-shirts."

"Did you ever go on a protest march?"

"A few times. I still would if I felt it would do any good."

He'd do anything he felt was necessary for what he believed in, Rennie guessed. "So would I," she said.

Grant stood up and said, "I have some work to do. Thanks for sharing your music."

Chapter Ten

At the start of the school holidays, Rennie asked Grant, "What are you doing about Christmas?"

"I hadn't thought about it," he confessed. "Jean used to invite me over for Christmas lunch. For the children's sake. She provided presents that I paid for, and put them under the tree to be opened when I arrived. It was a bit of a strain for Jean and me, but the children seemed to enjoy it. In the evening I give my mother a meal at a restaurant. And on Boxing Day I usually take the children to see her."

Rennie had never met his mother. He had visited her with the children while Rennie spent some time at home. Ellen had been inclined to cry when told that Rennie wasn't accompanying them, but without the hysterical behaviour she had shown previously, and she had yielded eventually to Grant's patient explanation that Rennie sometimes had other things to do.

"Why don't you all come to us for Christmas Day?" Rennie suggested. And, seeing the dubiousness in his face, she added, "Mum says she'd love to have you. There are

always lots of people for Christmas at our place. Stray un-
cles, people with no family, overseas students—Ethan and
Celeste may be coming, too."

"Leaving their idyllic island?"

"Didn't you know they're back for a while? Celeste sells
lots of stuff just before Christmas. She's been working on
new things to restock the shop."

"I haven't seen them since they left Auckland after their
honeymoon."

"Neither have I. But Mum's been keeping in touch."

"Well, thank Marian for the invitation. It may be a good
idea. If we stay here for the day the children are bound to
miss their mother. Could I ask you to buy some presents for
them? I'm afraid I've no idea what they'd like."

"I'll drop some hints and find out. Maybe even take them
window-shopping."

"Where?" Grant queried sharply.

Not, of course, to the department store where their
mother had been taken ill. "A mall," Rennie suggested.
"It's all right. I've taken Ellen to shops before." Ellen had
clung, but lately they had safely managed a couple of trips
to the local shopping centre. Her panic reaction to going out
was definitely fading.

Grant firmly sent Rennie home on Christmas Eve, keeping Ellen happy with the promise that next day they would
be joining her.

When they arrived the children presented her with a large
gift-wrapped parcel that proved to contain a heart-shaped,
pink quilted satin night-dress case, heavily beribboned and
lace edged, which they had chosen themselves. Ignoring
Grant's rueful glance over their heads, she thanked them
extravagantly and promised to use it every day. Unobtrusively, he handed her a smaller parcel and said, "Open it
later."

Ellen was wearing the black, lemon and hot-pink striped
socks and clutching the big orange-haired, freckle-faced rag
doll that Rennie had bought for her on Grant's behalf, and

Toby proudly showed her his calculator with a games facility. She admired it obligingly as though she had never seen it before and had not spent ages agonising over which make and model he would prefer.

For a little while Ellen seemed overawed by the number of people they were introduced to, but she was soon glowing as everyone admired the doll and some even mentioned the socks. Taking Rennie quietly aside, Grant said, "Did you have to buy her those striped abominations?"

"You said, whatever they wanted within the sum of money you gave me. She loved them."

"Yes. I couldn't persuade her not to wear them."

Rennie laughed. "Did you try to persuade her not to wear the blue dress and red sandals with them?"

"I'd already had an argument over the dress. I thought it looked nicer to go visiting in than the overalls she wanted to wear, too small for her and covered in paint splashes. And the sandals were a present from Sally's family."

"Well, I think she looks terrific," Rennie said firmly. "You shouldn't try to smother her fashion sense. In fact she probably has better taste than you do."

"Is that so?" His eyes gleamed. "Then you'll be glad to know that she's named that monstrosity of a doll 'Rennie.'"

Rennie choked. "I'm . . . I'm flattered."

Grant laughed unkindly.

"I have some presents of my own for the children," she told him. "I'll fetch them."

She had bought an easy board game for them to share, and small separate presents as well. After they had opened them and thanked her, she handed Grant a little parcel. "And this is yours."

"I didn't expect—"

He was interrupted by Marian coming into the room. "Ethan and Celeste have arrived. Now we're all here."

Grant slipped the parcel into his pocket as Ethan and Celeste walked in behind Marian. Celeste came straight over to hold out her hands to him, accepting his kiss on her cheek.

"You look well," he said, still holding her hands and smiling down at her.

"Ethan!" Rennie hugged Celeste's husband enthusiastically. "How nice to see you! And Celeste," she added, turning to smile at the other woman as Grant released her. "That's a terrific dress. One of your own designs?" It was painted silk, in muted peacock colours.

"Yes. I'm glad you like it." Turning to Grant again, Celeste said, "How are you, Grant? Things must have been difficult since Jean—"

"We're getting used to it, now. Come and say hello to the children. I told them you'd be here."

As they turned away, Ethan smiled affectionately down at Rennie. "And how are you, young Rennie?"

"Fine. Terrific."

"And the studies? This time next year you'll be a fully fledged lawyer, won't you?"

"Not quite. I'll have completed my fourth year but I have to work for a legal firm for several months and then take professional exams before I can call myself a barrister. And of course I'll still have a lot to learn."

"I can't imagine you in a wig and gown. But I suppose I'm feeling my age."

Rennie smiled. "Rot. Most people are a year or so older before they qualify," she admitted. "Comes of being born at the beginning of the school year, the right time for a fast track through the education system, you see."

"Mmm. That and brains. And hard work." Ethan shook his head nostalgically. "Seems only yesterday you were a carroty-haired kid swinging upside down from the old tree out there."

"Don't you start!" Rennie sighed. She hoped he wouldn't compare notes with Grant.

"What are you doing with the holidays?" asked Ethan. "Got a job?"

"Yes, looking after Grant's two children."

Ethan looked over to where Celeste was talking to them. "Really?" He turned a thoughtful look on her. "Bit of a change. I thought you needed to find something in a legal office?''

"I've already done most of my field hours.''

Marian looked over at her and raised her eyebrows, and Rennie said, "Excuse me, I've got to help Mum serve the food.''

Lunch was set out buffet-style on a long table. The guests helped themselves to cold chicken, turkey and ham, a variety of salads, hot new potatoes dripping with butter, steaming, golden-fleshed kumara, fresh beans and sweet minted peas. For afters there were plum puddings with cream or ice cream, fresh strawberries and fruit salad. Frank poured wine for those who wanted it, and soft drinks for the half-dozen children and for those adults who preferred no alcohol. Toby held out his glass for wine and amid laughter was told firmly by his father that he was to have a soft drink instead.

After helping with the clearing and washing up everyone sat around while Shane and another young man cracked nuts, and the children handed them to the adults. Ellen, on Rennie's knee, almost went to sleep, and Rennie whispered in her ear, "Would you like to lie down on my bed for a little while?''

Ellen nodded, her eyes drooping, and Rennie picked her up and made for the door.

Grant came to her side as she reached it. "Let me take her,'' he said. "She's too heavy for you.''

"No, we're fine,'' Rennie assured him, but he followed her into the bedroom, and watched as she put Ellen gently down and removed the red sandals, then pulled the light cover over her.

"She's asleep already,'' he commented. "They were awake before six. Bouncing all over my bed.''

"I remember doing that to my parents on Christmas morning,'' Rennie said, taking her eyes away from the sleeping child. "Don't you?''

"It was too long ago,'' he said, turning away.

"Didn't you have Christmas stockings?''

"Yes, of course."

"And your father played Santa Claus?"

"He wasn't into that sort of thing. My mother used to fill the stockings, I think, and leave them by the fireplace."

"Were you and your brother close?"

"There're eight years between us."

"That's a big age gap."

"He left home before I ever got to know him."

"When did your father die?" Rennie asked.

"I was twenty-one. Old enough to cope."

"What about your brother? Was he here, then, in New Zealand?"

"No, he'd gone to live in Australia when he got married. They came over for the funeral, of course."

"So you looked after your mother?"

Grant shrugged. "I lived with her until I married. She's quite independent, but with her heart—"

"It was bad, even then?"

"We knew she had a problem, yes."

"It must have been a responsibility, at twenty-one."

"I was brought up to cope with responsibility."

"I've always imagined you being like Toby as a child," she said.

Grant looked quizzical. "With his tendency to bossiness, I imagine," he said drily. "Believe me, I never got the chance."

"Did your brother bully you?"

He shook his head. "Nobody bullied anybody. We were— too civilised for that. Never a raised voice in the house."

"Never?" Rennie queried disbelievingly.

"I don't believe my parents ever had a row in their lives."

"They were that close?"

He laughed rather harshly. "Actually, I'm not sure they even liked each other very much. I never saw them deliberately touch. I wasn't even sure they liked me, but my father was at least proud of my brother. They were alike in looks and temperament. One son was enough for my father. I was an afterthought, probably a mistake." He gave a wry, self-mocking smile. "I used to fantasise that my father—wasn't, really. But I can't imagine my mother having an illicit affair. And her grief when he died surprised me. So maybe I got it all wrong. She's never spoken of her feelings for him. But in spite of that, I believe she's been happier since he died. I'd hoped—"

He stopped abruptly, and Rennie said, "What did you hope?"

"That I'd do better in my own marriage, I suppose. Better by my children."

"You are doing that," she assured him, "for the children." She dared not comment on his marriage. But his love for Toby and Ellen was patent.

"You haven't opened your present," she reminded him.

He smiled. "No, I haven't. You didn't need to buy me anything."

"I know I didn't need to. I wanted to."

He took it from his pocket and carefully stripped off the paper, revealing an audiotape in its plastic case and a long, narrow box. He glanced up at Rennie, opened the box and took out the silver ballpoint pen.

"How did you know I needed one?"

"I remembered you hunting one day for a pen, and mentioning that you'd had a silver one but lost it somewhere recently."

"It's very kind of you, Rennie." He replaced it in its box and put it back in his pocket. Then he turned over the tape in his hand and looked up into her slightly anxious eyes.

"You said you liked the album I played for you. This is their latest."

He smiled. "Well, thank you!"

"You weren't just being polite? Be honest!"

"Cross my heart," he promised. "I'll look forward to listening to it." He tossed it lightly in his hand. "Have you opened your present?"

"No. Stay here, I'll fetch it."

She slipped into the kitchen where she had left it when the dishes were done, catching a glimpse of Toby and another boy making their way toward the tree house, each with something hugged to his chest.

"Toby's made a friend," she reported to Grant as she returned to the bedroom. "I think they're smuggling some giant-size bottles of pop out to the tree house."

"I hope he doesn't make himself sick," Grant commented as she began peeling tape off the parcel. "What was it? Orange?"

"I couldn't see. Don't worry, they can't drink a whole two-litre bottle each. Their eyes are bigger than their tummies. Oh, Grant, this is lovely!"

The bracelet was silver and enamel, subtly coloured in greens and golds. She had to look closely to see that the pattern was made up of tiny butterflies and flowers.

"Put it on," he said. "I hope it fits."

"It will." She slipped it over her hand and held up her slim wrist for him to see. "It's beautiful, thank you!"

She turned to him just as his eyes moved from her wrist to her face. He was quite close, and it seemed natural to put her hands on his shoulders and kiss him lightly.

His hands clamped on her waist as her lips left his. For a second they stood like that, her head tipped back, her eyes widening as she read the sudden blaze in his. Then he pulled her roughly against him and covered her parted lips with his mouth.

Rennie's arms slipped about his neck and she kissed him back, her body curving into his. One of his arms was about her waist, while the other hand roved over her back, shaped her hip, slid up her spine and finally buried itself in her hair, holding her as he coaxed her mouth wider and insistently explored it. There were stars wheeling behind her closed eyes, points of light dancing through her entire body. She went on her toes, arching herself closer still, and felt him bend over her, wanting the same thing....

She could hardly bear it when he suddenly relinquished her mouth and moved away from her, only keeping a steadying hand on her waist.

His face was flushed, as she knew hers was, but while she watched him with dazed eyes, he paled. "I'm sorry, Rennie," he said, and wiped his hand over his mouth as though he was embarrassed. "And I don't even have the excuse of mistletoe."

"Why be sorry?" she demanded. "I didn't mind. You must have noticed."

"Yes, but I have no right—I should—"

Rennie impatiently put her fingers on his lips. "Don't say that," she ordered. "And don't be sorry. It's Christmas. I won't let you say anything to spoil it. We needn't talk about it now."

He hesitated, then nodded. "Yes, you're right. But I think we should go back to the others."

She smiled at him almost as she would have smiled at Toby or Ellen. "All right," she said. "If that's what you think best."

It was some time later that a series of high-pitched giggles from outside penetrated to the house. Marian looked out the window and said, "Toby and Alan are having a great time out there. Oops! Toby nearly missed the ladder, but he's okay."

As she turned back into the room, Grant got up idly and went to the window himself. He smiled, then began to frown, and after a few seconds abruptly swung round and went striding toward the door.

Rennie broke off her conversation with one of her brother's friends who had called in after lunch, and hurried after him. By the time she got outside, he was racing across the lawn.

Toby was lying on the grass a few yards from the tree house, while Alan regarded him owlishly from a perch on the ladder.

"Did he fall?" Rennie gasped as she joined Grant, who was feeling Toby's forehead. The boy's eyes were open, but looked peculiarly unfocused, and he was very flushed.

"No. Yes," Grant said. "He got down the ladder and started walking, but he walked very oddly—and then he just fell over. How do you feel, son?" he asked Toby.

The little boy blinked and said, "F-f-funny."

"What kind of funny?" Rennie asked anxiously.

"Jusht funny," Toby said, and giggled.

"I feel funny, too," his young friend announced. "Can you help me get down?" he added plaintively.

"You're big enough to get down on your own," Grant said, barely throwing him a glance. "Toby, do you hurt anywhere?"

Toby's head slowly moved from side to side.

"Well, can you get up, then?" Grant put his hand under his son's shoulders and brought him to his feet. "Okay?"

Toby nodded his head and suddenly clutched at Grant's sleeve. "Daddy, I c-can't walk."

Grant went totally white. Rennie darted from his side, just in time to catch Alan, who missed the last few rungs of the ladder and collapsed as she broke his fall.

"Both of them?" Grant said, turning a stunned and desperately worried face to her.

"Apparently," Rennie agreed. She set Alan on his feet, and he subsided immediately to a sitting position on the ground, grinning foolishly at her. "Just a minute," she told Grant, and grasped the ladder, quickly ascending it to disappear into the tree house.

"Rennie, we haven't time to—" he shouted at her, gathering Toby up in his arms.

But she had already reappeared in the doorway. "Look," she called to him.

He looked at the two bottles she held, both of them half empty, and the colour slowly returned to his face. "Not pop," he said. "Wine. Champagne-style, no less. The little devils!"

"Yes," Rennie said, grinning. "Aren't they? Thoroughly drunk little devils!"

"Daddy?" Toby said. "Are you angry?"

Grant hastily wiped an answering grin from his face. He put Toby carefully on his swaying feet, holding his shoulders and squatting to his level. "I told you the wine was for the grown-ups, didn't I?"

Toby nodded. "I think I'm going to be sick."

Grant said, "I'm not surprised. Too much alcohol is bad for people, especially children. Now you know why I didn't want you to have it."

Toby nodded vigorously, and then threw up. Grant moved his feet in their polished shoes out of the way just in time and held his son's head until it was over. Alan looked on with interest, and shortly afterward followed suit.

"I'd better tell his parents," Rennie said. "Come on, my lad."

"Do we have to tell?" Alan whined, reluctantly accepting her guiding hand, as Grant wiped Toby's mouth with a handkerchief.

"Yes, because you might be sick again, and they need to know why."

"I won't be sick again," Alan declared, and promptly proved himself wrong.

By the time he was finished, his mother had come flying out of the house, and Rennie explained what had happened.

"I don't think they've had enough for it to be dangerous," she said. "But you'd better watch him, in case."

"Thank goodness it was nothing worse," the woman said. "And thanks for looking after him. We'd better take him home. Do you mind holding the fort while I round up the rest of the family? Now, Alan, you stay here a minute. I don't want you messing up Auntie Marian's carpets. Honestly, I can't take you anywhere!"

She was back in a few minutes, as Grant and Toby joined Rennie. "I'm sorry if my son led your boy into mischief," she told Grant. "I thought my husband was keeping an eye on him. You can't leave him alone for a minute!"

"Not at all," Grant assured her. "In fact, I'm grateful."

His eyes met Rennie's in a look of pure understanding as the harassed mother stared in complete noncomprehension.

"It's a long story," Rennie said, taking pity on her. "But sometimes a total lack of mischief can worry parents, too."

"Oh, yes?" the woman said in polite disbelief. "Tell me about it!" But she didn't wait for an explanation, ushering her erring son before her round to the front of the house.

"We'd better be going, too," Grant said, as he and a pale, subdued Toby joined Rennie. "I'll take Toby out to the car now, and come back for Ellen."

Rennie wanted to offer to come with them, but knew he wouldn't let her. He had vetoed her suggestion that she should look after the children while he took his mother out for her customary Christmas dinner. Mrs. Morrison understood, he told her, that he had to be with the children. And Rennie should spend Christmas with her parents.

"Shane tells me you've both been invited to a party tomorrow night," he added. "You didn't mention it."

"I don't mind missing it."

"You haven't had much social life since you've been working for me. Go to your party and enjoy yourself. And you needn't come back the day after. I don't have to go to the office until after New Year. We can cope."

"I know Ellen's much more independent of me than she was, but don't you think ten days is too long a break, so soon?"

"Your family must be missing you, and I'm well aware that you've seen almost nothing of your friends lately."

"I think," she told him roundly, "that this sudden change of plans is for another reason entirely."

He looked away from her, his gaze absently resting on the house behind her, then returning to her face. There was a bleakness in his eyes that made her want to put her arms around him, but at the same time warned her off. He said quietly, "Don't push it, Rennie."

"All right," she said as he turned away. "But promise me one thing."

Reluctantly, he faced her again, his expression impatient.

"Promise," she said, "that you'll call me if Ellen's fretting. Or Toby."

He nodded. "Yes. Yes, the children must come first. Don't worry, I will."

Chapter Eleven

Grant called three days after Christmas.

"Ellen?" Rennie queried. "Is she all right?"

"She's fine. Beginning to miss you but she isn't fussing about it. Something's come up, though."

"What?" Rennie asked sharply.

"It's okay. Nothing bad. A friend of my mother's has a beach house in Northland. It was booked for the holidays, of course, but the family that was supposed to have it over New Year has cancelled. My mother suggested that we take it—it's a big house and there's a downstairs room with its own bathroom where she could be away from the children. And three bedrooms upstairs, one with bunks."

"It sounds ideal."

"Yes. I'd like to get away from here for a few days. Also it's a chance to wean the children from this place. Make it a bit easier for me to move them to another house later on. And they're dead keen."

"Ellen is?"

"Yes, even Ellen is." He paused. "On condition that you come with us."

"Of course I'll come," Rennie said immediately. "If that's what you're asking me."

"Yes, I am. Um—my mother thinks you should come, too. I don't think she trusts my expertise with children, she's afraid that she'll have to look after them if there isn't another female on the premises."

"She won't have to do a thing," Rennie promised. "Tell her I'll take care of everything."

She danced toward her room, hugging herself. Marian, coming out of the kitchen, smiled at her with raised brows. "Good news?"

"Great news!" Rennie told her. "We're having a holiday by the beach—Grant and the children and me. Oh, and his mother. We leave tomorrow morning."

"You'll be well chaperoned, by the sound of it," Marian commented.

"Yes, I will." Rennie laughed. "I expect that's why he didn't mind asking me. I guess his mother's supposed to protect him."

"Rennie!" Marian followed her into the bedroom. "What are you up to?"

Rennie sat down on the dressing table stool, smiling. "Nothing," she said innocently. "But I think I may be in love!"

Marian came over and put a hand on her shoulder. "Rennie, darling," she said gently. "Do you know what you're doing?"

"Yes. Well, maybe not entirely. I've never felt quite like this before. But oh, isn't it great?" She turned and put her arms about Marian's waist.

Looking down at her, Marian stroked her hair. "Yes," she said. "Of course it is. Only remember what I said about not rushing into anything. Do you know how Grant feels about things?"

"He thinks he's too old for me."

"He could be right, you know. He'd be closer to my age than yours."

Rennie lifted her head. "What does that matter? *I* don't care!"

"No, darling, but maybe *he* does. It might not be just that he's too old for you. Perhaps he also feels that you're too young for him."

Rennie's eyes clouded. "Not when he kisses me," she said defiantly.

"Has he kissed you often?"

Rennie shook her head. "He thinks he shouldn't. But when he does, I know how he feels."

Her mother said, "I know it isn't fashionable to say so, but men *are* different from us, Rennie. Whether it's biological or cultural isn't really an issue here. They can make love where they don't love much more easily than most women. And if you force or manipulate Grant into that situation, you could be doing yourself more harm than good. You do understand what I'm saying?"

"Yes." Rennie sighed. "I hear you. But it doesn't make any difference to *my* feelings."

"I know. Just think about what you're doing though, before you do it, hmm? You've got an excellent mind under that flaming hair, in very good working order. It doesn't have to go into neutral every time your emotions are engaged."

Ellen came running to meet her when she arrived, with Toby not far behind. Putting Ellen down, she held her arms out for the boy. "Am I allowed a hug today?"

He smiled and flung his arms about her, mussing her hair. Grant came out of the lounge and stood in the doorway. She felt unaccountably shy with him, and fussed over the children to hide it.

"It's nice to have you back," he said, standing aside as they pulled her into the lounge.

"It's nice to be back." She looked at him and wanted to go on looking, and he too seemed to be having trouble dragging his gaze from hers, seemed to be drinking in the sight of her as though he couldn't get enough of it. But Toby and Ellen were talking, and she smiled down at them, scarcely hearing what they said.

"Hey, calm down, you two!" Grant ordered. "You'll give Rennie a headache, both talking at once."

There was a momentary silence while the children turned to look at him. Then they began to chatter again. Grant raised his eyes, and Rennie laughed. "It's better, though, isn't it?" she asked him softly. These two cheerful, talkative children were worlds apart from the solemn, worried boy and the tearful, frightened little girl they had been only weeks before.

Grant's mother was a small, precise lady with white-winged brown hair, who sat in the front seat of the car clutching a handbag that contained several bottles of pills and, among other mysterious objects and papers that made it bulge prodigiously, a gold powder compact with a mirror in the lid, that fascinated Ellen. Introduced to Rennie, she had given her a slight, gracious smile and a kindly, "How do you do, my dear?"

Rennie wondered if she ought to curtsey.

She sat in the back with the two children, mindful of her responsibility to keep them amused and reasonably quiet.

At first it was easy. As the car travelled over the high curve of the Harbour Bridge, they pointed out to each other the yachts and launches busily darning the water below, and at Albany they were intrigued when Grant had to stop at a set of traffic lights to let a group of horses and riders cross the motorway.

"Is it a pedestrian crossing for horses?" Toby asked.

"That's right," Grant answered over his shoulder. "An equestrian crossing. There are a lot of pony club riders here, most of them children, and the local people insisted when the road was put in that there must be a safe place for them to cross."

Some time after that, Ellen began wriggling uncomfortably and whispered in Rennie's ear.

Rennie said, "Grant, we need a comfort stop soon."

"And I would like a cup of tea," Mrs. Morrison announced. "I know a very nice restaurant at Orewa."

The car descended a steep hill, went over a bridge where several people were fishing from the sides, and entered the township, strung out along the shoreline.

"I want to go to the beach!" Toby said excitedly, glimpsing the blue water separated from the road by a strip of grassed reserve. "And play on that!" he added, seeing a group of children scrambling about a large, undulating wooden climbing frame. "And the slide!"

"There's a beach where we're going," Grant reminded him. "And we can't spend too much time here. We've a long way to go."

Toby looked disappointed. Rennie said, "Why don't you and your mother have some morning tea while I look after the children? I'd quite enjoy a short walk on the beach, myself."

Grant looked relieved, and his mother gave her an approving smile. Rennie let the children have their heads, scrambling about the play equipment and running along the sand shouting to each other. The beach was long and wide, and even the houses and motels crowded along most of its length couldn't spoil its beauty.

Grant had bought them cold drinks and a bag of potato chips, and having had a chance to stretch their legs, the children were content for some time. At Kaiwaka he drew up at a shop advertising Dutch-style cheese.

The children, intrigued by the huge cheeses on shelves behind the counter, and the opportunity to taste, helped him to choose three from which the Dutch proprietor cut large wedges. Grant bought some exotic sausages, too. On the way back to the car he said, "Kaiwaka's aptly named."

"What's aptly?" Toby asked.

"Suitably," Rennie explained. "It means it has the right name. Kai waka means 'the food canoe.'"

"You know Maori?" Grant asked.

Rennie shook her head. "Very little. A few common words like that. I'd like to, though. We did a bit at school. I've always meant to learn it properly."

"Me, too. Like most people, I haven't got around to it."

Apparently inspired by the sight and discussion of food, Ellen said, "I'm hungry."

Grant glanced at his watch. "We could buy some sandwiches at the take-away over there and have a picnic a little further on."

They had it at a wooden table set in the shade of black-barked kahikatea and dainty small-leaved kowhai on a grassed space off the road. A tui called throatily from the trees, and the sound of rushing water in a nearby stream alternated with the sound of traffic passing on the road. Mrs. Morrison produced a thermos flask of tea which she offered to share with Grant and Rennie, but they declined, settling for canned drinks instead. Rennie tried to keep her attention on the children, helping them with their meal, and Grant seemed to be concentrating on his mother with equal determination.

The children found a path going towards the water, and Rennie got up to go after them as they disappeared into the trees. Grant followed within seconds.

"I'll look after them," Rennie said. "You stay with your mother."

"My mother's fine," he answered. "Watch out!" The path was muddy, and he shot out a hand to steady her as her shoes slipped on the soft ground.

She straightened and moved rapidly ahead of him. The children had disappeared round a curve, and she called, "Toby! Ellen! Wait!"

She caught up with them before they reached the broad, stony stream, and took their hands as they approached the water. Grant accompanied them, and watched while the children bent to dabble their fingers, exclaiming at the cold. The water flowed fast and was overshadowed by trees. Ferns layered the bank opposite, and slim mottled trees dipped their branches almost into the water.

Toby said, "Look—stepping stones." He raced off to try them, and Grant went striding after him, while Rennie and Ellen followed more slowly.

Toby was already on the second stone, gauging the distance to the next one. Grant glanced at Rennie and put his foot on the first stone.

There were eight of them, and Toby successfully negotiated the lot to scamper up a narrow path on the other side as Grant reached the bank behind him.

"I want to go, too," Ellen said.

Her legs were not as long as her brother's and Rennie had to help her, since she refused to be carried. Standing on one flat square and trying to swing Ellen over to her from the previous one was no easy task. On the very last one, Rennie lost her balance, let out a gasping cry and landed awkwardly in the water, soaking her jeans.

Ellen, safely ensconced on the stepping stone, regarded her solemnly and said, "You splashed me, Rennie."

Grant's voice said urgently, "Are you hurt?" He'd come racing back down the path with Toby on his heels. Regardless of his shoes and trousers, he waded in and as Rennie started to scramble up, put a hand on her arm to help.

"I've probably got a bruise," she said ruefully, "but otherwise I'm okay."

"Rennie fell in," Ellen said.

Grant glanced at her. "The child's brilliant," he confided to Rennie, surveying her. "We'll make a lawyer of her yet. Sure you're okay?"

She nodded. "*You* didn't need to get wet. I can see where Ellen got it from."

He acknowledged the dig with a hint of a smile. "Luckily we've both got clean clothes in the car."

Ellen said singlemindedly, "I want to go where Toby did."

Seeing Grant was about to veto the idea, Rennie said, "I can wait."

"Show her, Toby," Grant said resignedly. "But don't go any farther than we did before."

Toby took his sister's hand and Grant offered his to Rennie. "Can I help you get back?"

"I don't need help," she told him, slightly offended by the assumption. "I only fell in because I was trying to get Ellen across."

They sat on the bank trying to wring out their clothes until the children came back and Grant went over to swing Ellen up on his shoulders.

Once across the stream again, he put her down and she looked Rennie over critically and pronounced, "You're wet," before running up the path with Toby.

As they disappeared out of sight, Grant said, "I apologise for my daughter's lack of feeling."

Rennie shook her head, laughing. "You're as delighted as I am to see her getting back her independence."

He smiled at her and held out his hand. "Come on, let's get you back and into something dry."

The look in his eyes as he ran a glance over the wet, clinging jeans made her breathless. She passed him without taking the outstretched hand. "I'm not hurt," she said in excuse. "Honestly."

She hurried up the path ahead of him, emerging from the trees in time to hear the children giving Mrs. Morrison a highly coloured version of Rennie's mishap.

"And Daddy jumped in to save her!" Ellen finished.

"Nothing so dramatic," Grant said, going to the car to lift out a couple of bags. "The stream's less than a foot deep." Encountering his mother's curious stare, he added, "But Rennie might have hurt herself on those stones. And you, young lady," he added lightly to Ellen, "should be grateful she managed not to drop you in the water at the same time."

Ellen looked doubtful.

Retiring into the trees, Rennie made a quick change, emerging to find Grant already wearing dry trousers and stowing wet things into the car.

Soon they were winding over the Brynderwyns, topping the summit and finding a magnificent view of hills and ocean laid out before them, glittering in the sun. After descending to sea level and passing through the little town of Waipu, they could see the ocean from the road, a shining sheet of blue with small rocky islands silhouetted stark against the sky.

"Is that our beach, Daddy?" Ellen enquired.

"No, we're not there yet, but it won't be long now."

At Whangarei, a small city enclosed by hills and harbour, they didn't stop, but continued up the Tutukaka coast on a winding road, where they lost the sea. They found it again when Grant turned down a switchback side road that skirted several little bays and eventually arrived at a huddle of houses along a white, curved foreshore where the water came gently in to rest.

Grant slowed the car, while they peered out at a mixture of modest and often shabby cottages and newer, more permanent homes.

"There it is! Shaw." His mother pointed at the name on a letterbox outside a substantial Mediterranean-style house. She started digging in her handbag for the key.

The house was just as impressive inside. The children discovered that their room had four bunks, so they could each have a top one, and Grant gave an exaggerated sigh of relief. "I had visions of arbitrating on that one."

His mother's room was large and comfortable and quite private, with a sofa set facing the sea, as well as a bed. Grant gave the children a strict injunction that they were not to visit her unless specifically invited.

"Choose a bedroom for yourself," he instructed Rennie, giving her the choice of a twin or double room, and she chose the twin, which was marginally smaller, leaving the other one for Grant.

The lounge had large windows right across the wall that faced the beach, and Rennie, having quickly unpacked the children's things and her own, stood admiring the view for a few minutes while Grant brought out the cheeses he had bought and cut some slices for the children.

"Sit down at the table and eat," he admonished, and called to Rennie, "Want some?"

"No, thanks," she answered dreamily. She was hypnotised by the sunlight on the water, the sudden, surprising lift of white along the edge of each wave as it reached the sand, the clouds drifting on the horizon.

He came to stand beside her, a piece of cheese held in his hand. "Gorgeous, isn't it?" he commented.

Rennie didn't answer. She turned to smile at him, and saw the answering smile in his eyes, and experienced one of life's rare moments of pure happiness.

Mrs. Morrison rested for the remainder of the afternoon, which Rennie and Grant spent with the children on the beach, swimming, building sand castles, and exploring the rock pools on the headlands when the tide receded.

"Look!" Toby cried, fishing something out of one of the pools and displaying it on his hand. "An orange starfish!"

"So it is," Rennie agreed, impressed. "Isn't it lovely?" It was brilliant orange with black markings. "Put it back carefully, now," she said when they had all admired it. "It will die if we keep it out of the water too long."

Toby slid it back into the pool, and he and Ellen watched as it slowly fastened itself to a rock.

"There's a *blue* one!" Ellen said, hushed as though afraid of frightening it. "A tiny little one. And a bigger one, see! And look, a fish!" She started as a tiny silver fish went shooting across the pool and hid under an outcrop of rock. "And—oh, look, Rennie! A hedgehog!"

"It's a kina," Rennie explained. "A sea-egg. Or sea-urchin, some people call them."

"It looks prickly."

"Yes, it is, but you can eat them. Lots of Maori people love them."

"Not the prickles!"

"No, the insides."

Toby said, "Ooh, yuck!"

"It's not so different from eating fish," Grant said.

"I don't like fish."

Grant laughed. "Anyway, we're going to leave them right where they are." He straightened, and Rennie, getting up from her haunches at the same time, slipped a little on the wet rock, cannoning into him.

He put a strong arm about her, and her hand came up to steady herself, the palm against his chest. His heart was beating strongly, and she glanced up, caught the sudden glitter in his eyes before he put both hands on her arms, gripping them hard as he eased her away.

"Okay?" he enquired casually. His eyes were cool now, and she wondered if he thought she had engineered that moment of closeness.

"Fine," she said, pushing her hair from her eyes. "Thanks."

He watched her movement, his gaze slipping downwards to her thin white T-shirt, his mouth going tight.

Rennie flushed, feeling a stirring of anger. She wasn't being deliberately provocative and it was unfair of him to think so.

"It's about time we were getting a meal," Grant said, transferring his gaze to the children. "Is anyone hungry?"

After the children were tucked up in their top bunks, the three adults sat in the lounge. Mrs. Morrison, her feet propped on a stool, was reading one of the half-dozen library books she had brought with her. Grant, on the cane sofa, opened a newspaper he had bought at Orewa, and Rennie curled up in a roomy cushioned wicker chair with a paperback that Shane had given her at Christmas, a romantic thriller by one of her favourite authors.

Grant said, "Anyone want the radio or the TV on?"

Rennie shook her head.

"Not until the ten o'clock news," his mother said.

At about nine, Grant put down the paper and said, "I think I'll go for a walk."

His mother looked surprised but said only, "All right, dear." Rennie, lost in a world of intrigue and romance, scarcely looked up from her book.

Half an hour later, Mrs. Morrison said, "Rennie, dear, would you care for a cup of tea or coffee?"

Rennie looked up. "If you want one, I'll make it."

"Thank you. You will join me, though? And perhaps a biscuit."

When Grant returned, Mrs. Morrison was drinking tea, and Rennie a mug of coffee.

Rennie got up, saying, "What would you like?"

But Grant waved her back to her chair. "I can get my own. Stay there."

Rennie finished her drink and went to the kitchen to rinse out the mug. "I won't wait for the news," she said. "I think I'll go to bed." She was quite tired, and besides, Mrs. Morrison probably wanted some time alone with her son. She collected her toilet things from her room, and as she walked along the short passageway to the bathroom, she heard the older woman say, "...certainly a nice enough girl, and good with the children. But I still think that..."

"I told you," Grant answered patiently, "I had no choice. It's only temporary. She has to go back to university in a month or two, anyway. The children will be more settled by then, and I'll have had time to find someone more suitable."

Rennie entered the bathroom and shut the door quietly behind her. Suitable! What's unsuitable about me? she thought. What does he *want,* for heaven's sake? I've done the job well, I know I have. And if the children are settled by then, it'll be *because* I've done a good job! Admittedly the house wasn't always as neat as it might be, and meals were sometimes late, but the children were happy, he couldn't deny that, and surely that was the most important thing. So I'm not Jean! She felt a sudden stab of pure jealousy. I can't compete with his wife. But he didn't want Jean in the end—or she didn't want him. And neither do I, she lied to herself. Stuff him.

She turned on the shower and stripped angrily, stepping under the hot water to scrub at the sand that dusted her body. She was still seething when she slid into her bed and pulled up the sheet.

The next day she took the children for a long walk to a neighbouring bay, partly overland and then along the beach while the tide was low. Grant offered to come along, but she told him coolly that she could manage, and that she was sure his mother would appreciate his company. Grant looked faintly bemused, but acceded readily enough to the suggestion.

In the afternoon, while his mother rested, Grant said he would watch the children and Rennie could have some time to herself.

"I'm being paid to look after them," she reminded him. "And they didn't drown or break any limbs this morning, did they?"

Grant's brows went up. "You're entitled to some time off," he said. "Take it this afternoon."

She bowed her head. "If you say so."

She took her book and climbed the headland, finding a place in the shade of a large windblown ngaio tree, where she could alternately read or sit staring at the sea, or lie back against the harsh, dry grass and drowse.

"Feeling better?" Grant enquired when she returned to the house.

She gave him a deliberately surprised stare. "I feel fine, thank you. How was your afternoon?" she added politely.

"No problems. Ellen had a nap. She and Toby are sorting out their collection of shells and stones in their room, now. Finish your book?"

"Nearly. I didn't spend all the time reading. Did you know there are gannets here? I've been watching them dive for fish."

"Yes, I've seen them. Spectacular, aren't they, the way they go straight into the water. What are you reading, anyway?'' He plucked the book from her hand when she held it out to him, and looked at the cover picture of a young man and woman fleeing hand in hand from a man with a gun.

He looked up at her, smiling quizzically. ''This is what you like?''

''Sometimes,'' she said, taking the book from him. ''It's very well written.''

''I'll take your word for it.''

''You can borrow it when I've finished, if you like.''

''Thank you, but I don't think so.''

Rennie shrugged. ''Please yourself.'' Obviously he thought her taste in literature was beneath contempt. Snob, she thought angrily, as she went to put the book away in her room.

Most of the houses along the beach were occupied for the holidays, and during the day there were usually a couple of dozen people sunning themselves or swimming, and a few more fishing from the rocks that bounded the bay. Toby and Ellen made friends with another family who regularly rented a large house for the summer holidays.

The Townsends had a combination family. The three olive-skinned youngsters whose ages fitted neatly around Ellen's and Toby's had a blond stepbrother and stepsister of about Rennie's age. They obviously got on very well with their father's young Maori wife, and treated her more like another sister than a stepmother. Their father, a tall, balding man with kind blue eyes, offered to take Grant fishing in his aluminium dinghy. Grant accepted the offer, apparently surprising his mother, and that evening he brought back a couple of snappers for dinner. Even Toby, in spite of his professed dislike of fish, tucked into his father's catch with relish.

Afterwards Grant started to help Rennie wash up, but she said shortly, ''You must be tired. I can manage these.''

''I don't mind,'' he said. ''You must be tired, too, after having the children all day on your own.''

"It's what you're paying me for," she reminded him. "Why don't you go and supervise their showers? They're likely to have water all over the bathroom."

He put down the tea-towel he was holding and gave her a long look. "Okay," he said finally. "If that's what you'd prefer."

After the children had gone to bed, Grant seemed restless. He switched on the radio for the first time, and twiddled with the knobs, but in less than ten minutes had switched it off again. The reception was bad, and the choice of stations limited. He stood up and went to the window to look out at the fading sunlight on the sea, and then picked up the paper, shuffled through the pages and put it down again.

"Why don't you go for a walk, Grant?" his mother suggested at last.

"Yes, I think I will." He stood up. "Come with me, Rennie."

She looked up, startled. "I don't think—"

"Come with me, Rennie," he repeated, making it sound like an order.

"The children—"

"My mother can keep an eye on the children, can't you, Mother?"

"Yes, dear. Of course." She looked almost as startled as Rennie, her glance going from one to the other of them.

"Come on," Grant said peremptorily. "You needn't change. It's still warm outside."

Rennie rose, her cheeks a little flushed. She wore a T-shirt and light cotton pants, and her feet were bare. For walking on the sand, she never wore shoes.

He stood back to let her go down the stairs first, and she took a quick peek at his face as she passed him. He looked grim.

He opened the door at the bottom of the stairs, and they walked side by side over springy buffalo grass to the short incline that led to the beach. Usually Rennie jumped it, but tonight she took it more slowly. There was a dinghy with an outboard motor heading out to sea, a night fisherman, no doubt. And a couple of Maori women with a bucket were digging for shellfish at the edge of the water, while some children with a dog played about nearby.

Grant touched her arm to lead her in the other direction, towards the dark rocks under the headland. "So. What's it all about, Rennie?" he asked her as they reached the firm sand bared by the receding tide, leaving their footprints on its smooth surface.

"What's all what about?"

"Don't play games with me! You're sulking, and I want to know why."

"I'm not sulking!"

He stopped, so that she had to stop, too. "What would you call it, then? All this cold shoulder. You're hardly speaking to me, quite apart from the Jane Eyre act."

"I don't know what you're talking about!" He quirked an eyebrow, and she mumbled, "Well, I thought that was what you wanted." She hunched her shoulders and turned to continue walking.

"Is this all because I kissed you and didn't follow it up?" he demanded.

"No, it isn't!" She turned on him. "It's because—"

"Well?"

"Because you—you don't give me credit for *anything!* Not for looking after your kids, or—"

"What do you mean, I don't give you credit? You told me not to keep saying that I was grateful!"

"I suppose you are. Any port in a storm, and you were pretty desperate, weren't you?"

He frowned. "This is nonsense. How can you think that I don't appreciate—"

"I heard you talking to your mother," she said. "As if I'm some kind of stop-gap, a second-best solution until you find something better!"

He shook his head, looking resigned but enlightened. "I didn't mean it to sound like that, Rennie. All I meant was that the arrangement is a temporary one, and I'll have to find a permanent solution before you return to university. My mother thought you were too young for the job before she even met you, as soon as I mentioned you were a student. I suppose I was feeling defensive."

"I'm not that young," Rennie said. "Even teenagers have birthdays. And they don't stay teenagers for ever."

"You've had a birthday?"

"I will have. On New Year's Day."

"Congratulations," Grant said. "So you'll be nineteen."

"Twenty."

"Twenty?"

"Legally adult."

"Legally."

"That's right. So you can stop treating me like a child, okay?"

"Maybe," Grant said. "That depends on whether you're going to act like one, doesn't it?"

"For instance?" she challenged him, stung at the accusation.

"For instance, sulking."

"I told you I was not sulking! I was trying to remember that you're my boss. I thought you wanted some...distance between us."

"Oh, I do," Grant said softly. "I need some distance, Rennie."

"Well," she said, looking him in the eyes. "There you are, then."

He sighed. "You don't know anything about half-measures, do you?"

"I've never had much time for them," she said scornfully.

"All or nothing at all?"

"Yes."

The sea lapped at their feet, but neither of them noticed. The light was dying, leaching the colour from the water. Along the sand the dog barked. A car door slammed, the engine roared and the car took off. The beach was deserted now, except for them. Grant said, "It can't be all, Rennie."

She nodded, then turned and looked out at the ocean, her hands jammed in her pockets. "Okay." She was trying hard to sound indifferent. "If that's what you want."

"Rennie—" He tried to take her arm, but she shook him off.

"Don't!"

"This is silly!" he said angrily. "I know your feelings are hurt, but we can be friends!"

"No, we can't," she said. "And you may be years and years older than me, but you don't know anything! Not about me! So don't even try, okay? I'm your employee, you pay me to do a job for you, which I'm doing and I'm damn good at it, too! I'm not being paid to be *your friend*, as well. And my feelings are none of your business. So just do me a favour and leave me alone. That's all I ask."

Grant stepped back, tightlipped. He spread his hands in capitulation. "I won't argue with that. You have every right—I just wish it could have been different."

"So do I," Rennie answered him bleakly. "May I go back to the house, now? I'm tired."

He pointedly stepped aside, watching her stride past him with her head held high, her bare feet leaving emphatic imprints in the sand.

Chapter Twelve

On New Year's Eve the Townsends were having a party. "Some of Huia's relations are coming over," they told Rennie. "They're going to put down a hangi near the beach. And we're having a barbecue as well. Tell Grant you're all invited. The kids, too."

Toby and Ellen, of course, knew all about it from their young friends, and watched as Huia's relatives dug a pit for the hangi, tipped in some rounded beach stones, and lit a roaring fire to heat them, before the foil-wrapped food was placed on top and the pit covered over with sacking, corrugated iron, and sandy earth.

All through the afternoon the children kept dragging Rennie back to the site to feel the slowly warming earth over the pit, asking her when the pork, chicken, fish and vegetables they had seen go into the umu would be cooked.

Grant had run out of reading matter, he said, politely rejecting his mother's offer of one of her library books. He looked at Rennie and said casually, "You offered me one the other night—have you finished it?"

"Yes. I'll fetch it."

He settled with it on one of the loungers set on a terrace overlooking the sea. When Rennie and the children returned from their fourth check of the hangi, he had read a quarter of the book and seemed engrossed. By the time the party started, he was half-way through, and reluctant to leave it.

Somewhat smugly, Rennie said, "Enjoying the book?"

He shrugged. "It's fast paced and action packed. I must admit I have to keep turning the pages. It's okay for whiling away a holiday afternoon."

"I thought that was exactly what you wanted." Rennie was slightly nettled by the faint praise.

Grant raised his brows. "Did I say different?" he queried. "It's fine. I'm enjoying it. Is that what you want to hear?"

Something like that. She smiled at him innocently. It wouldn't do him any harm to relax now and then with something that wasn't a book of statutes. She didn't think she'd ever seen him reading fiction before. Perhaps he thought it was slothful.

Even Mrs. Morrison joined the party, sitting on a chair which Grant carried down from the house for her. Picking at steamed pork, potatoes and cabbage from the hangi, and a small piece of barbecued steak, she smilingly but firmly refused the offer of a bite of Ellen's sausage wrapped in a slice of bread and dripping with tomato sauce. The children sat among their friends, eating with their fingers from paper plates and thoroughly enjoying themselves. Rennie wiped their greasy faces and hands with paper towels and shook her head when Grant suggested she might like to join the teenage contingent who were gathering round the barbecue fire on the sand with a tape player and a guitar.

Grant shrugged and said, "I'm taking my mother up to the house."

When he returned, Ellen had fallen asleep against Rennie, and Toby, although he protested for form's sake when his father suggested it, looked ready for bed, too.

"Stay there," Grant told Rennie, as he lifted his daughter into his arms. "I can manage them."

"I'll come, too—"

"I said, stay here!" Grant repeated softly, but with an edge to his voice. "And that's an order."

There was no doubt he meant it. Rennie subsided to the sand, wondering if he intended to come back.

Everyone was drifting over to the fire, now. "Rennie!" Larry Townsend called from the group of young people, waving her over to join them. He was a good-looking young man, with longish curly hair and a gold ring adorning one ear. "Come on! You don't want to sit there by yourself."

She joined the circle, Larry shifting over to make room for her.

When she saw Grant next, she was singing along with the others, swaying from side to side in time with the song, and Larry's arm was casually draped about her shoulders. Grant was standing outside the circle talking to Larry's father. He lifted a hand to her and went on talking.

The guitarist laid aside his instrument and got up, stripping off the sweatshirt he was wearing with shorts. "I'm going for a swim."

"Coming?" Larry asked Rennie. Several of the others were following.

"Yes, okay." The water would be warm, and with a group of them going in, perfectly safe. Rennie stood up and unbuttoned her cotton skirt, letting it drop to the ground, then tugged off the big T-shirt that hid her bikini.

As she tossed it down on top of the skirt, she noticed that Grant was standing alone now. And he was watching her. She couldn't see the expression on his face, he was outside the circle of firelight, but there was a tenseness in his stance that made her self-conscious. She put a hand to her hair, pushing it back, and saw him make an abrupt movement. Then he turned away.

* * *

The water was warm from the day's sun, and the stars brilliant overhead, the moonlight almost like day. Rennie splashed about with the others, and joined in a game with a beach ball that someone had tossed into the water. But she felt cold, and when she came out and ran up the sand to fetch her towel, she was shivering. Huia was sitting in the circle of her husband's arm chatting to some friends. She said, as Rennie towelled herself dry and pulled on her clothes, "Have you got a sweater or something, Rennie? Come into the house and I'll get one."

Over Rennie's protest that she'd soon warm up, the other woman insisted. "I was just going to check on the little ones, anyway. It's my turn."

Inside, Rennie accepted the loan of a roomy sweatshirt, and waited for Huia while she looked in on the younger children, who had been put to bed.

"Sound asleep," Huia reported, smiling, as she rejoined Rennie. "Are you warmer now?"

"Yes, thank you. Has Grant gone home?"

"He said he was afraid his mother wouldn't hear if the children called. But to tell you to stay as long as you wanted."

"Still, maybe I should go—"

"It doesn't take two of you," Huia said. "He seemed to want you to stay. Come on." She put her arm about Rennie's waist. "Enjoy yourself."

She stayed until after midnight. When the cheering and kissing and singing were over, she slipped away and trod along the sand on her own. The light was on in the lounge, but it wasn't until she had quietly climbed the stairs that she realised Grant was still up. He must have been sitting on the long sofa, and as she entered he stood up.

"Have a good time?" he asked.

"Yes, thank you. Huia told me you said for me to stay—"

"Yes. It was only a question, not a criticism. Happy Birthday."

"And a Happy New Year to you."

"If I'd realised, I wouldn't have taken you from your family. You should have said."

"I didn't want a fuss. I won't be able to avoid a party next year, though." She saw the bottle and glass on the small table beside him. "Have you been drinking alone?"

"A bit. Do I sense disapproval?"

"Of course not. I don't have the right, anyway. It can't be much fun, though."

"Join me if you like. It's wine. I didn't bring any whisky."

"All right," she said, coming into the room. "I'll get a glass."

She fetched one from the kitchen. When she came back he was standing where she had left him, but he had the bottle in his hand. He poured for them both, then lifted his glass. "To you, Rennie."

"Thank you."

He drank some of his wine in silence, then turned away from her to gaze out of the big window. Rennie went to stand beside him, but he didn't look at her. She had finished her wine before he tossed off the rest of his drink in one go and put the empty glass on the table.

As he straightened, she held hers out to him, and he said, "More?"

Rennie shook her head. "No. I should go to bed."

"Yes. You certainly should."

She glanced up at him and didn't move. There was a sudden tension in the room.

He said, "Where did you get the sweatshirt? You didn't take one with you."

"Huia lent it to me. She's nice."

"They're a nice couple."

"Yes. And happy, in spite of the difference in their ages." She dared to look at him then.

"You can tell that," he asked mockingly, "on a few days' acquaintance?"

"I think so. They seem a very happy family."

"Do you know what people said when Jean and I broke up? 'We always thought you were such a happy family.' I don't know how many times I heard that."

"I'm sorry."

"For me? Don't bother. It was as much my fault as anyone's. Ellen was our last desperate bid at mending the cracks. But that was a mistake. In the end, as Jean pointed out when she was feeling particularly bitter, it only meant that she was left with two children to care for instead of one."

"She didn't want them with her?"

He shook his head. "It wasn't that simple. She would have fought me tooth and nail if I'd gone for custody. She loved them both. She also resented the fact that they existed. And I shouldn't be talking to you like this. On your birthday, too." He gave her a faint smile. "It's the advent of the new year. Makes me think back over the old one, and the ones before. Vain regrets."

Rennie shook her head. "I don't mind. I hope you won't have vain regrets about this year."

"So do I."

"You shouldn't have seen it in on your own," she said. "The children would have been all right."

"I know. Mother said she'd leave her door open. But I didn't want to go back there and watch—"

He stopped abruptly.

"And watch what?"

"Nothing. Just wasn't in the mood for partying, that's all."

She crossed her arms in front of herself and plucked at the baggy sweatshirt. "Well . . ." She took a step forward. "See you in the morning."

He nodded stiffly, and she obeyed an insane impulse and stopped before him. "Happy New Year," she said huskily, and put her hands on his shoulders and pressed her mouth briefly to his.

His lips were cool and unresponsive, but as she stepped away his hands suddenly clamped on her shoulders through the cotton knit. His eyes blazed, and then her head was forced back by his kiss, his fingers biting into her flesh with almost bone-breaking strength. His mouth was ruthless, an invasion and a chastisement, and when he finally released her, she fell back with a hand to her aching lips, her eyes wide with shock.

"You're all grown up, now," he told her harshly. "Old enough to know better than to play with fire. Now go to bed."

Rennie swallowed, dropping her hand. "You had no need to do that!"

"Yes, I did," he said, his eyes still glittering. "And you asked for it, little girl. So don't expect me to apologise this time!"

"That's your whole trouble," she flashed. "You know I'm not a little girl! You just won't accept it!"

"If I accepted it," he said between his teeth, "the way I'm feeling at the moment, believe me, you'd wish that I hadn't!"

Hurt and disappointed at the way he had broken the mood, she lifted her chin and refused to back down. "Try me!"

There was a heartbeat's silence, while she wondered if she was quite, quite mad. Because it didn't take a genius to work out that Grant was nearing the end of his tether, and if she pushed him she wasn't sure how far he might go. An echo of her mother's warning sounded in her mind, and she drew a breath, ready to retract the rash words.

Too late. She heard the hiss of his indrawn breath, saw the sudden taut decision in his expression. Then he smiled, but it was a smile that brought to mind icy steppes and prowling wolves. And his voice shivered down her spine as he said, "All right. Yes, if that's what you want."

She shut her teeth as he reached for her. He was right, she'd asked for it, and she wasn't damned well running away now, begging for mercy like a frightened virgin.

Which was exactly what she was.

He lifted her in his arms, and carried her easily the few steps to the door of his room, shouldered it wide and then shoved it closed behind him.

He dropped her on the bed, and she was shamingly glad that he hadn't turned on the light. In the distance she could dimly hear the sounds of the party still going on, and moonlight shafted through the window. Grant sat on the bed beside her, pulling off his shoes. Then he leaned across and, with his hands on the borrowed sweatshirt, said, "Let's have this off, first. Not the sexiest thing I've seen you in, darling."

The endearment should have reassured her. Instead, she had an immediate, irrational desire to cross her arms, which she conquered with difficulty as he hauled the sweatshirt off. It was a moment before she realised that the T-shirt underneath had gone with it, leaving only her bikini top and the skirt that had already ridden up past her knees.

Making to lower her arms as he tossed the shirts to the floor, she was stopped by his hands on her wrists, holding them on either side of her head as he studied her in the white moonlight.

Looking back at him, she saw a face that seemed all shadows and angles, the face of a predator. It came towards her, and she closed her eyes, spurning a craven instinct to turn her head aside, waiting for his mouth on hers.

Instead, she felt his lips on her throat, moving over her skin, hot and fierce. She took a harsh, gulping breath, trying to say his name, and he muttered something that sounded angry and let go her wrists to place his hands under her, lifting her a little as his mouth travelled down to the curve of her breasts above the bikini top.

Rennie stiffened in nervous anticipation, and when she felt the scrape of his teeth on the tender flesh she flinched and gave a startled little sound.

He lifted his head. "Did I hurt you?"

"N-no," she admitted, but her heart was beating wildly with fear and excitement.

He said, "Good." But his hands on her ribs and back were not gentle. He had found the fastening of her skirt, and impatiently parted it, pushing the folds roughly aside as he muttered, "I want to see you."

He had seen her before, on the beach, dressed—or undressed—as she was now. But it had been very different then. She felt his eyes sear her, even in the semi-darkness, and when he reached for the lamp switch above the bed she said sharply, "No!" Then whispered, as he paused, "Please!"

"Not so bold after all, Rennie?" he taunted quietly, but his hand lowered until it rested on her shoulder, the thumb stroking over the bone.

She bit her lip, unable to think of an adequate reply, and his hand skimmed over the bikini top, across her midriff to her hip, firmly shaping her thigh. He shifted down on the bed, and she felt his open mouth on her navel, the tip of his tongue exploring the little spiralling grooves.

She felt herself flush all over, her breath quickening. She moved restlessly and he stopped what he was doing and sat up, one hand still caressing her hip. "Don't you like that?"

"I—yes, I think so—"

His quiet laughter had an underlying harshness. He slid a finger inside her top, moving back and forth over softness, the tip meeting a hardness at the centre. "I think you do, too," he said.

He slid his hand round to her back, following the line of the fabric, and finding the fastening, tugging at it. He sat up on his elbow and said, "Take this off for me, Rennie?"

She wished she could discount the implacable note in his voice, forget that so far he had not kissed her since they left the lounge. But after only the briefest hesitation, she reached behind her and unfastened the catch. The top loosened, and she took a quick, calming breath and pulled it off. And closed her eyes.

She had the impression that for a long moment he was holding his breath. Then he said, "Yes. Oh, yes."

She felt his hands cover her, and her lips parted involuntarily on a muffled moan. She whispered, "Please, Grant, kiss me!"

He did, with his hands still warm on her breasts, and she thought she would die with the sweetness of it. She opened her mouth to him, and felt his tongue thrust demandingly against hers and then his hands moved round behind her and lifted her up to him, her body taut and curved against his.

Her veins were rivers of fire, her heart a soaring bird. He shifted again, taking her with him so that her head was at the edge of the bed, her long hair flowing almost to the floor, her neck arched. His mouth was leaving a slow trail of heat as it burned down her throat, and then to her breast.

When it fastened there, warm and moist and urgent, she cried out, she couldn't help it. Grant lifted his head and said, "Shh. What is it?"

"It's all right!" she whispered frantically, but suddenly she was aware of the children sleeping in the next room, of his mother downstairs. Trying to blot them from her mind, she repeated, "It's all right, I'm—I'm just not used to this—"

His hand scooped into her hair, lifting her head, and he looked down into her bewildered, passion-darkened and slightly frightened eyes.

His own eyes glittering with a complex mix of emotions, he said, "No, you're not, are you?" And eased her head onto the pillow before removing his hand. He looked away from her into the darkness of the room for a moment, then back at her, making a slow, deliberate, regretful inspection of her near-nakedness. And suddenly rolled on his back.

He heaved a long breath into his lungs and said, "I must have been mad. Or I've drunk more than I realised. I didn't mean to go so far."

She eased herself up on the pillow to look at him, fighting an urge to cover herself, feeling terribly exposed now that he was no longer touching her. "If you're mad," she said, "so am I. What did you mean to do?"

He sighed. "Teach you a lesson," he said.

He'd been angry, she knew, perhaps more with himself than her. And he'd meant to frighten her off.

"I'm a fast learner," she said huskily. She didn't scare so easily, and she didn't believe he'd ever have really hurt her—except emotionally. But she'd been nervous of the edge of anger in his lovemaking.

His laugh came bitterly. "I noticed. Hoist with my own petard." He suddenly swung his legs over the other side of the bed, turning his back on her. "Get dressed and go, will you?"

He was throwing her out. Relief and sharp disappointment mingled. "Class dismissed?" she asked, surprised at the accusation in her own voice. She knelt on the bed to touch his shoulder. "Grant—"

He shook her hand off and stood up. "For God's sake, Rennie!" he said savagely. "Can't you see I'm not in a fit frame of mind now to initiate a virgin?" He swung about to face her. "Get out of here while you still can!"

She held his eyes for a second, then scrambled for her clothes, holding them in front of her as she stumbled out of the room and fled to her own. She flung the clothes into a corner, pulled on her nightshirt and huddled herself under the blankets, furiously wiping hot, stinging tears from her eyes.

In the morning she woke with a thundering headache, and her mirror told her she looked pale and hollow-eyed.

Grant, when she saw him at breakfast, didn't look a whole lot better. At least she had concealed some of the ravages with makeup, a remedy not available to him. When she offered to take the children for a swim he didn't suggest coming with them.

By lunchtime she was feeling better; her headache was gone, and the sun had warmed her skin. She managed to get through the meal without looking once at Grant.

Afterwards he said, "This is our last day. I thought I'd go for a drive this afternoon, see some of the other bays, perhaps. Mother doesn't want to come, but I'll take the children, Rennie, and you can stay here or come with us as you like."

"I'll stay," she said hurriedly. "Thank you." In the car she'd have no chance of avoiding him, even with the children there as a buffer.

After checking that Mrs. Morrison didn't want anything, she went for a walk round the rocks, followed by a swim, and then settled on the beach with a book. It wasn't until a long shadow fell across the page that she realised Grant was standing by, watching her.

"Oh, I didn't know you were back!" She looked at her watch and began to scramble to her feet.

"No hurry," he said. "The children sent me to fetch you," he added dryly. "They have a surprise for you."

"What kind of surprise?" She pulled a wraparound skirt about her waist over the swimsuit she was wearing, and tied it firmly. "Did you tell them it's my birthday?" she asked suspiciously.

He shrugged. "It might have slipped out."

"I didn't mean anyone to know. I told you—"

"You know how children love birthdays. You wouldn't deprive them of this small pleasure, would you?"

She bent to pick up the book from the grass, as he did the same. He relinquished it and they straightened together, standing close. She stared into his eyes. They were concerned, even worried.

"Rennie," he said, "I didn't intend to hurt you."

She said, "I thought that was just what you did mean to do."

He stepped back, shaking his head. "Momentarily. But I had no right to take out my bad temper on you."

Dimly she understood that her presence had been just the catalyst. He'd been drinking, not a lot but enough to skew his judgement and unbalance him from his normal, rational self. And he'd been brooding, over Jean's death and their failed marriage, over a lot of things, perhaps, that Rennie knew nothing about.

"It's all right," she said generously. "I know you didn't mean it."

Any of it, she thought bleakly. Not only the anger, but the passion had been directed less at her than at the demons from the past that were tormenting him.

Grant nodded. "I hope we can forget last night. It should never have happened."

"Sure." She shrugged to hide her hurt. With only the slightest hint of sarcasm, she added, "It's forgotten."

Fat chance, she thought. Shooting a glance at his face, she deduced with some satisfaction that he wasn't going to find forgetting so easy, either.

He soon proved it. As she preceded him across the hot sand, he ran a finger over her shoulder blades. "You've burnt a bit," he said. "Didn't you use sunscreen?"

"I couldn't reach there," she said.

"Where's Larry today?"

"How should I know? And why should I, anyway?" She quickened her pace but it was difficult in the soft, warm sand.

"You seemed to be getting on last night," Grant said.

She turned her head to stare at him. "Getting on?"

"You looked pretty close to me."

In the shade of one of the pohutukawas that overhung the beach where it met the grass she stopped short. "I'm not *close* to every man who casually puts an arm around me!"

"How many are there?"

Rennie blinked. He was jealous, she thought blankly, then with a sense of triumph. *Jealous!* The realisation was so heady that she smiled. "Dog in the manger, Grant?" she challenged him.

He moved forward so suddenly that she backed into the rough tree trunk behind her, gasping at the impact. Grant stopped abruptly, and she saw a quick flood of colour come into his face. "Don't push me, Rennie," he said. "You already know where that can lead."

"You started it!" she accused him quickly, breathlessly.

His lips clamped. She saw him making an effort at control.

"You're right," he said colourlessly. "I was out of line." He reached out to take her arm in a hard grip. "Come on. They're waiting for us."

The children were with their grandmother at the table, and the minute she walked in they started singing "Happy Birthday." They had bought sweets and ice cream and pink wafer biscuits, and a cake with yellow icing on which the children had stuck candles. "I wanted to make you a birthday cake," Ellen confided, "but Daddy said we didn't have 'gredients, and besides it wouldn't be a surprise, then."

"I'm sure you'd have made me lovely birthday cake," Rennie said, "but this one looks delicious."

She had to blow out the candles, and then Ellen and Toby presented her with a huge box of chocolates. "Daddy said it's from all of us," Toby said. "And you don't have to share."

"I couldn't possibly eat them all by myself. I hope you'll help me."

"If you like," Toby said, trying to sound offhand. "I like the ones with the gold paper on."

"You should have told us it was your birthday, dear," Mrs. Morrison admonished. "How do your parents feel about your spending it away from them?"

"I already told them I don't want a party," Rennie said. "And we'll have a special dinner one night after I get back."

"Grant says you're twenty. You don't look it. He thought you were a year younger."

"A year's neither here nor there at her age," Grant commented.

"It means I'm not a teenager," Rennie reminded him.

"That's just the age when it does seem to make a great difference," his mother said. "Heavens, I was married at twenty."

"Were you?" Rennie asked, and shot a glance at Grant.

"My husband, of course, was much older."

"Really?" Rennie felt slightly breathless. "How much?"

Mrs. Morrison gave her a frosty look. "A number of years," she said. "The children are waiting for you to cut your cake."

The next day, Grant dropped off his mother first, then headed for Rennie's home.

"I can go home with you, if you like," she offered without much hope.

"That won't be necessary. I'm sure that the children and I can manage on our own tonight. I have to work tomorrow, though. Can you be there by eight o'clock?"

"Yes, of course. I'll see you in the morning, then." She was afraid that he would tell her she needn't stay at nights any more, but he said nothing about it.

He began sending her home every weekend, though she stayed during the week. She was sure he was avoiding being alone with her as much as possible, and felt an odd mixture of exasperation at his scruples and a tingling excitement that he evidently found her so hard to resist. Most nights he said he had work to do after the children were settled, and sat at the kitchen table with a pile of papers. Once she went in to make herself a drink, and found him staring into space.

"Coffee?" she asked.

He looked at her as though he hadn't heard, and she repeated the question.

"Yes, I'd like one." He pushed the papers to one side and sat back, rubbing the nape of his neck with one hand, and watched her absently while she prepared the coffee.

"Thanks," he said, when she handed the cup to him.

She hesitated, and he said, "Sit down."

"Do you have a problem?"

"Problem?"

She indicated the piles of papers.

"Oh, that! Nothing I can't handle there." He was staring into his cup.

"Well, then?"

He looked at her. "I have to get another carer for the children," he said. "Before you go back to university."

Impulsively she said, "I've been thinking. Supposing I don't go back?"

"What do you mean?"

"Would you like me to stay on?"

He put down his cup so hard that it splashed a few drops of coffee onto the typewritten pages on the table. "*No,* I would *not!*"

Hurt at his vehemence, she said, "The children have got used to me—"

"And they can get used to someone else. You are going back to university to finish your degree. And that's final."

"You can't dictate what I do!" she protested.

"I never heard such a crazy idea! Three years of work and you're going to throw it in just like that! You can't give up now!"

"Surely I should be the judge of that?"

"On what grounds do you base that statement?" he asked her sarcastically.

Mulishly she said, "It's my life—"

"Yes, and you're about to ruin it—"

"—and it's my choice, not yours!"

"It's *my* choice that I don't want you looking after my children after the start of term. Your job ends right then. Understood?"

Rennie swallowed. "Understood."

Softening a little, he said, "I didn't mean to snarl, Rennie, but believe me, I know what I'm talking about."

"Because of your *age,* and *experience,* I suppose," Rennie said.

"You could say that."

"And *I* know what I *feel!*" Rennie said, a clenched fist at her chest.

"Yes," Grant said. "That's the crux of the matter, isn't it?"

"What do you mean?"

His face was pale, his expression strained. He'd been overworking, she thought. "When did you decide to chuck it in?" he demanded. "Four weeks ago? Six? Two?"

Rennie shrugged. "What difference does it make?" She hadn't decided anything, but if the children—and Grant—needed her she could at least think about giving them a year or so from her life. She'd expected a discussion, not a sudden flare-up from Grant.

"I should never have kissed you that night," he said flatly.

"Which night?"

He made an impatient gesture. "The night I took you out to dinner. And proved to my own satisfaction that you weren't, after all, infatuated with Ethan. It never occurred to me that I ran the risk you'd—"

"I'd what? Become infatuated with you, instead?" Rennie stood up, trembling. "That's what you think, isn't it? That I have an adolescent crush on you!"

Grant leaned back in his chair, his eyes hard and his face expressionless. "Can you deny it?"

"Yes!" Rennie said fiercely. She knew that the emotions she felt now had nothing to do with the romantic fantasising she had indulged in at puberty. This was something different. But she could see there was no hope of convincing him. "I deny it," she said. "Absolutely."

He was smiling, a faint, disbelieving smile. Rennie, goaded beyond bearing, said, "And what about you? You can't tell me you feel nothing for me!"

"No, I won't try," he said. "I don't deny your sexual attraction for me. Particularly since you've made it plain that it's mutual. That's a powerful aphrodisiac, and very flattering. But I'm not about to lose my head over a lovely adolescent, even one well over the age of consent and legally adult. Frankly, it could lead to more trouble than it's worth."

Rennie whitened. He spoke so coolly, as though delivering a legal opinion. She couldn't remember when her confidence in herself had been so shaken. She felt small and insignificant, and very, very young.

Grant removed his eyes from her stricken face, and shuffled the papers before him, shoving his half-empty coffee cup into the middle of the table. "And now, if you'll excuse me," he said in the same tone, "I really have a lot of work to get through."

Rennie walked into the other room and noticed she was holding an empty cup. She felt as though she'd been flattened by a steam-roller, her mind a blank. After a while, when it began to function again, she was shaken by the realisation that there were three more weeks to the end of the holidays. And she didn't know how on earth she was going to get through them.

Chapter Thirteen

Survive she did, somehow. It was made easier by her continuing anger with Grant, and his own distant manner. Also the frequent excuses he made for going out after the children were in bed. Work, she assumed.

But one night when she was about to go to bed, he came in and was not alone. The woman he introduced as Lorna Fielding, a colleague from his office, would have been in her early thirties, Rennie guessed. She wore a white shirt, slim black skirt and very high heels with black stockings, and her blond hair was sleekly shining, falling against her jawline. She greeted Rennie pleasantly and seemed politely regretful when Rennie said she was going to bed. But long after turning out the light, Rennie could hear her voice and Grant's in the lounge, with occasional bursts of laughter. Then there was a long silence broken only by music which she eventually identified as an etude by Scriabin which she didn't recall seeing in his collection. Apparently this wasn't a business meeting. Eventually she pulled a pillow over her head and went to sleep.

* * *

Over breakfast she said casually, "I didn't know you owned Scriabin's Etude in D sharp minor."

"You know it?" Grant looked up from his coffee in surprise.

"I'm not a total bimbo, you know," Rennie told him with a hint of sharpness. "I listen to all kinds of music. Actually that's one of my favourite pieces."

"Feel free to play it," he said. "There are other pieces of his on the tape. I only got it yesterday."

And had brought Lorna Fielding home to share it with him. Or had she given it to him?

Inexplicably hurt, Rennie asked, "It wasn't your birthday, was it?"

"No." He looked blank. "I have to go."

He got up and bent to kiss the children as usual. Ellen said, "Why don't you kiss Rennie, Daddy?"

She cast him a mocking look, and with a faint glint in his eye he approached her and bent to brush his lips impersonally against her cheek.

The next evening, while the children were in the bath, Grant answered the telephone and called, "Rennie! It's Larry Townsend, for you."

"How did he know this number?" she wondered.

"I gave his father my card. He had a small legal problem and asked if he could look me up after the holidays."

"I've got two tickets for Alice and the Amaranthas for tomorrow night," Larry told her. "Thought you might like to come to the concert with me."

"Alice and the Amaranthas?" It was one of her favourite pop groups. "How did you get those? They were booked out months ago!"

"I have my ways," Larry said modestly. "Well, are you coming?"

"Um, yes," she said, for some reason thinking of the laughter she had heard last night when Grant and his woman friend were alone together. "I'll have to ask, though. Wait."

"Yes, of course you can go," Grant told her. "I'll make a point of being home. Don't worry about the children. Tell him he can pick you up here."

"I can meet him in town."

"You can meet him here."

"Even my parents don't insist on that!"

For a moment Grant looked tight-lipped. Then he said, "Well, if you're sure. But get him to bring you home, anyway. Or use a taxi."

"Will you mind if I invite him in afterwards for coffee?"

"Of course not." He sounded rather clipped. "If that's what you usually do at home."

When she ushered Larry into the house the kitchen light was on. He followed her into the brightly lit room, where Grant was still sitting at the table, his shirtsleeves rolled up, his eyes a little tired.

"I'm making coffee for us," she told him. "Would you like some?"

"Thank you." He pushed the papers away and asked, "How was the concert?"

"Fabulous," she said.

"Grr-eat!" Larry crowed, closing his eyes and waving a fist for emphasis. He was wearing heavy boots and a long coat over jeans with a purple shirt, and the gold ring gleamed in his ear. "You should have seen it when they did 'Turkey Red.' Man, that was *rad!*" He launched into an imitation, swaying from side to side and then stepping into the middle of the room to do a twirl, the coat flapping and swirling about him.

"I'm sure it was wonderful," Grant said when he had finished.

"Yeah, pity you missed it," Larry sympathised.

Grant's lips twitched wryly. "I'll live, I think."

"Coffee," Rennie interrupted. "Are you coming through to the other room with us, Grant?"

He looked from her to Larry. "No, thanks. Far be it for me to intrude on love's young dream."

"Huh?" Larry took a cup from Rennie as she thrust it into his hand.

She banged another down in front of Grant, giving him a wordless glare. "Come on, then," she said to Larry, scooping up her cup. "Grant has work to do."

Half an hour later she let him out, and closed the front door behind him. Grant came out of the kitchen, and she said coolly, "I hope we didn't disturb you." Larry had still been on a high from the concert, and she had laughed a lot.

"Not at all," Grant answered. "I wondered about the children, though."

"They haven't woken. And we weren't that noisy. No more so than you and *your* friend the other night."

"Did we disturb *you?*"

"It's your house."

"Yes."

"But that remark of yours was quite uncalled for."

"Which remark?"

"'Love's young dream,'" she repeated sarcastically. "A cheap crack, don't you think?"

He shrugged.

"Larry's a friend. Nothing more."

"Your choice, not his."

"How would you know? He never attempted to make a pass."

"One day he'll pluck up courage. Just remember what happened to you once before—or nearly happened."

"Larry doesn't drink much."

"Good for him. It isn't only drink that can drive men to madness."

Rennie snorted. "Good heavens, we are getting melodramatic, aren't we? I'm not Helen of Troy!"

A reluctant smile tugged at Grant's mouth. "You don't need to be," he said cryptically.

Rennie said huskily, "Thank you—I think?"

"As if you didn't know." His gaze slipped over her clinging shirt and tight jeans. Almost to himself, he said, "I don't believe Helen was half as sexy."

The flush now encompassed her whole body. And that wasn't all. Her gaze riveted on him, she thought, *How can he make me feel like this, without even touching me?* And closed her eyes.

"Don't do that!" Grant's harsh voice brought them wide open again. He had moved closer, but halted abruptly as she looked at him. She saw his chest rise and fall once. "You'd better get yourself off to bed," he said.

"The cups," Rennie said. "I should wash them—"

"Leave them. They can wait until morning."

Rennie swallowed. "Well, good night, then," she said lamely. She had to walk past him. She didn't look at him, but she knew he was watching her all the way to her bedroom.

She had begun spending more nights at home so that the break wouldn't be so noticeable for the children. Toby seemed to take the impending change in his stride, but Ellen had begun sucking her thumb again, and Rennie spent much time reassuring her.

"I've told Ellen that I'll visit her and Toby often," she said to Grant one night as they were finishing their coffee after dinner. "I thought it would help her get used to the change."

"That's good of you," he said formally, putting down his cup on the table. "I'm sure you're right, but I hope it doesn't cut into your social life, or your studies. Thank you," he added.

"That's all right. I'll try not to intrude on you."

With a hint of impatience, he said, "Of course you won't be intruding. Toby and Ellen are fond of you, and anything that will help them is fine by me, you know that."

"You're a very good father," Rennie said impulsively.

Grimly rueful, Grant answered, "Not particularly, until I was forced into it by circumstances. Then I didn't have much choice. As a matter-of-fact, I was a bit shaken by the way they—particularly Ellen—depended on me after their mother died. Ellen was a baby when I left, I hadn't even had time to get fond of her. I was all they had, but it was a frightening responsibility.''

"Well, you're doing a good job now. And it's worthwhile, isn't it?"

He looked faintly surprised. "Yes, I haven't taken the time to think about it, but I've derived a great deal of pleasure out of those two, as well as worry. Oh, I meant to tell you, I've cancelled the advertisement for a nanny-housekeeper, so you needn't answer any more calls. I had a call from Mrs. Beddoe. Her daughter is out of hospital and progressing nicely at home. Mrs. Beddoe is coming back to Auckland next week, and she'd like to continue in the job. She said to give you her regards."

"Oh, I'm so pleased!"

"Yes, I thought you would be. The children liked her, and they haven't forgotten her, either. I imagine even Ellen will find the transition quite easy."

And so will you, she thought bitterly. Rashly, she said it aloud. "You'll be relieved to see me go, won't you?"

He looked at her across the table. "Don't be silly."

"I'm being honest. Why can't you?" she challenged him.

His mouth was wry. "That's your forte. Perhaps I don't dare."

Rennie looked at him scornfully. "You mean you're a coward?"

His lips went tight. "Stop it, Rennie," he warned. "You could get more than you bargained for."

She leaned across the table. "Just once, why don't you let yourself go with your feelings?"

"I did, just once," he reminded her, softly jeering. "And you were scared stiff."

Rennie swallowed, trying not to blush. "That's an exaggeration. I was nervous, that's all. And anyway, you—meant to scare me, then. You said—you said you wanted to teach me a lesson."

"You want another one?" The jeering note was stronger now, the curve of his lips almost cruel.

Rennie swallowed. "I just want you," she said baldly. "And I know you want me." She saw his face close, his fist on the table clench, and said hurriedly, "And it isn't just sex and—and flattery with you, either. You're not that sort of man." Before she could lose her courage, she went on. "I think you're in love with me. Why don't you want to admit it?"

He was looking down at the table, but then he raised his head and she almost flinched at the blaze in his eyes. Anger, obviously, but desire, too?

He got up suddenly, and she held her breath, but he slammed away from her towards the sink, for a moment leaned his hands on the counter, his head bowed, and then turned to face her. "Listen to me," he said. "It's a first time, for you. At your age, being in love is enough. You think it's so simple, that love can move mountains, overcome all obstacles. It's not like that, Rennie. Not in the real world, where I live."

"You think I don't—?"

Brutally he reminded her, "I've been in love before, Rennie. When Jean and I met she was eighteen and I was ten years older. I was," he said deliberately, "madly in love with her, then."

Rennie steeled herself not to flinch as he continued. "My father was sixteen years older than my mother. My parents' marriage wasn't exactly a glowing testimonial to the state of matrimony, but I didn't give the parallel much consideration." He paused.

"What does that have to do with us?" Rennie demanded stubbornly.

"There are too many similarities. You are almost the same age that Jean was when I first met her."

"And I'm studying law—" Rennie conceded impatiently.

"Yes, an A student—"

"You need them to get into law school at all. I had to work for them."

"I'm not implying otherwise. You're bright, and ambitious, and young—just as Jean was."

"I'm not Jean!"

He looked at her, and she saw pain in his eyes, but with a sinking heart she knew intuitively that he wasn't seeing Rennie, alone. Her image in his mind was overshadowed by the indelible memories of his marriage and his ex-wife.

She said, "You really think the fact that you were older was the reason for the break-up of your marriage?"

"Perhaps not," he conceded after a moment. "But it did seem to accentuate the problem. I'm sure Jean felt that a younger man would have been more competent in the house, and she certainly thought I was too far removed from my own childhood to be any good at child rearing."

It sounded to Rennie as though Jean had flung at him whatever came to mind when they were arguing. And probably Grant had accepted the accusations with that stoic calm which Toby had inherited. His own arguments would have been incised with an infuriating logic, but his wife's accusations had bitten deep. Grant was almost morbidly aware of his own shortcomings.

He said, and there was pain in his voice, too, "I think we both hoped that Ellen's birth would perform some sort of miracle for us and restore our marriage. But by then it was too late. Jean was always tired, and when I tried to help—my efforts weren't very welcome."

Tired and irritable, Rennie thought. Giving herself too much to do, setting unrealistically high standards and refusing help, but at the same time resenting the workload. And resenting the drastic change of direction in her life. "She was punishing you," she said slowly.

"Perhaps," he acknowledged. "Certainly I felt guilty, and I guess we both felt cheated. She wasn't the loving, passionate girl I had married, and she must have felt that I'd forced her into a role that she hadn't been prepared for but was determined to make the best of. And my attitude didn't help her. I began to feel shut out. By the time Toby was two I'd found my own compensation."

Rennie's head lifted. "You were unfaithful?"

"Not in the way you mean. I threw myself into my work. I wasn't home much—it seemed better that way. But naturally, Jean became fed up with it. She thought I was taking her for granted."

She had to respect his unwillingness to criticise his ex-wife. No doubt both he and Jean had been partially to blame for what had happened to his marriage. But his awareness of past mistakes had changed him.

"Rennie," he said. "Try to understand. I can't risk it all happening over again. Don't ask it of me."

She got up and walked towards him. She took his arms and looked up into his taut, determined face. "Look at me, please! Please, Grant," she said, trying to get through to him, blinking away tears. "You don't have to send me away out of some silly notion of self-sacrifice."

For a moment she saw the longing in his expression, and his hands came out to clamp on her arms. She lifted her face to his, thinking she had won. Then he pushed her away from him. She saw the effort he made to steady himself, to wipe all expression from his face, and her heart contracted with love and hurt.

When he spoke his voice was harsh but even. "You don't understand," he told her. "It isn't self-sacrifice, Rennie. It's self-preservation. I'm not prepared to go through all that again."

He was rejecting her, finally and completely. Knowing how she felt, tacitly admitting his own feelings, he was turning his back on them. Furious and appalled, Rennie swallowed a fierce desire to hurl herself at him and attack him with her fists. That would only convince him all over again of her childishness. Instead, she looked him right in the eye. "Then you are a coward, after all. And a fool, too. You're like Ellen, afraid to set foot outside of your self-imposed, loveless prison because you might get hurt again. But Ellen's just a little girl, and you are supposed to be all grown up."

But if she hoped to goad him, it was useless. He had himself well in hand now. "Thank you for that analysis, Rennie," he said equably. She detected a spark of temper in his eyes, but even so he managed a faint, superior smile that made her long to hit him. "Maybe you should take up psychology after all." Then he gave her an ironic little nod and walked out of the room.

Mrs. Beddoe came in the afternoon of Rennie's last day, bringing an overnight bag. "Mr. Morrison asked if I could stay overnight occasionally," she explained. "We thought I should for tonight."

Ellen was shy with her at first, but by the time Grant came home from work she seemed quite happy with the situation. She pressed into Rennie's hand an unidentifiable object made of paper, ribbon and some pictures cut from a magazine, and said, "I made it for you."

"It's very pretty, Ellen," Rennie said sincerely, restraining herself from asking what it was. "I'll keep it in my room at home."

"And I made you something at school," Toby told her, producing a parcel wrapped in crumpled paper. At least she recognised his gift as a pin-cushion, and thanked him warmly, promising to use it.

"Mr. Morrison said not to bother with dinner, he'll bring something in and run you home afterwards," Mrs. Beddoe said.

Rennie crushed a pang of jealousy that the message had been given to the other woman, not to her. Out with the old, and in with the new, she told herself. She toyed with the idea of going home by bus before Grant arrived. But it would be impolite, and perhaps cowardly. And the children would want to know why.

He brought Chinese food with him, much more than they could eat, and while Mrs. Beddoe put the children to bed, he said, "I'll take you home."

She fetched her small bag, which he took from her and swung into the back seat before opening the passenger door for her.

She was doing up her safety belt when he got in beside her. She thought he hesitated an instant before he started the car, but she was still adjusting her belt, not looking at him.

He drove in silence, seemingly concentrating on the traffic, and she could think of nothing to say. A small, cold wad of misery was lodged somewhere in the region of her heart.

When he drew up outside her house, he said, "You'll be glad to be home again."

"I'll miss... the children."

He glanced at her, then looked away, fishing in the breast pocket of the suit he wore. "Your wages," he said, handing her an envelope. "And a bonus."

"Thank you. I didn't expect any bonus."

"You've earned it."

She sat fiddling with the envelope. He reached across her and flipped open the glove box. "And this is—well, something extra. I hope you'll like it."

It was much more expertly wrapped than the children's presents. She removed the silver paper with its looped bow, and opened the box inside, to lift out a crystal suspended from a gold hoop that curved round to form a circular stand. It was simple and beautiful. She held it on the palm of her hand, and he touched the crystal with a finger, making it dance and glint, even in the gathering dusk.

"You didn't have to give me anything," she said, blinking away tears.

"I wanted to. I didn't buy you a birthday present. Chocolates don't count." He paused. "You don't like it?"

"Yes, of course I do. I love it."

She replaced the lovely thing carefully in its box, trying to put off the moment when she had to say goodbye.

He watched her hands, and when she looked up again, he gave her a faint smile, and touched her cheek with the back of his index finger. She turned her head against his hand,

and somehow his fingers were tangled in her hair. His face was very close. He was holding himself still.

She said, "You could at least kiss me goodbye."

His smile was crooked. "Not a good idea, Rennie."

She moistened her lips with her tongue. "Well, Mahomet—" She curled her hand behind his neck, and lifted her face until her mouth found his. She felt him go rigid, and slid her hand down his neck inside the collar of his shirt, and dug her nails into his skin, at the same time opening her mouth with a desperate, angry passion, her teeth closing momentarily on his lower lip.

Grant made a low noise in his throat, and the hand in her hair convulsed and tugged painfully, pulling her head back.

"What do you think you're doing?" he demanded hoarsely, his eyes ablaze with furious desire. "Have you any idea what you're asking for?"

"Yes. I'm *not* a child, Grant."

"The hell you're not!" he groaned. And then his mouth was on hers, his hand in her hair, their breath mingling. He trailed a finger down her throat and a moment later firmly cupped her breast in his palm, making her heart treble its beat. She arched toward him with her arms about his neck, and felt his hand sweep down to her hip, her thigh, then up to her waist under the edge of her loose T-shirt, stroking the heated skin. A finger traced the line of her backbone from waist to nape and back again, and his palm found her breast once more, this time with only a thin layer of nylon and lace between them. Her head was pressed against the back of the seat, his tongue mercilessly exploring her mouth. She freed one hand and burrowed under his jacket, trying to hold him closer to her. His hand was inside her bra now, touching her, reminding her how it had been lying almost naked with him on his bed, and she made a long guttural sound of pleasure and satisfaction.

And yet it wasn't enough. Even as she moved against his hand, abandoned to that sweet caress, she knew that it wasn't going to be enough.

Then the pleasure unexpectedly spilled over and she cried out against his open mouth so that he lifted it from hers, and she shuddered in his arms, hearing his shaking voice in her ear saying, "Rennie? Rennie! I don't believe this. Darling..." The last with a kind of stunned amusement.

Her head had fallen against his shoulder, and she was filled with a delicious lassitude and slowly fading pleasure. He smoothed her hair, his lips on her temple, and whispered, "Rennie? Are you all right?"

She nodded.

"You are quite a girl."

"That was quite a kiss," she said drowsily.

His chest shook with silent laughter. "You could say that."

"That never happened to me before."

"No?" he enquired tenderly.

She shook her head again. "Never."

"Well, it's bound to happen again. Though not necessarily in the same way."

There was a grim sadness in his tone that made her raise her head from its comfortable resting place. "And not with you?" she asked painfully.

She was ferociously glad at the look of torment in his eyes. "You're not making this easy for me."

"No," she said, cruelly obdurate in her despair. "I don't want to make it easy."

He nodded, almost smiling. "That's my girl."

"But I'm not," she said. "Am I? In spite of—everything."

"You can't be! For your own sake—"

"You don't need to dress it up in self-sacrifice. The truth is, you want me, you—love me, but not enough." She moved away from him. "That's it in a nutshell, isn't it?"

He had shifted back, too. His hand was clenched hard on the steering wheel. It was dark now, and she couldn't see his eyes. "You have a neat ability to cut through to the kernel, Rennie." He shrugged. "What more can I say?"

She was too proud to cry. It was nothing she hadn't known all along, and she would probably think herself lucky, some day, that he hadn't been the sort of man who would have taken what he could get and then discarded her. Because surely that would have been worse. If anything could be worse than what she was feeling now.

He stooped and picked up the box with its torn wrapper that had dropped to the floor of the car. "Here," he said, and closed her hands over it very gently. "I'll get your bag."

Chapter Fourteen

It was going to be a long year, Rennie told herself on the first day of the new term. But she would get through it. And at the end of it she would have a law degree. Three months later she'd have professional exams to sit, and at twenty-one she would be eligible to be admitted to the bar, as planned.

Her friends would have said that in her last university year, Rennie had a high old time. On beach trips it was she who swam out to sea the furthest and climbed highest on the cliffs. When a group decided to go to Ruapehu to ski, Rennie was first on the slopes, and the last to give up and return to the ski hut, where she led the singing in front of the stove for hours. At parties Rennie was always there, tossing her impossible hair over her shoulders and talking, laughing, flirting until nearly everyone else had gone home. If there was dancing, Rennie was first on the floor and the most energetic performer, outlasting all her partners.

Her mother looked at her askance a few times, and hinted that if she wanted to talk . . .

But Rennie just hugged her, gave her a husky, "Thanks. I know." And kept her own counsel. She was long past the stage where her mother could kiss the hurt better.

She visited Toby and Ellen often, after her daytime lectures and before Grant came home. She was surprised at how much she missed them, at the rush of love that always came over her when they greeted her with hugs and clamoured to tell her what they had been doing since she saw them last. Her heart ached a little at the small changes that she noticed between visits, Toby becoming less solemn, developing a mischievous sense of humour and telling terrible jokes learned from his friends, Ellen losing the last of her baby fat and talking about going to school. They were growing up so fast, and she had a passionate desire to be with them, not to miss any phase of their development.

But she forced herself to make the visits further apart. Just before the May holidays she phoned Grant and asked for his permission to take them out for a day. He gave it coolly, asked how she was, made arrangements for her to collect the children, and said a firmly pleasant goodbye.

When she went to fetch Toby and Ellen, they met her at the door and took her into the lounge. Grant stood up with a glass of something in his hand and said, "Hello, Rennie, how are you? You remember Lorna, don't you?"

Lorna Fielding was there, smiling and looking very much at home, her blond hair as sleek as the first time Rennie had met her, but her smart businesslike clothes replaced by equally smart casual slacks and a loose but beautifully styled shirt.

"I'm all right," Rennie said. She wrenched her eyes away from the strangely intent look Grant was giving her and said hello to the other woman. With some difficulty she managed to conduct a polite if stilted conversation and, refusing a drink, got the children away as quickly as she could. She deduced that Lorna and Grant were looking forward to a quiet day together.

Extravagantly, she took the children to Kelly Tarlton's Underwater World. She knew Grant had taken them there once or twice, and Toby was keen to go again. Ellen held her hand for a good deal of the time they were in the tunnel via which the aquarium stingrays, sharks and other sea life were viewed. But she didn't seem frightened.

Afterwards Rennie bought them milkshakes and a snack, and they walked a little way along the waterfront, watching the ferries and sailboats on the harbour, and having a look at a cruise ship that was in port, before boarding a bus to go home.

When they returned there was no sign of Lorna. Grant met them at the door, asking, "Had a good day?"

The children proceeded to tell him exactly why. Rennie said, "Well, I'll be getting along," and was in the act of turning when he said abruptly, as though he hadn't meant to, "Don't run off just yet. Come in for a few minutes."

She shook her head, but he reached out and took her arm, and she found herself in the hallway, then being led into the lounge.

"Sit down," Grant said. "Can I get you some coffee? A drink?"

"I should be getting home," she said.

"I'll drive you. The children can come along. You've already been on enough buses today. And with two kids in tow."

"Do I look tired or something?"

"Not particularly. You look remarkably fresh and quite— beautiful." His voice was suddenly husky.

She hadn't expected him to say anything like that. "Flattery will get you anywhere," she responded. "That is, it would if you wanted it to," she added gloomily.

Grant laughed, and the tension relaxed a little. "You can't be kept down, can you, Rennie?"

"That makes me sound like some kind of noxious weed."

He shook his head. "An exotic plant, perhaps. Definitely not a weed."

"The definition of a weed is a plant that's growing where it's not wanted, isn't it?"

She thought she probably fitted the description rather well, but Grant just shook his head and said, "Sure I can't get you something?"

"All right," she said. "Coffee." He would have to go into the kitchen to make it, and that might give her a chance to gather her defences.

By the time he brought it, the children had disappeared to play outside. "You don't have to do this," she said, stirring in sugar.

"I wanted one for myself, anyway. How did *you* enjoy the outing?"

"Very much. I love being with them. They seem to have got over any problems they might have had about their mother's death."

"I think they're both managing well. I heard Toby once explaining to Ellen exactly what I'd told him."

"About him and his sister not being responsible?"

"Yes. I think eventually it sank in."

"It must be awful for a child to feel guilty about something like that."

"Yes. It's bad enough for an adult."

"Do *you* feel guilty?" Rennie asked. "About Jean?"

"I was guilty of a lot of things. I can't dodge that. At the same time, it's no use dwelling on what can't now be mended. The main thing is not to make the same mistakes over again."

"You mean you won't ever marry again."

His eyes rested on her enigmatically. "It's unlikely."

Because, she thought, after one failed marriage, he didn't want to risk another. He'd been hurt, and seemed to feel worse about the fact that he'd hurt his wife. He'd lost confidence in his ability to sustain a permanent relationship, was still flailing himself for the breakdown of his marriage. Still brooding over his own failure and his part in his wife's unhappiness. The anger she had felt with him after his rejection of her love shook her again. She tried to despise him for his lack of trust in himself, in her. Instead, she felt a wave of love and pity.

She thought about Lorna Fielding. Did she hope to be the second Mrs. Morrison? Or would she settle for something less?

"Did you enjoy *your* day?" she asked him.

Perhaps he had followed her train of thought. His eyes crinkled at the corners. "Very much," he said. "It was nicely restful."

Lorna looked a restful sort of person. Was that what he wanted? Someone composed and self-possessed and mature, as Rennie imagined Lorna to be, rather than volatile and unpredictable and sometimes disastrously impulsive, like herself?

Feeling suddenly depressed, she finished her coffee and said, "I'm ready to go whenever it suits you."

She and Shane had both been invited to a twenty-first birthday party that night. Shane wanted to borrow their parents' car for the occasion and as he hadn't long had his licence their father was a little reluctant to give permission.

"He won't worry if you're with me," Shane assured her. "Come on, Ren, say you'll come."

It was noisy and crowded, and there wasn't anyone there over twenty-five. All the men appeared youthful and boringly full of themselves. Rennie tried to shake off a feeling that she had been to umpteen parties just like it, and that there were more interesting things in life than listening to tapes played at top decibel level, conducting a shouted conversation with people only inches away, and trying to dance on the minuscule bit of floor space that was left by the several dozen people squeezed into three quite small and not very comfortable rooms. Drink flowed freely, and at eleven o'clock the owner of the flat had a loud argument with one of the neighbours, after which the tape player was turned down for a time, but Rennie suspected that someone later inched it up again.

Kevin was there, ignoring Rennie either because he was embarrassed about his drunken attempt at making love to her at last year's legal ball, or because he was too engrossed in his partner.

The girl at his side looked about fifteen, and was wearing a miniskirt that barely covered her hips. As the evening wore on, Rennie noticed her getting progressively gigglier, apparently trying to keep up with the number of drinks Kevin was having.

It was none of her business, Rennie told herself, but when she went to the bathroom and found the girl vomiting into the toilet bowl, she couldn't retreat and leave her to it.

She found a cloth and wet it with cold water to wipe the girl's pale, sweaty forehead. Then, as she patently couldn't stand up, Rennie helped her to lean back against the wall, her thin legs sprawled on the vinyl floor.

"Thanks," the girl said weakly. "What's your name?"

"Rennie. What's yours?"

"Amanda. Oh, I suppose you wanted the bathroom. Sorry." She tried rather unsuccessfully to get up, and had to hold onto the washbasin, swaying.

"Maybe you should lie down."

"I just want to go home!" Amanda wailed, putting a hand to her head. "Could you find my boyfriend for me, and ask him to come and get me, do you think?"

"He drove you here?"

Amanda nodded, then clapped a hand over her mouth. "Mmm."

"Are you going to be sick again?"

"Yes," Amanda gasped. "No." She gulped in some deep breaths. "No, I don't think so. If you fetch Kevin for me..."

"Okay," Rennie agreed doubtfully. She returned to the other room and made her way to where Kevin was leaning heavily on the young man next to him, waving a beer can splashily and hazily eyeballing another man standing less than a foot away.

She plucked at his arm, and tried to ignore the leering grin he gave her as he turned and recognised her. "Amanda," she told him, "wants to go home. She's sick."

He guffawed. "Sick? She's shickered, that's what. Told her she couldn't keep up with me. Silly bitch. Anyway, don't want to go home jus' yet. You tell her."

Rennie itched to slap him. Maybe her childhood instincts had been correct, after all. Turning on her heel, she went back to the bathroom. Amanda had subsided to the floor again, and was leaning against the wall with her eyes closed.

"Kevin isn't going to be much use, I'm afraid," Rennie told her. "I wouldn't trust him to drive a car tonight, and I don't think I'd trust him in any other capacity, either."

"You mean he's drunk," Amanda said, without opening her eyes. "So am I. My mother'll kill me! I've never had more than two or three glasses of anything. Only Kevin dared me. Oh, God, I feel sick!"

Rennie said, "Tell you what, I've had enough of this party, anyway. My brother and I will drive you home."

"Oh, I couldn't ask you to—he'll think it's an awful cheek, won't he?"

"You didn't ask. And I'm sure he won't mind."

Shane showed surprisingly willing and competent, helping to remove Amanda from the bathroom to his car with a minimum of fuss, and even firmly calming Kevin, who was inclined to be belligerent at what he apparently conceived as some infringement of his rights.

"I'd drop that nerd if I were you," Shane advised Amanda as he helped her into the rear seat. "If you ask me he's got a big fat hole where his brains ought to be."

As Rennie climbed into the front beside him, he added, over his shoulder, "Where do you live, kiddo?"

Amanda told him and he nodded. "Not far from our place."

When they got there Shane helped Rennie get Amanda up the path. She threw up again on the doorstep. Then her father flung open the door and seemed to think Shane was responsible. Amanda was too busy being sick to talk, and the man wouldn't listen to Shane's explanation or Rennie's.

Her mother came out and helped her inside, and Shane hastily backed off while her father shook a clenched fist in his face and threatened to have his guts for garters—and other parts of him for less mentionable things—if he ever set foot inside the gate again. Rennie followed, still futilely trying to explain what had happened.

"And we were just doing his little darling a good turn!" Rennie sympathised as they climbed into the car.

"Oh, well," Shane said philosophically, "it's all experience, I guess."

Shane won two tickets to an Oscar-winning film in a phone quiz run by a radio station. "Want to come with me?" he asked his sister. "The tickets are for tomorrow night, and every girl in my little black book is booked up."

She knew he didn't have one, that he was rather shy about asking girls to go out. "Okay," she said. "How can I refuse such a gracious invitation?"

In the foyer afterwards, as they made their way from the theatre, they were discussing the film's excellence when a warm feminine voice said, "It's Rennie, isn't it?" And she turned to see Lorna Fielding smiling at her, one hand hooked into Grant Morrison's arm. Rennie's hand clenched in the pocket of her light jacket, and she carefully refrained from looking at Grant.

Grant said, "Good evening, Rennie. Hello, Shane." The four of them stood discussing the film for a few minutes. Then after a slight pause Grant said, "We were going to have some supper. How about you two joining us?"

"Do come with us," Lorna said, smiling at them both.

"Thank you, but—" Rennie started to say.

Grant added, "I'm paying."

Shane leapt in with, "Thanks. That'd be great."

Shane was hardly starved at home but he had a healthy appetite and an appreciation of food—good, bad or indifferent. The chance of a free supper in a good restaurant rarely came his way. Rennie looked at his eager expression and nodded. "If we're not too long. I have an early start tomorrow," she reminded him.

"How's the study going, Rennie?" Grant asked when they were seated around a table in a small, comfortable supper restaurant.

She risked a glance at him, thought he looked slightly strained in spite of the air of neutral interest he had adopted. "Okay," she said. "My tutors seem pleased."

"Good." A waiter approached with menus, and after they had all made their choices the talk turned to the film they had just seen.

As they had coffee, Shane said, "I forgot to tell you, Rennie, that girl came round yesterday, before you got home."

"What girl?"

"The one we did the rescue act on—What's'ername— Amanda."

Grant said, mildly interested, "Who have you been rescuing, Rennie?"

Shane explained, and added, "She must have remembered me pointing out our place when we passed it taking her home. She was on the doorstep when I got home yesterday from school. Said she wanted to thank me—us—properly, and apologise for her father."

Rennie thoughtfully noted his slight embarrassment. But he was saying to the other two, "Her father thought I was the one who got her drunk, you see."

"Went after you with a horsewhip, did he?" Grant enquired.

"If he'd had one, I reckon he would've."

Rennie said, "She seemed like a good kid, really."

Looking at the quirk of his lips, she could tell what Grant was thinking. But she had felt much older than the other girl.

"Yeah," Shane said.

"Something bothered you?" Grant asked shrewdly.

"She had a bruise on her face."

"Do you think her father beat her?" Grant asked, frowning.

Shane looked worried. "He was pretty angry. And I was sorry for her, you know. The way she thanked me, you'd think I was some kind of knight in shining armour. All I did was drive her home."

Grant said, "It sounds as though the girl's set to develop a bad case of hero worship. She could turn into a real headache, and you'll end up having to hurt her. Which is bad news all round."

Rennie didn't look at him, but she felt herself going hot. Bending her head, she fiddled with the spoon in her coffee cup, waiting for the tell-tale flush to subside.

"But if her parents are ill-treating her—" Lorna objected.

"We can't jump to conclusions on the strength of one bruise," Grant said. "The girl wasn't afraid to go home. She was with a boy at the party? Maybe he hit her."

"Very likely," Rennie said. She decided not to mention that he knew Kevin.

Shane said, "The bastard!"

Shane was one of the most non-violent people Rennie knew, but he looked positively murderous now, his fists clenched on the table, and a furious scowl on his face. Seeing their surprise, he said sheepishly, "She's a skinny little kid, you know? Brings out a man's protective instincts."

"I know the feeling," Grant said dryly. "Believe me, those instincts can bring a man a whole heap of trouble."

This time Rennie did look at him, sure that he was deliberately needling. There was a gleam of affectionate humour in his eyes, inviting her to laugh with him. He was reminding her of the revenge she had planned after their first meeting. But too much had passed between them since then. She gave him a frosty, indignant stare, and the humour was replaced by a rueful sadness.

"It's time we were going," she said abruptly. "Thank you for the supper, Grant. And it was good to meet you again, Lorna."

It had been, too. Lorna was a nice, caring person, capable of showing concern for a girl she'd never even met. Rennie scolded herself for allowing that to depress her.

Chapter Fifteen

Several days later Rennie was curled up on her bed with a stack of study books when Shane came into her room.

"It was the boyfriend," he said. "Kevin."

It was maybe a second before she made the connection. "You've been talking to Amanda."

"I phoned her. Met her downtown. Got her to talk to me eventually. She told Kevin she didn't want to see him again, and he hit her."

Rennie made a disgusted exclamation and Shane said, "Yeah, I was tempted to go and sort him out, myself. But you know me. One of nature's little cowards."

"You're not!" Rennie said loyally. "But it wouldn't have done any good."

"I know. He'd have beaten me to a pulp. As far as fighting goes, I hardly know my right fist from my left. Anyway, Amanda won't be seeing him again."

"Good," Rennie said. "That's very sensible of her." She wondered if Amanda was going to be seeing her brother, instead.

* * *

Each time Rennie visited Grant's house she was overwhelmed by a sense of his presence, even when he wasn't there. And she kept looking for signs of him in his children, in Toby's grave and considering expression, in Ellen's smile.

She was just making things harder. She was pretty good at dispensing advice, she told herself, but maybe she ought to put her own life in order. She had to stick to her decision to ease herself out of Toby and Ellen's lives. But it was very hard letting go.

All the final year students were beginning to look hollow-eyed and haunted. Rennie curtailed a social life which she had to admit had not filled the empty spaces left by Grant and his children.

Glad that mid-year exams required her concentrated energy, Rennie tried to push all thoughts of Grant from her mind. When the exams were finished and she surfaced from a sea of text-books and lecture notes and timetables, her mother said casually one day, "What are you planning to wear to the legal ball this year, Rennie? Your father's offering to subsidise a new dress."

"I...hadn't thought about it." The legal ball. Where she had met Grant a year ago. Only a year. But it seemed an age. So much had happened in that year. She had grown from a girl into a woman, for one thing. Learned to love a man. And to go on living after losing him. "I don't think I'll go," she blurted out.

"But we always go. And now, in your final year? Why don't you want to?"

"I just don't feel like it," Rennie said vaguely. "I'm tired."

Her mother looked at her shrewdly, and Rennie was almost tempted to tell her everything—or nearly everything.

"You've worked very hard this year," Marian coaxed. "Maybe a night out is just what you need. Shane's coming, too. I think he wants to impress Amanda."

Amanda and Shane had been a twosome for a while now. Rennie recalled his relief when he'd told her that Amanda was actually seventeen. "I asked her mother," he said. "And her father finally agreed to meet me."

He, too, seemed anxious for Rennie to attend the ball. "The only balls I've been to are school ones, and they don't count, with the teachers egging you on to ask every dog in the hall to dance...and Amanda's...well, I want her to have a good time."

"Mum and Dad will be there."

"Yeah, and they'll be surrounded by people. Older people! We won't know anyone in our age group."

"Okay," Rennie finally capitulated. "I'll go if you want me that much."

It wasn't until some time later that she wondered if their mother had put him up to it.

Ethan and Celeste arrived in Auckland again a few days before the ball, and when they called round, Frank offered them tickets.

Ethan glanced at his wife. "Shall we go? A sentimental occasion? If it hadn't been for the legal fraternity and their annual celebration, we might never have got together again."

Celeste smiled. "Yes, I'd like to."

"Fine. You'll join our party, of course," Frank said.

Rennie was glad there was to be a party of them. After some thought, she had invited Larry Townsend to accompany her. She had been seeing him now and then, but kept the relationship casually friendly. It wouldn't have mattered in the least if she went to the ball on her own, except that Grant might be there. Somehow for him to see her without an escort would be galling.

It was also, somehow, necessary for her to appear as dazzling as she possibly could. She accepted gratefully her father's offer of help to buy a dress for the ball, and spent a lot of time choosing one.

Black, she decided. Black with her creamy skin and flaming hair would be dramatic. And also sophisticated. She found just what she wanted, a ruched chiffon sheath with a beaded bodice, that hugged her curves and showed off her legs and had a long floating scarf that fell over one shoulder and left the other bare. She wore it with a row of fine gold bracelets and no other jewellery, and twisted her hair back from her face, letting the ends fall free.

Even Shane whistled when she appeared, holding a beaded black evening purse. "Knock 'em dead, Sis!" he advised.

Larry had obviously made an effort, too. In a hired suit and with his hair trimmed for the occasion he was a very presentable escort.

Shane was riding with them, and they were to pick up Amanda on the way. "Shane," Marian had said to Rennie, a smile in her eyes, "would really appreciate not having to pick up his date in his parents' car. At least, not with the parents in it. We're taking Ethan and Celeste with us, so I thought Larry might oblige."

In the event, they all arrived more or less at once. The evening was already underway, the band playing while several couples circled the floor. Many of the tables were occupied, and there were people congregated at the bar. Others milled about on the carpeted area at the entrance to the hall, waiting for friends or debating on the best place to sit and whether they should visit the bar first or not.

Shane introduced Amanda to Ethan and Celeste, and Rennie did the same for Larry, with rather less anxious enthusiasm.

Frank, taking charge, said, "Over there. That's James Powell waving at us."

Following the others through the crowd, it wasn't until they arrived at one of the tables that Rennie saw James and his doctor wife, who was seated alongside their son and his girlfriend. There were other people as well, some of the men busy moving two tables together for the enlarged party. Near James stood Grant Morrison, looking very distinguished in evening clothes. And at his side Lorna, elegant in a cream silk dress. Rennie's mouth dried and she took a quick little breath to steady herself before looking at Grant. She was sure she had felt his eyes on her, but when she raised hers he was smiling at her mother.

James beamed at them all and there was a flurry of introductions. "You know Grant Morrison?" James assumed. "And Lorna—sorry, love, can't remember your last name. Frank—Marian—you can congratulate these two on their engagement."

Chapter Sixteen

I've never fainted in my life! Rennie told herself fiercely.
And she wasn't going to do it now. But this sudden clammy
dizziness certainly felt remarkably like what she imagined
fainting to be.

Grant wasn't looking at her when her eyes flew to his face.
Ethan's hand was on her arm, even as she distantly heard
James Powell saying, "My son here is getting married."

Ethan moved, blocking off her view of Grant. "Hey!
Isn't this our song, Rennie?" he asked. "We can't let that
pass. Excuse us, everyone! We'll join you later."

And his arm was about her, solid and comforting, as he
urged her the few steps to the dance floor, which was quite
crowded now, and turned her to face him, that arm holding
her, bracing her against him so that she couldn't fall. After
the first few fumbling steps her feet automatically followed
the dance. She let her head rest on Ethan's warm shoulder,
and the cold dizziness gradually receded.

She said, "Our tune?" And raised her head.

He smiled down at her, very kindly. "It was all I could think of. Better now?"

"How did you know?"

"I happened to be looking at you. Everyone else's attention was on the happy couple. You rather gave yourself away, I'm afraid, young Rennie. For a minute there you thought it was Grant Morrison who was getting married, didn't you?"

She bit her lip. "You don't think anyone else noticed?"

He shook his head. "I shouldn't think so. Your mother, maybe. But she could hardly ask you to dance."

Rennie gave a wavery ghost of a smile. "No. Thank you, Ethan. I'm grateful for the rescue."

"Any time." He kissed the top of her head. "He's a lot older than you."

"Oh, don't you start on that!"

"Sorry. Your parents?"

"Not them. Grant. He seemed to think there was something immoral about me being so much younger."

"So it wasn't entirely one-sided," Ethan said thoughtfully.

"No. Not entirely." Although Grant had not felt a tenth of the emotion she had expended on him. If he had, he would never have been able to let her go.

"Have you been having an affair with him?" Ethan asked bluntly.

"No such luck," Rennie confessed forlornly.

"Rennie!" His shock was tempered with amusement. "I must admit, it would have surprised me. I'd guess he's an honourable man. Hardly likely to seduce a young girl living under his roof."

"An honourable man. Oh, yes. It sounds almost biblical." Rennie made an effort at a smile. "Are they sitting at our table?"

"I'm afraid so. You'll be all right. You've got guts. And you have friends." He smiled down at her as the music stopped. "Okay?"

She took a deep breath. If nothing else, she had her fair share of pride. "Okay."

Ethan gripped her hand. "That's the way."

"Please, can we get a drink first?"

He laughed sympathetically and steered her to the bar, where he accepted without comment her demand for a large gin and tonic, and got himself a glass of wine.

Slipping into the chair by Larry she said, "Sorry, I didn't mean to desert you. Ethan is a very old friend." Across the table Rennie saw her mother looking at them anxiously. Oh, shoot, she thought. Was I that obvious?

The worst of it was, Grant might have noticed, too. It was a humiliating thought. She lifted her chin. Pull yourself together, she admonished herself. And smile!

The band was warming up, and had started belting out a tune with a heavy beat, bringing the younger contingent onto the floor.

"This music is too good to waste," she suggested to Larry. "How about we get on the floor?"

"Sure," he said, getting up immediately.

Rennie threw herself into the dance, relying on the music thrumming in her ears, and the movements of her body, to numb her mind and her emotions. When the tune finished she applauded loudly, and as the musicians launched into another, she took up the beat with renewed energy, moving her feet, hips, shoulders to the music.

She saw that Grant was dancing with Celeste, and dragged her gaze away from them, smiling at Larry and tossing her head back, the loose curls swinging against her shoulders. Larry grinned back.

But when the bracket closed with a drum roll and the band took a break, she followed him back to their table.

Grant was talking to Celeste and Ethan. He glanced up as she sat down, giving her a piercing look, but she returned him a bland, determined smile before lifting her gin and tonic.

The music began again. She held on to her glass, both hands curled around it. Grant got up and moved across to her.

"Dance, Rennie?"

She wanted to say no, she had to say no. But what excuse could she make, in front of all these people? She turned to Larry, hoping that somehow he would rescue her, but he totally misunderstood.

"Go ahead," he said generously. "I don't mind."

Grant said with dry courtesy, "Thank you." His hand was on her arm, lifting her from the chair, guiding her to the dance floor.

Then his arm was around her waist, his other hand holding hers close to him, his breath stirring the short tendrils of hair at her temple.

"How have you been, Rennie?" he asked. "Really?"

She was sick of telling people she was fine, fine, fine. What if she told him how she really felt, screamed out her rage and pain at him, right then and there?

But of course she couldn't. And anyway, he wasn't to be blamed for her feelings. Or his lack of them. The pain was entirely her own fault. And she had no right to be angry with him. He had never tried to deceive her about how he felt. He had never said he was in love with her, although he hadn't denied it either. He had, by implication, told her that being in love was not an incurable condition. And he'd presumably had an antidote in Lorna.

She said, "I'm fine. And you, obviously. Are you and Lorna a twosome?"

His gaze flicked over to the table where Lorna was talking to Rennie's father. "You could say that."

"She's a lovely person."

"I think so, too."

She wanted to ask, *Do you love her? Do you kiss her the way you kissed me? Make love to her as you never would to me? Does she love you the way I do?*

She glanced up fleetingly, and saw that he looked troubled. Pity, she thought sinkingly, and guilt. Humiliation made her squirm.

She laughed. It sounded genuine. "Of course, you were quite right," she said. "Much as I hate to admit it. I had a crush on you." She grimaced. "I got over it, just as you predicted when you thought I was yearning over Ethan."

"Did I?" he asked. "I seem—" he paused to clear his throat "—I seem to remember that you thought I was fairly crass in saying so."

"I've grown up since then."

"Yes," he said. "I've noticed."

And about time! she thought. For once he was looking at her as though she was more than ten years old.

They danced in silence for a while, and she let herself relax in his arms. The lights were low, only flickering colours playing across the dancers, and the tempo had slowed. She closed her eyes and allowed a bitter-sweet pleasure to take over.

His hand moved on her back, and she snuggled closer. And felt his sudden withdrawal, his hand stilling.

Rennie drew away. She said, "How are the children?"

After a moment he said, "Good. Both well. You haven't been round in a while. They—we all miss you."

"They're all right, aren't they?" she enquired anxiously. "You said they're well."

"Yes. They're not distressed about it. I told them you were busy. How did the exams go?"

"Okay. The finals are coming up fast."

"I'm sure you'll pass with flying colours. Next year you'll be qualified."

"Yes. Will you be pleased?"

"Of course I'll be pleased for you."

"Are you going to marry Lorna?" she asked suddenly, without thinking. Hastily she tacked on, "She'd be a good mother."

"I know she would," he said in a strange tone, his eyes searching hers. "The children like her."

Rennie felt sick. What are you doing to yourself, girl? she thought wildly. Digging your own grave? "That's nice," she said brightly. "So, are you going to announce *your* engagement?"

"I haven't asked her yet," Grant said.

Yet. The sick feeling grew in intensity. "I see."

"Do you?" His eyes looked cold now. He had distanced himself. She couldn't tell what he was thinking. "And you're still seeing Larry," he commented.

"Now and then. I see a lot of people."

"Men?"

Her heart skipped a beat. She smiled into his eyes. "Some of them."

"You will be careful, Rennie, won't you?"

"Not to get myself raped, you mean? I've learnt my lesson. You made sure of that. You taught me a lot that I'm not likely to forget."

"Rennie—" He hesitated, searching her eyes. His weren't cold any more, they were troubled again and there was something in the depths of them that made her want to cry.

Still smiling, she said, "I'm sorry, I shouldn't tease."

"Is that what you're doing? Teasing?"

"What else? I can't help it, sometimes, when you're being—"

"Pompous?" he suggested, a glint of grim humour in his eyes displacing the disturbing sombreness.

"I didn't say that."

"You'd better not even think it!" He was smiling, too, making an effort to keep things light.

"Or else—" Rennie finished for him. "What?" she asked innocently.

But equally suddenly the humour disappeared, his face closing. "You are incorrigible," he said softly.

"And what are you?" she threw out recklessly. "Susceptible?"

"Evidently." His tone was clipped.

So he still wasn't completely indifferent to her. But even though she could momentarily get under his skin, he wasn't about to lose that iron control of his. Unless . . .

She danced closer to him, linking her arms about his neck, her eyes challenging. Her body moved against his.

"Cut it out, Rennie." His face went tight, almost as if he was in pain.

"Does it bother you? Larry likes it."

His jaw clenched. "I said, cut it out!" His hands closed on her wrists, pulling them away.

"What a prude you are," she mocked him.

"I wouldn't start name calling," he warned her. "You might hear a few you wouldn't like."

"That's a horrible thing to say," she flashed.

"Self-defence."

Her smile this time was real, although there was a complicated adrenaline-fed anger behind it. "Oh, pooh!" she said, making a face at him. "I'm no threat to you. You can't tell me I've cost you any sleep."

He stopped dancing suddenly, looking down at her, and she caught her breath, gazing back at him. His hands tightened on her. His voice very low, he said, "All right. I'll tell you. I've lost sleep over you for weeks at a time, especially when you were in my house and I knew I had only to walk down the passageway and be welcomed into your bed. You don't have any idea of the nights I lay awake trying not to think about that, and despising myself for doing so. You make my blood run hot just by looking at me, and when I hold you I want nothing more than to take you to the nearest bed and make love to you until morning, and the morning after, and the one after that, until we're both so spent we fall asleep in each other's arms. I was besotted over you. You're my middle-aged erotic fantasy—does that please you? But fantasies have nothing to do with reality. Fortunately for all of us I was never quite mad enough to take you too seriously. If I invite a woman into my life I have to consider the children. What I need is a mother for them, not a pretty, tantalising nymphet who's nearer Toby's age than mine. As you pointed out, Lorna would fill the bill admirably."

Then he said, "I'll take you back," even though the music hadn't stopped, and walked her across the floor with his arm about her waist. He put her in her chair, and then turned and left her.

And Rennie sat and deliberately didn't watch him go to Lorna's side and bend close to speak to her, then take her into his arms to dance. She listened to Larry talking, and smiled and nodded and even laughed once or twice, then got up to dance with him, and didn't feel a thing. Not a thing.

Chapter Seventeen

That came later. She was astonished at how much it hurt. Lying awake in bed she said to herself wonderingly, against the pain, You never really believed it, did you? That he could turn his back on you and decide cold-bloodedly to marry someone else. You thought that somehow it would all come right. Like in the story books. Kidded yourself you were doing great without him, when all you were doing was marking time and waiting for him to admit that he couldn't do without *you*. Well, he could. And this time it's for real, you have to accept that it's over, finally. And if you truly love him you'll hope that he *will* live happily ever after. With Lorna.

She thumped her pillow and tried to will herself to hope that. But all she could think was, *But I want it to be me! Why couldn't it have been me?*

This time it was harder. When she appeared at breakfast, pale and puffy-eyed, her father asked if she had a cold, and her mother looked at her searchingly.

"Too much gin last night, more likely," Shane said. "She was knocking it back like nobody's business." But his teasing grin was strained and almost apologetic. He was covering for her.

"I might be getting a cold," she agreed. She didn't want any discussion of what was really ailing her. The wounds felt too new and raw. While grateful for her family's concern, she knew she was going to have to get over this by herself.

Life had to go on somehow. Over the following months, she immersed herself in study, swotting for her finals, actually forgetting Grant for hours at a time. Except for a nagging, hollow ache that never quite went away and that she learned to live with. Then exams were on her again and she made a gut-wrenching effort to banish Grant's memory while she tackled them. By the time they were over she was blessedly tired, and for days at a time nothing seemed to matter any more. Not the exam results, not her projected career, not even her blighted love life.

At the end of the year she applied for a job with a legal firm. She received a letter asking her to come for an interview and bring references from any previous employers.

That was something she hadn't thought of. References from her father, who had sometimes given her field training, wouldn't be very telling, she supposed. She had several character references, but in terms of employment experience, a vital one was missing. And time was getting short.

She had to do it. The day before the interview, she phoned Grant at his office.

"Rennie?" He sounded reserved as he answered.

"I'm sorry to bother you. But I need a reference. I wondered if you'd mind—"

"Of course I don't mind!" Was that relief she heard in his voice? "I'll be happy to write you a glowing testimonial. You want me to post it to you?"

"No." She paused. "No, there isn't time, I'm afraid. I have to produce it for an interview tomorrow. Sorry it's such short notice, but I wondered if I could pick it up from your office on my way to the interview."

"Yes, certainly."

She was sure he sounded decidedly cool, now. Did he think she was making an excuse to see him?

And aren't you? an inner voice jeered. If you'd contacted him earlier he could have posted it, and you'd have no need to call.

"You could leave it with your receptionist," she suggested, trying to match his tone. "I won't need to bother you."

"No bother. What time do you expect to call?"

"About twelve-thirty," she said, "but I could make it earlier if that time is inconvenient." He could legitimately be out to lunch then, she thought. "The interview is at one."

"Twelve-thirty is fine," Grant said. "I'll see you then."

She dressed for the interview carefully if listlessly, choosing a dark green skirt and an apricot blouse that looked both pretty and business-like, and slipping her feet into a pair of medium-heeled Brazilian leather shoes. She pinned her hair back and applied a little eye makeup and a touch of lipstick, and hoped she looked both capable and mature.

When she gave her name to the receptionist at Grant's office, the woman said, "Yes, Miss Langwell. Mr. Morrison is expecting you. Come right on in."

She got up to open the door, withdrawing and closing it behind Rennie when she had entered the room.

Grant rose from the desk and said, "Come in, Rennie. Have a seat." He had glanced at her briefly, but now he didn't seem to want to look at her.

"Thank you." She sat on the edge of the chair he indicated. "But I can't stay. I don't want to be late."

"No, I understand. You may want to read what I've said about you, though." He took a piece of paper from the desk, and got up to come round and hand it to her, leaning back against the desk while she read.

"Thank you," she said. "It's very—flattering." Glowing was hardly the word for it. Trying to smile, she added,

"You've made me sound like a cross between Florence Nightingale and the Angel Gabriel."

Grant laughed. "Every word is true. I hope it gets you the job," he said, taking it from her and folding it into an envelope.

She stood up quickly, holding out her hand, expecting him to move aside as he gave her the envelope.

But he didn't. And that made them very close. So close she could smell his masculine scent, see the fine lines about his eyes, hear his breathing. Outside the traffic hummed, and someone put on their brakes with a protesting squeal. But the room seemed locked in stillness and quiet.

"Rennie?" His fingers brushed her cheek. "Are you really all right?"

His hand was resting lightly on her neck now, his thumb lifting her chin. She thought what she saw in his eyes was some kind of longing, but she reminded herself of the way he had flayed her last time they met, of what he thought of her, really. *Does that please you?* he'd asked bitterly, as though she were a shallow tease who had led him on for some kind of teenage ego trip of her own. And he had described his own feelings minutely enough. Lust, for which he despised himself. Something he thought ugly and unworthy. Because he was a man on the wrong side of thirty-five, with two children, and she was—had been—an attractive nineteen-year-old with an undisguised passion for him.

"Of course I'm all right. Why shouldn't I be?" Her voice was brittle. She wished he would stop touching her... No she didn't. She wished he would go on touching her and never, never stop...

He shrugged, and dropped his hand. "I just wondered if you...I thought...you look thinner."

"Do I? Maybe it's the hairdo. You've no need to worry about me."

He shook his head. "I can't help being...concerned for you." He looked down and said huskily, "Rennie, let's stop pretending. I hurt you, and you don't know how deeply I regret that."

"I told you at the ball," she said. "There's nothing to worry about. I'm sorry if I embarrassed you with my adolescent maunderings—"

"I wasn't embarrassed," he said. "I'm . . . honoured that you gave me a little of your love, even if it was only for a while." Softly he added, "Be happy, Rennie. I hope that with all my heart." He leaned forward and kissed her cheek, and then at last moved away, allowing her to go to the door.

"Thank you, Grant," she said. At this moment she felt she would never be happy again. Which was a ridiculous outlook, she knew. But knowing it didn't alter anything.

Lorna was talking to the receptionist in the outer office. She smiled. "Hello, Rennie."

Rennie's lips stretched. "Hello." Lorna was the last person she wanted to see just now. To be polite to. "I've just been collecting a reference from Grant," she said, surprised at how normal her voice sounded.

"Yes, he told me about it," Lorna said.

Of course he would have. He probably told her everything.

Please, God, not everything! No, he wouldn't. Not about the fact that his young baby-sitter had thought she was in love with him. Not about kissing her. Not about how she could make him feel, in spite of his good intentions.

"I'm sorry if I kept you waiting," she said to Lorna.

"Not at all." Lorna headed towards the door to Grant's office. "Nice to see you again." She nodded pleasantly and went in without knocking.

Out on the street, Rennie took several deep breaths. The traffic seemed noisier than ever, and what she was breathing in was not so much fresh air as exhaust fumes.

She tucked the envelope carefully into the bag hanging at her shoulder, and glanced at her watch. Plenty of time.

She went back to the pedestrian lights, crossed, then retraced her steps on the other side of the street, resisting the urge to glance up at Grant's office window. If she could see him, he would be with Lorna. Would they be standing close—kissing, perhaps?

Stop torturing yourself.

"Rennie! Ren!" Shane caught at her arm. He had Amanda with him.

"Sorry." She smiled at them both. At least someone was happy in this world. "Hi, Amanda. How are you?"

"Okay." The girl smiled back briefly, but her face looked pinched and pale. "How're you?"

"We might have a bit of a problem," Shane said.

"I think Kevin's after me," the girl said.

"She thought she saw him just a while ago," Shane added. "Back there."

"I'm sure he was following us!" Amanda shuddered. "I'm scared."

Shane put his arm about her, pulling her close.

"After all this time?" Rennie was sceptical. "It's months since you broke off with him."

"I think he's done it before. I told myself I was bound to bump into him, but... And there've been phone calls at home. At first he used to abuse me if I answered, now he just hangs up. But I know it's him."

"Go to the police," Rennie said.

"You think so?" Shane looked up.

"He's already hit her once. I think you should ask the police to check it out. Look, I'm sorry, but I've got to go. Talk her into it," she advised Shane tersely. "Let me know what happens."

She turned along the street, brushing her way through the crowd. A man started out of a shop doorway, also in a hurry, she thought vaguely as she sidestepped to avoid him.

Rennie stopped dead. It was Kevin. He had a peculiarly intent expression as he scanned the street behind her, then walked on, not seeing her at all.

Coincidence? Surely not. He *was* following Amanda.

If she turned back after him, to warn Shane and Amanda, she'd be late for her appointment. With all these people about, what harm could he do? He was probably playing a particularly cruel game with poor Amanda, deliberately showing himself now and then but being careful not to do anything criminal that could get him into trouble.

Rennie's flesh crawled. He really was a nasty piece of work.

She started back the way she had come, almost running, scanning the bobbing heads in front of her.

She bumped into someone, murmured a hasty apology and kept going. She could see Shane now. And Amanda, still snuggled against him, as they stood close to a big display window full of women's shoes, Shane earnestly talking, dropping a kiss on her hair.

And then she saw Kevin quite close to them. Rennie broke into a run. "Shane!" she yelled.

But she was too late. Kevin lunged, grabbed at Amanda, shoving her aside. Then his fist smashed into Shane's face, and Shane slumped to the ground.

As Rennie reached them, Amanda launched herself on Kevin, shrieking, hitting out at him. He felled her with the back of his hand, just as Shane, starting groggily to his feet, swung wildly and ineptly at the other man, before Kevin knocked him flying again, and drew back a booted foot.

Amanda flung herself across Shane's prone body. Rennie shot into the fray and gave Kevin a hard push. People had stopped, some frozen in shock, one or two beginning to move cautiously forward. Someone said, "Call the police!"

Kevin rounded on Rennie, astonishment in his face, and then murder. *"You!"* he said. "You bitch! I'll fix you, too. I'll fix the lot of you!"

She saw his fist coming at her, and tried to dodge, her hands automatically going up to defend herself. She twisted away, saw her own frightened face reflected in plate glass, oddly mixed up with rows of shiny new shoes. And then something slammed into her, and she knew he had hit her, before the world went black and she felt herself falling and heard a terrible crashing all around her. But she never felt the plate glass smash on the impact of her body, never felt the deadly slivers slice into her raised arms, her shoulders, her back. And her face.

When she became conscious again, her face felt stiff. Both arms and her right hand were bandaged, and after a while she realised there were bandages on her head, too, and dressings covering half of her face.

"Sore?" A nurse bent over her, feeling her pulse.

"Not specially." Her voice sounded strange. She asked for a drink of water.

When she had sipped at it, the nurse put the glass down on the bedside cupboard. "Your mother's outside. I'll send her in, shall I?"

Marian came in, smiling but pale. "You look better," she said.

"You've been in before?"

"Mmm. You were pretty groggy, though. You don't remember?"

"No." There had been dreams. She thought they were dreams. Grant had been in some of them. Grant, Shane, her parents.

"Do you remember what happened? Why you're here?"

"Kevin," Rennie answered. "Is Amanda all right? And Shane?"

"They're both okay. Shane was kept in overnight and then discharged. You got the worst of it, I'm afraid. Shane's inclined to blame himself for that."

"It wasn't his fault. I went through the window, didn't I?" Rennie asked, looking at her hands. She could see several small red nicks not covered by the bandages. "How bad are the cuts?"

"They can't tell yet. Fortunately the glass missed your eyes." Her mother sounded reassuringly matter-of-fact.

"He must have been crazy," Rennie said. "Kevin. With all those people about—"

"I could wish some of those people had reacted a bit faster," Marian said.

"Didn't they do anything?"

"Oh, yes. But only after he'd knocked you through that window. Then a couple of men held him until the police got there. And the ambulance."

Rennie moved her right arm, and winced. "You must have been worried. Getting a call from the hospital—or was it the police? I suppose that would be worse."

"Actually, Grant phoned me."

"Grant? How did he—"

"It happened right across the street from his office," Marian reminded her. "When the ambulance arrived, naturally he looked out to see what was going on. He recognised you—well, your clothes—as they were putting you on the stretcher. He went down, insisted on going with you to the hospital, then phoned me. When I arrived he was with you. You don't remember?"

Rennie shook her head. "I thought I'd dreamed—" Grant holding her hand, stroking her hair, whispering words of comfort and love into her ear. That part she must have dreamed. "That was kind of him," she said. "Please thank him for me."

Marian hesitated. "I have, of course, for all of us. But you can do that yourself when you're feeling better," she added.

"I don't want to see him."

"You don't want to see him? Or you don't want him to see you?"

"Does it matter?" Rennie felt tears gathering in her eyes. "Please! Please, keep him away from me!"

Marian got up and took her hand. "All right, I'll explain that you're not up to having visitors except family, okay?"

"Thank you." The tears were trickling down her cheeks, now, soaking into the dressings and bandages.

"Shh." Her mother smoothed her hair. "It's all right, Rennie. Everything's going to be all right. I promise."

It won't, Rennie thought. But she was childishly glad of her mother's comforting presence, and in a little while the tears stopped and she went to sleep.

Chapter Eighteen

She had to agree to see Grant. It was unreasonable not to, and he had been asking to visit. She didn't dare say that she couldn't bear him to bring Lorna, but when he arrived he was alone, bearing only messages from her. And flowers. She was glad of the yellow roses, because the business of thanking him and smelling their perfume and asking a nurse for a vase helped her to get over the initial greeting.

"They tell me you stayed with me on the way to the hospital," she said. "I don't remember, but thank you."

"I only wish I'd realised sooner what was going on," he said tautly. "If I'd looked out the window before it happened..."

"Even if you had been watching," she said, "there was nothing anyone could have done. I've had enough guilt to deal with from Shane and Amanda. Don't you start."

His smile was strained. "They got off lightly."

"I was the unlucky one," she agreed. "I must have been a mess."

He said, his voice hoarse, "You were, rather. I've never seen so much blood in my life."

Rennie looked down at the blue hospital coverlet. "I'm sorry if I gave you a fright."

"I was scared out of my mind."

"Maybe it's just as well I was unconscious."

"Rennie—why didn't you want to see me?"

"Don't take it personally. I'm not exactly pretty just now. I guess I was just self-conscious."

"You looked much worse in the ambulance. Compared to then, you're a raving beauty now, bandages and all!" He smiled, but not with his eyes, which were anxious.

"Yes, I s'pose. How is Lorna?" she asked. "And the children?"

"Lorna's well," he said shortly. "The children . . ." He hesitated. "They wanted to visit, but . . . oh, I forgot. They made cards for you." He took an envelope from his pocket and handed it over. Her bandaged hand fumbled with the opening of it and he had to help her.

Looking at the childish drawings, and the painstakingly printed messages, she blinked back tears. "Thank them for me," she said. "I can't write to them with this—" She moved her bandaged hand. "And you're right, it's probably better if they don't visit."

"Rennie—" He stretched out his hand to hers, and she said sharply, "Please don't touch me, Grant!"

He sat back, looking at her strangely. She thought he had paled.

"It hurts," she explained, and tried to smile. "I have cuts and bruises all over. I just—don't want to be touched. Nothing personal."

"No," he said woodenly. "Of course, nothing personal."

"It was kind of you to come," she said.

"I came because I—because I wanted to."

"Thank you," she said. "Give my love to Ellen and Toby. And Lorna," she added with an effort.

His mouth was wry. "Are you dismissing me?"

She said, "I am rather tired. I'm sorry."

"Don't apologise," he said. "I should be doing that."

She didn't know what for. She didn't ask.

He looked at her for a few moments, rather helplessly. Then he said, "Get well, Rennie." He leaned over and very gently kissed a spot on her forehead that wasn't bandaged, turned abruptly and left the room.

She had to make a statement to the police. But there was no need to appear in court. Kevin had decided to plead guilty, they said, so the case would be wrapped up quite quickly.

Shane came to tell her about the verdict.

"Is he going to jail?" she asked him.

"He got a suspended sentence, on condition that he remains under supervision and gets some treatment," Shane said. "And Amanda has taken out a court order against him molesting her. So if he goes near her he'll be rearrested and have to serve his sentence."

"I see." So he wasn't to be locked up. Rennie shivered. Her left arm had been freed of its bandages. The right one was lightly bandaged and in a sling. She was having physiotherapy for damage to the tendons of her right hand, but a certain amount of stiffness would probably remain. The dressings on her face were lighter and smaller than they had been. She'd had further surgery and would need more in a few months' time.

She was allowed home in time for Christmas. The bandages and dressings came off, and she nerved herself to look in a mirror. The smaller cuts were healing nicely and would soon disappear, but there was a nasty purple scar on her temple, which she could comb her hair over, and another on her right cheek, jagged and uneven.

On Christmas Day only relatives were invited. Rennie knew her mother was being tactful. She forced herself to appear at lunch, but afterwards pleaded tiredness and said she wanted to rest. No one dared suggest a birthday party to her. Her mother told her that Grant was asking to see her. She said no. She knew her family was worried.

When visitors came she fled to her room. One day Ethan and Celeste's car drew up outside, and she retreated from the window muttering an excuse as her mother went to let them in. From her bedroom, she heard Ethan's footsteps in the passageway, and then he knocked on the door, calling her name.

She didn't answer, but he came in anyway, bringing her scrambling resentfully off the bed, facing him with angry eyes.

"Rennie," he said gently, putting both arms around her. "Your parents are worried sick. You do realise you're suffering from depression?"

Rennie nodded. She wanted to tell him it was more than that, but that name would do for now.

"We know something about that, Celeste and I. Sheerwind is a good place to be when you need emotional healing. We want you to come back with us."

"Sheerwind?" The magical island she had dreamed of visiting. A place where no one would know her. A thousand miles across the Pacific, a thousand miles from Kevin. And from Grant.

"We'll check with your GP and the hospital," Ethan said, "but we have a semi-retired doctor almost next door on the island. Henry will be glad to keep an eye on you. The only other near neighbour is a writer, and he's away just now researching a book in New Guinea." He was telling her there would be almost no one she had to meet.

Her mother helped her to pack, and arranged her hair to fall across the scarred cheek so that it wasn't so obvious. Rennie didn't have the heart to tell her that really it didn't matter.

The flight was quite short and uneventful. Celeste and Ethan fussed over her unobtrusively, and when they arrived on the island Celeste insisted that Rennie should take the front seat next to Ethan so that she could see the scen-

ery. There was only one town, Conneston. They soon passed
through it, and followed a road bordered by tall rubber trees
with glossy leaves, a few palms waving above everything
else, and lots of shrubby scarlet and yellow hibiscus.

The road eventually rounded a hillside to a small bay
sheltered by a steep, tree-covered slope. Ethan's house was
nestled on the slope, a magnificent wall of glass giving the
maximum impact from the spacious living room. The sea
opened out from the bay and stretched away limitless to the
horizon. Today it looked very calm, a great spread of crinkled dark blue with sequin glints sparking off it.

"It's just as you described it," Rennie said, turning to him
as he carried in her case. "I feel better already."

The days went by, then weeks. Rennie swam and sun-
bathed, and watched Celeste painting silks in her studio,
trying to show a normal amount of enthusiasm. But she
overheard Celeste and Ethan discussing her once, when they
were sitting on the terrace outside the house, unaware that
their voices carried in the evening air, all the way to the trees
where Rennie was climbing the path from the beach after a
quick swim.

"...a vivacious girl. It's not like her to be this quiet,"
came Celeste's voice. "Is it?"

"She certainly isn't herself. Better, though, than when she
arrived here. Give her time," Ethan said easily.

That night she dreamed. Saw a face behind her, reflected
in glass, distorted by hatred. And then she fell and the face
disintegrated into a thousand pieces, and pain sliced into
her.

She woke with a scream, and found strong arms around
her, pulling her close, and a deep voice saying, "Shh. It's all
right, Rennie, it's only a dream."

"Grant!" she gasped, and clutched at him, shuddering
with relief. "Oh, Grant!"

"No, not Grant," Ethan said in a strange voice. He turned his head, and Rennie, lifting her hot forehead from his comforting chest, saw Celeste was standing by the bed.

Celeste took her hand. "Did you want Grant?" she asked quietly.

"Yes! No, I just thought...I was asleep. I thought he..."

"He was in your dream?"

"I don't know. Sometimes it's him. First it's Kevin, and then it's him. It changes. That's why it's so frightening."

"But you weren't frightened when you thought I was him," Ethan pointed out.

"Oh no! I knew I'd been dreaming then, and I thought..." She moved back onto the pillows. "I'm sorry, I woke you both. It's just a silly dream."

"A recurring one?" Ethan asked, standing up. He was wearing a short dark robe. Celeste was in her nightdress.

"Yes," Rennie said. "But it hasn't come so often since I've been here. I dream about...about going through the glass. The odd thing about it is, I don't actually remember that part at all. Kevin had knocked me out before it happened."

"Would you like a drink or something to help you go back to sleep?" Celeste asked.

"No. I'll be fine now."

A few days later she was helping Celeste to mix some paints in the studio when the other woman said casually, "Did you mention your bad dreams to Henry?"

"I haven't had any since that night I woke you."

Celeste said, in the same casual tone, "Grant's not a man who would want to hurt someone on purpose."

"What makes you think that he did?"

"That dream isn't so hard to figure out, Rennie," Celeste said. "Kevin injured you quite deliberately. In the dream the man sometimes changes from Kevin to Grant."

Rennie said, her hands stilling, "I saw Grant just before—the other thing happened. I suppose that's why they've got muddled in my mind."

"I see."

Rennie looked up, and saw that she did. Celeste didn't need to know the details. But she knew about the pain. Rennie blinked, trying to hold back the tears, but Celeste put down the paintbrush in her hand and said, "Oh, my dear." And held out her arms.

Rennie went into them and cried her heart out.

Chapter Nineteen

Rennie had received letters from her family and sent back brief, cheerful replies in a slightly wavering hand. She was feeling better, the island was beautiful, Celeste and Ethan were being very kind, Dr. Palmer was keeping an eye on her health...

She wrote to Toby and Ellen, too, telling them she was having a holiday on a lovely Pacific island, and thanked them again for their card. She didn't want them to think that like their mother she had disappeared from their lives. Folding the page into an envelope, she brushed away tears. She had a sudden longing to hold Ellen's warm little body close, to be the privileged recipient of one of Toby's rare hugs.

She borrowed a bicycle that Janice Palmer, the doctor's wife, had stored in her garage. "I used to ride it," Janice told her, "but the old bones are a bit creaky now. You're welcome to it as long as you're here."

She found beaches, and a deserted bay where the waves crashed around jagged black rocks and there was no beach to speak of, only a small shelf of black pebbles that rolled and drifted under the receding water and made little clicking noises. There were spiky spiral shells and spotted cowries among the stones. And she picked some of the tropical flowers from the trees and took them home to put in vases. But they didn't last.

The local people were friendly, and though sometimes her scars drew curious looks, nobody stared or asked questions.

She went into town one day with Ethan to collect the mail. When they got back Celeste was on the terrace. Ethan kissed her and tossed a pile of letters into her lap.

Rennie was sitting on the steps reading a letter from Shane when Celeste said, "I've a message for you, Rennie."

Rennie looked up, meeting Celeste's slightly troubled eyes.

"From Grant. He sends you his love."

Rennie felt a quiver of expression cross her face. "Thank you," she said distantly.

She wished he had not sent that careless, conventional greeting, crass in the circumstances, and unlike him.

She examined her feelings, probing as one might probe a tooth that had a tendency to ache, trying to find the spot that hurt.

Nothing. She felt nothing. Just a strangely numb blankness. It had stopped hurting.

That was good, wasn't it? This hollow emptiness had to be better than the seesaw emotions that had plagued her ever since meeting Grant Morrison. She was really on the way to healing now.

"Are you all right, Rennie?" Ethan was looking at her piercingly.

She smiled at him. "Yes, of course. Would you two like me to cook tonight? I know a great chili con carne recipe, and we could eat it out here on the terrace. It's going to be a beautiful evening."

* * *

They sat on the terrace after dinner until the stars came out and the sea lost its sunset glow and turned to dark pewter.

Ethan said, "How about a swim?"

Celeste smiled at him. "Lovely idea."

"And you, Rennie?"

"I'll go and change," she said promptly. Then paused as the other two exchanged a glance of secret amusement. She looked at them, and guessed, "You don't wear swimsuits?"

"Not always. It's accepted here," Ethan said.

"It's okay, Rennie," Celeste told her as she hesitated. "It took me a while to get used to it. I'm coming in to change, too."

The water was incredibly warm, and seemed to caress her body as she entered it, following Ethan and Celeste. They swam close to each other, and Ethan warned her, "Don't go out too far. You can lose your bearings at night."

Rennie splashed about lazily, then turned on her back, looking at the stars flung prodigally across the sky. The water lapped at her shoulders, and her hair floated on its surface. From the land came a faint perfume of flowers that she had never noticed in the daytime.

When Ethan said, "We're going in," she went with them reluctantly. Her limbs felt pleasantly relaxed. She could have stayed out there for hours.

Ethan had his arm about his wife's shoulders as they left the water, and he picked up a towel and put it round her. "Warm enough?" he asked.

"Yes. It isn't cold. I love the beach in moonlight."

Rennie rubbed at her hair, and wiped her arms and legs. She saw the look that Ethan gave Celeste, and her suddenly lowered lids, before he slowly picked up his towel, wrapping it about his waist. Celeste lifted a corner of hers and bent her head to dry her hair.

"I can find my own way back," Rennie said, "if you two want to stay here for a while and enjoy the moonlight."

"Take the torch," Ethan said. "We know our way in the dark."

"Ethan," Celeste remonstrated. "We can't let Rennie—"

"It's okay," Rennie assured her. "It's lovely here, but I'm tired."

She heard Celeste's low, laughing reproaches as she climbed the path with the torchlight bobbing ahead. Ethan's deep, teasing voice answered, and then there was silence. She smiled, a little sadly. Glad for them, in their obvious contentment with each other. Sad for herself. But one day, perhaps there would be someone for her, too. Someone who would make her feel again. Even make her feel the way she had when Grant kissed her and held her. And who would feel the same way about her.

"Do you think I could get a job here?" she asked Ethan and Celeste.

Surprised, Ethan said, "What about your bar exams? You need to take them in a few months, don't you?"

Rennie shrugged. "I thought I might take a year off. I've missed out on the job I was hoping for, anyway. I don't want to outstay my welcome, but if you can put up with me a little longer, once I'm working I'll find board in Conneston."

They protested that of course she was welcome to stay as long as she liked.

In a few months she was scheduled for more plastic surgery, but she would think about that when it was time.

She was drowsing in the shade after a swim, her wet hair drying on her shoulders, when she became aware of someone else on the beach. She lifted her head, expecting to see Ethan or Celeste, or perhaps Henry Palmer and his wife. They usually took a stroll at low tide, or in the later afternoon.

The newcomer was wearing grey slacks and a short-sleeved blue shirt. Perhaps the other neighbour had returned. Celeste had taken her to see his house, perched among the trees on the side of the steep slope.

But this man was standing at the foot of the path to Ethan and Celeste's house, shading his eyes with a hand, looking along the beach away from her. Then he turned, and she gasped with shock as his eyes found her, and he started to walk in her direction.

Her heart began pounding like a jackhammer. *What was Grant doing here?* She scrambled to her feet, casting round wildly for some sanctuary. She took two steps back, then turned and fled.

"Rennie!" He called twice, but she took no notice. Her feet raced along the sand, her breath sobbing. There was a path ahead, winding into the trees and uphill. The path to the writer's house. There wasn't anywhere else to go. She took it.

"Rennie!"

She ran up the slope, slowing as she reached some steps. She tripped on one, fell and scrambled to her feet again. She could hear Grant's footfalls on the path.

She was at the top of the steps before he caught her, swinging her round with a hand on her arm, his expression incredulous.

"Rennie, what the hell is all this about? You're not *frightened* of me?"

Not hearing the pain in his voice, she tried to push him away, panting, flinging her head back and turning from him, her damp hair swinging into her eyes and across her face.

He grabbed her other arm, gave her a little shake. "Rennie, for God's sake! Stop it!"

He wasn't letting her go. She went still, her head averted from him, trying to take in the fact of him being here. Trying not to think what it meant.

His voice suddenly gentle, he said, "Is it the scar?"

She didn't answer, and he lifted one hand and pushed the hair back from her face, and turned it so that he could inspect the ugly mark.

"It doesn't matter," he said softly. She shivered as he dipped his head and deliberately put his lips to the scar, with the utmost tenderness. "I don't give a damn what you look like."

"And I don't give a damn what you think!" Rennie flashed. She twisted away from him and retreated up the path, making their eyes almost on a level. "What are you doing here, anyway? Ethan and Celeste never mentioned you were coming."

He put his hands into his pockets. "I have a standing invitation," he said. "Like you, I decided to take them up on it."

"I'm using the spare bedroom."

"Celeste says she has a couch in her studio that I can use."

"Did she invite you?" Rennie demanded, feeling betrayed.

He seemed to hesitate. "No. Not exactly."

"Then *why did you come?*"

"To see you." He watched her, looking for her reaction.

"Okay, you've seen me," she said stonily. "Now leave me alone!"

He said, after a moment of bewildered silence, "This isn't quite the welcome I expected."

What *had* he expected? That she would fall into his arms? Fat chance, she thought scornfully. Her days of mooning like a schoolgirl, making a fool of herself over a man—particularly this man—were over. She said, "Tough. We don't always get what we expect in this life."

"No," he said thoughtfully. "Well, that's what makes it interesting. Where does this path lead to?"

"A house. It's empty just now. The owner's away."

"So you weren't running to him for protection."

"I wasn't running *to* anything."

"No. You were running away, weren't you? From me."

She debated saying she hadn't recognised him. But he wouldn't believe her. He had called her by name and must know she had heard.

He said, "An interesting reaction, if a bit disconcerting."

"You startled me," she said. "It was just an instinct."

"Blind panic? Not like you, Rennie. Surely you've always been the type to rush headlong *at* problems, not away from them."

"Yes," she said, "and look what it got me!" She touched her scarred cheek. "I've learned my lesson, thank you."

He frowned. "I'm sorry," he said slowly. "I didn't understand."

"You still don't. Will you get out of my way, please? I'm cold and my shirt and towel are on the beach."

He stepped aside, and followed her as she walked back down to the sand. Trying to ignore his presence, she pulled the cotton shirt on over her swimsuit, and picked up the towel.

He said, "This may not be the time, but I need to talk to you."

"It certainly isn't," she said shortly. "And whatever your needs are, I don't know that I want to hear about them."

She made to leave and he caught her hand. "Rennie, your parents are wondering why you don't want to come home—"

She jerked away from him. "When they ask me why, I'll tell them!"

"I'm asking why."

"It's none of your damned business!"

He nodded curtly. "I accept that. But I've come a long way to talk to you—"

"Did they ask you to?"

"No."

"And neither did I," she told him cuttingly. "I admit that there was a time when I'd have been over the moon at the idea of your travelling a thousand miles just to talk to me, but I grew out of that. I'm not the naïve teenager who thought you were God's gift. I'm a different person now. And if you've had a change of heart, it's a bit late."

She left him standing on the sand, and climbed the path to the house on her own.

"I hope we haven't embarrassed you, Rennie," Celeste said, coming into her room later.

"It's your home," Rennie answered. "You're entitled to invite whatever guests you like. Grant said he has a standing invitation."

"He does." Celeste looked a little uncomfortable. "But I should confess that I...hinted you might like to see him."

Rennie said, "I know you meant well."

Celeste sighed. "Ethan told me not to interfere. Oh, Rennie, I *am* sorry! I can tell him to go—"

"No, of course not!" He was their guest, just as she was, and she knew they would hate to be inhospitable. Especially since Grant had come so far. "It's not that important," she said. "He can't stay long, surely? He has two children back home."

Over supper, she asked him about the children. "They'll be missing you," she added.

The way he looked at her indicated that the faint note of censure in her tone had not gone unnoticed. "They're fine," he assured her. "But they miss you, too," he added, turning the accusation back to her. "It was good of you to write to them. They were a bit worried. Mrs. Beddoe is living in temporarily, and Jean's unmarried sister is in Auckland for a few weeks. She had plans for outings with them, which they seemed to be looking forward to."

"It's none of my business," she said. "I'm just a little surprised that you feel able to leave them while you have a holiday."

She knew she was being unfair. Grant was a conscientious father and he wouldn't have left them if he hadn't felt confident that they could handle the separation.

"The children have come through this last year very well. You had a lot to do with that."

"I just did what I was paid for," Rennie said, and saw his mouth tighten.

Ethan cast her a glance of sharp amusement. "Don't be too modest, young Rennie," he advised. "Genuine compliments are rare currency, and not to be undervalued."

Rennie smiled at him. She must try to behave, and not make things awkward for him and Celeste. "How's your latest computer programme going?" she asked. "I heard you talking to yourself this afternoon in your workroom. Celeste says that's a bad sign."

He glanced at his wife's bland face. "Giving away secrets? Shame on you. I had a problem," he answered Rennie, "but I think I've solved it. I'll have to test it out tomorrow."

"What is it supposed to do, anyway?"

As she listened to Ethan's explanations with every indication of breathless fascination, Grant looked at her thoughtfully. Then he turned his attention quietly to Celeste.

She managed to avoid being alone with Grant for two days, but of course on the whole island there was not enough room to hide forever if one person was determined to track another down.

She had been fossicking among the rock pools near the beach below the house, watching the sea anemones waving their innocent-looking tendrils to attract unwary little fish, and the hermit crabs moving slowly across the rocky floor. There was a very large pool quite a long way around the headland that was great for swimming. The water freshened with each tide and warmed to almost body heat in the sun before the next tide came in. She slipped in and stroked lazily about for a while, then dried herself off and applied a coat of sunscreen before lying down on the flat, smooth shelf above the pool. No one would disturb her now. It was only possible to reach this particular place at low tide.

When she felt a shadow fall across her face, she thought it was a cloud passing over the sun. Then she heard a sound

that was different from the waves swirling about the base of
the rock, and her eyes flew open.

"Yes," Grant said, as he sat beside her and hooked an
arm about an upraised knee. "It's me."

"How did you get here?" she demanded, sitting up.

A wave rushed in to hiss and rumble around the rocks,
spray slapping onto the flat shelf.

Grant shrugged. "The same way you did, I suppose. Got
a bit wet in the process." He glanced ruefully down. The
drill trousers he wore were darkened with water.

"You could have got swept off your feet," she said
crossly. "Don't you know it's dangerous after low tide?"

"I'm a stranger in these parts," he drawled. "The water
wasn't all that high."

"It will be now. You can't go back for at least an hour."

"Neither," he pointed out, "can you."

She shifted uncomfortably under his gaze. Was that why
he had followed her here?

As if in answer to the unspoken thought, he said, "Perhaps now you'll have the time to listen to what I have to
say."

"I really don't care," she said. "I don't think that anything you have to say could possibly interest me." She got
to her feet, snatching up her towel. "I'm going."

"Where to?" he demanded, barring her way as she made
to pass him. "You said yourself there's no way off these
rocks until low tide."

"I can wait somewhere else," she said.

"And I can follow you."

"Stop harassing me!"

"Is that what I'm doing?"

"Yes! What else would you call it?"

She saw the effort he made to swallow his anger. "I just
don't understand . . ."

She said, "No, you don't, do you? Please get out of my
way."

She stalked off while he gazed after her. She went as far
along the rocks as she could, and sat watching the wild wa-

ter race into a narrow gap in the rocks, wave piling on wave, all foam and fury. Strangely, the endless pulling and sucking and pounding had a calming effect on her.

Gradually the water began receding, becoming shallower. She became aware of Grant sitting several yards from her. She didn't look up, ignoring him completely. For a long time they sat in silence, isolated from each other.

When most of the waves were coming in at only ankle height, she stirred, ready to get up. And Grant said quietly, "I can't make you listen to me, now. You can get up and walk away if you want. But I wish you wouldn't."

Chapter Twenty

She was looking away from him towards the white sand, the glossy trees shading the edges, red and yellow hibiscus and some white starry flowers like paint splashes against the green. She didn't turn her head, but she stayed where she was, sitting on her towel with her knees hunched.

He waited until another wave had hurried in from the sea, foamed and splashed and receded. Then he said, "Rennie, will you marry me?"

For an instant, shock stopped her breath. Then shock was replaced by a hot, flooding anger. She turned her head, her body tense. "What?"

"I'm asking you to marry me, Rennie. Will you?"

"No!" She sprang to her feet. "No, I won't marry you!" Once she would have given her right arm to hear him say those words. But now it was too late. Far, far too late.

He stood up, too. He looked slightly flushed, his eyes steady but with a disturbing glint in their blue depths. "You're very vehement," he said. "Whatever happened to 'sensible though I am of the honour that you do me...'?"

"Honour!" she said witheringly. "Do you really think it's an honour to be asked—now?"

"I certainly don't think it's an insult!" he said, obviously stung, although his voice was extremely level. "Not so long ago, you didn't seem to think I was so ineligible."

"I never asked you to marry me!" she reminded him, pride lifting her head and lending a bitter curve to her mouth.

"I see." The anger he'd been holding in check put a bite in his voice, now. "Was it just a quick fling you were after—some suitable candidate to relieve you of your virginity? I'm sorry I didn't take the bait you so temptingly dangled for me. Is that the reason for this sudden about-face? Wounded vanity?"

Rennie hit him. She didn't plan it, or even realise what she was doing until her hand connected with his face, and he flinched, and she felt the sting on her palm.

For a moment they stood staring at each other, Rennie feeling sick, Grant's face pale except for the red imprint of her hand. He swallowed, and said rather grittily, "I can't imagine any reason for this display of outrage."

"But then, you don't have much imagination, do you?"

He laughed, not very nicely. His cheek must have still been smarting, after all. "Where you're concerned," he said, his eyes running over her scarcely covered body, "my imagination has always run in overdrive!"

"You never had too much trouble controlling it, as I recall."

"It wasn't as easy as you seem to think, Rennie. Do you want me to prove it?"

"Don't touch me!" She stepped back from him.

"I haven't moved a muscle," he pointed out. He hadn't, but the frustration and fury emanating from him was palpable. "I just offered you what's usually considered the highest compliment any man can give to a woman."

Her lip curled. "What did Ethan say about a genuine compliment being rare currency? Only in your case the currency's debased, Grant."

"Would you care to explain what the hell you're on about?"

"It's pretty obvious. You wanted me before. You were even a little in love with me. But there was all that baggage you were hauling from your previous marriage, and you very sensibly and cold-bloodedly decided you didn't want to get into that again. So you smothered whatever feelings you might have had for me, and closed the door on our relationship. I was young and quite pretty, I'd find someone else, someone more my own age and therefore much more suitable, and I'd forget about you, because after all, at my age, what did I know about real love? What I felt for you was nothing more than a juvenile fancy." She added viciously, "Isn't that what you thought?"

"Something like that," Grant admitted tautly.

"And there was nice, suitable, attractive Lorna, who'd make a perfect wife and stepmother. You weren't in love with her, but you'd weighed it all up and decided that marrying her would be the best thing all round."

"As a matter of fact—"

But Rennie was racing on. "Did she turn you down, leaving you at a loose end again? No perfect wife and stepmother, after all? And then you got a letter from your old flame—"

"My *what?*"

"Celeste. Don't tell me you weren't carrying a torch for her at one time."

"Whatever gave you that idea?"

"I'm not dumb! At her wedding I noticed the soulful looks you cast in her direction."

"Whatever you noticed, you misinterpreted. If I was looking less than madly joyful, it was because I remembered my own wedding, and how my marriage ended. Celeste and I," he said, "were never more than very good friends. And for the record, I never asked Lorna to marry me!"

"You thought about it. You told me!"

"Pride, Rennie," he said shortly. "*You* brought the subject up—in the same breath telling me that you'd got over your teenage passion for me. Throwing me a crumb because you didn't want me any more. Matchmaking's a specialty of yours, I believe. You seemed to think it was such a good idea, you almost had me convinced." A quick flash of bitter humour lit his eyes, and was gone. "Actually, it had never crossed my mind."

Scarcely listening, she rushed on. "Anyway, Celeste wrote to you that I seemed unhappy. You knew I'd been disfigured. Poor Rennie, you thought. She isn't nearly so likely to find herself a handsome young hero now. You remembered you were quite fond of me, in your superior way—" Ignoring the protesting sound he made, she went ruthlessly on, "—and you remembered I'd been head over heels in love with you, even if it was just an adolescent phase. Maybe you allowed yourself to admit that you found me quite desirable, too. Besides, I was so good with the children, wasn't I? Marrying me would be quite in keeping now, with your image of yourself—"

"What image?" Grant asked, his voice grating.

"The Sir Galahad image," she said caustically. "The white knight. You're good at rescuing the damsel in distress. You just can't admit that you might lust after her as well. Not when you think she's somehow unsuitable for your—attentions. There has to be another reason. Like compassion. What did Celeste say to you?" she asked. "In her letter?"

"She felt you had been very much hurt, not only physically. She thought you'd taken an emotional battering—"

"And you figured you were responsible?"

"Wasn't I?" He looked at her very directly.

Rennie met his eyes. "Yes. Partly. A lot of it was my own fault. And some of it had nothing to do with you." She said, "You don't have to feel responsible for me. Or sorry for me. I'll survive. Even this." She touched her cheek. "I'm sorry if it ruins your grand gesture, but you've no need to pity me. The doctors say that after the plastic surgery I'll be as good as new. Maybe a tiny white line, easily covered with a little makeup. They promised. They're that confident.''

"I already know that," Grant said. "I talked to your parents, I told you. Do you think I didn't ask? And *not*," he added forcefully, "because I cared one way or the other whether your face was going to be permanently scarred. Only I thought *you* might."

"Everyone thinks I do. Of course I was worried, but it wouldn't be the end of the world. Lots of people live with worse than that. There's my hand. It'll always be a bit stiff. But even that's not such a tragedy. I'm not a concert pianist, or an artist." She paused. "You knew?"

"Yes. So your theory just went up in flames." He sounded grim.

Bewildered, but with a strong conviction that she couldn't cope with any more tension, she shook her head, and turned her back on him to make her way down the rocks to the sand.

"Rennie!" He leapt down after her, catching her up before she had a chance to reach the other side of the narrow gap. Water lapped about their feet as he clamped his fingers on her wrist.

She pulled back instinctively, but he retained his hold.

"Let me go, Grant."

"Rennie, I *love* you!"

Whatever reaction he had expected, it wasn't her wild burst of laughter. He dropped her wrist like a hot coal and stared at her, a flush mounting to his cheeks.

She stopped laughing, taking a step backwards. "You are unbelievable! You know that?"

"I'm sorry!" he said angrily. "I've handled this all wrong."

"Yes, you have!" Her tone was cutting. "Has that fact just dawned on you?"

He made an exasperated gesture. "I've been clumsy, but surely if we love each other—"

"That's the crux of it," she said.

For a long moment he said nothing. ''You're trying to tell
me it's over for you?''

''Yes. That is what I'm trying to tell you!''

He was staring at her in a calculating way that she didn't
like. ''You feel nothing?''

''You've finally got it!'' she said.

''But for a woman who's quite indifferent, your reactions seem fairly extreme. Running away, slapping my
face—''

''*Now,*'' she said, ''you finally acknowledge that I'm a
woman, not a lovestruck little girl.''

''Why did you run, Rennie?''

''I thought you'd worked that out. I was embarrassed by
my scars. Didn't want you to see them. And I slapped you
because you fully deserved it.''

''Maybe I did. We were both angry. You know the corny
old line about hurting the one you love.''

''I don't love you!'' She swung on her heel and had a
hand on the rock face, ready to climb, when he pulled her
round to face him.

''Prove it,'' he said, and as her head jerked back, he tangled a hand into her hair and held her while his mouth descended on hers.

The towel fell from her shoulder as she bent back, failing
to avoid the kiss. She pushed against him, determined to ignore the insidious pressure of his lips trying to coax hers
open. He shifted his legs and then she had a new sensation
to fight, as well. For all the protection the swimsuit gave her
she might as well have been wearing nothing. She kicked
him but her bare feet did no damage, and she swayed off
balance, which allowed him to gather her even closer, his
mouth still keeping hers prisoner while one arm remained
clamped about her waist, and the other hand explored her
bare back right down to where the swimsuit ended, and then
continued over the smooth nylon-covered curve.

Rennie quivered—with rage, she told herself. No man had
a right to do this to her. But then she discovered her mouth
was flowering under his, her lips parting, softening, burn-

ing with sudden need. Her limbs felt heavy with desire, and
there was a hot, spinning sensation starting in her head that
spiralled right through her body. She wrapped her arms
about his neck, and both his hands swept down to her bare
thighs, lifting her against him so that she was on tiptoe when
the next shallow wave swept into the gap and swirled about
them.

As it receded, something large and soft coiled itself about
her ankles, startling her out of her absorption in the kiss.
She broke free and looked down to find her forgotten towel,
thoroughly wet and sandy.

Grant picked it up and wrung out the water. "Sorry," he
said. Then, his eyes alight as he looked at her, he said, "But
it was worth it, wasn't it?"

Rennie wiped the back of her hand over her lips. "It
doesn't prove anything. Except that you're good at kissing."

His hands stilled for an instant on the towel. Then he said,
"Thank you. You're pretty good, yourself." Quite pleasantly, he continued, "It's war then, is it? Okay. It's a long
time since I had a good fight."

Stiffly, she put out her hand for the towel. He shook his
head. "I'll carry it."

Rennie shrugged. This time he let her climb the rock
without interference. He followed, and walked beside her
until they reached the narrow cliff path, when he dropped
back, allowing her to go ahead. At the house, he relinquished the towel and she went to rinse it in the laundry and
hang it outside before going upstairs to shower and change.

At dinner that night his manner was blandly pleasant, and
she, mindful of her manners and unwilling to cause discomfort to Ethan or Celeste, tried to match it, while inwardly seething.

Next day she went to the beach straight after breakfast
and plunged into the water. When she came out the sun had
warmed the sand, and after using plenty of sun cream she

lay face down on her towel and tried to blank her mind and drowse. She didn't hear any birds, but the trees on the slope behind her rustled in a faint breeze, and when she got too hot she moved into their shade.

Her thoughts wouldn't stop racing round in her head, and she was restless. She was swimming again when she saw Grant come down to the beach. She stayed in the water longer than she had intended, hoping that he would go away. But instead, he sat by her towel, waiting. After a while he stripped off his shirt and trousers, revealing dark blue swim shorts. She went stroking swiftly away from the shore. If he meant to come in, she decided, she would be getting out.

Perhaps he had debated it, but he must have changed his mind. Next time she looked, he was sitting down again, with an air of contained patience.

She was tiring, and even in the tropical water her skin was turning a little chilly. She swam in slowly, and walked up the beach, flinging herself face down on the towel, her head turned away from Grant.

"You're turning blue," he commented. "You should have come out earlier."

She didn't answer him.

After a moment he said, "Still hating me, Rennie?"

"I don't hate you."

She felt him lie down beside her, lounging on one elbow. His hand pushed aside her wet hair. "Still . . . indifferent?" he whispered, his lips close to her ear.

Gritting her teeth, she said, "Yes!"

His teeth gently nipped her earlobe, then his lips were nuzzling the little hollow behind it.

A shiver of pleasure danced down her spine. She drew in her breath sharply and sat up, glaring at him.

He hadn't moved except to lie back on his elbows, appraising her. "You're looking great," he said. And when her mouth twisted and she instinctively turned her scarred cheek away from his gaze he added harshly, "That doesn't count.

You're beautiful, Rennie. This place has helped you, hasn't it?''

Rennie nodded. Ethan had been right. The island sun, and its tranquillity, was good for her, body and soul. Her pale skin had acquired a faint golden tinge. The scars on her body had become almost invisible, the superficial cuts on her left hand had completely healed and only a fine white line on her right hand and a continuing stiffness in her index and middle fingers remained as a legacy of the assault. She was careful not to let her face burn, using a complete sun block. The scar tissue there was tender, though not as fiery to look at as it had been.

She had also a new, hard-won serenity. Nothing was going to hurt her as she had been hurt in this last year, she had decided. Never again. Certainly not this man whose presence threatened to shatter that resolution to bits.

She lay back again, closing her eyes, determined to ignore him. The waves lapped at the beach, the sound advancing and receding with each wash of the water.

"How about taking me sight-seeing?" Grant said.

"What?" she asked suspiciously, opening her eyes.

"I'd like to see the place, now that I'm here. Ethan has a deadline to meet with his latest software programme, and Celeste is trying hard not to seem too busy but I can see she's in the throes of creation. Besides—" he paused, then went on "—I don't think Ethan has quite got over a faint, unfounded suspicion of me. I detect a definite coolness at the idea of his wife showing me round. That leaves you. I believe you know the island pretty well by now."

His reasoning was transparent. "You won't see much by car," she told him. "I use a bicycle." That wouldn't appeal to him, she thought. "And you don't need a guide."

"Scared, Rennie?" he taunted.

"Not of you!"

Something flickered sharply in his eyes. "You've no reason to be. But you're frightened to be alone with me."

"I'm not frightened. But after yesterday I'd be a fool to give you another chance to—"

"Kiss you? Make you admit that this indifference of yours isn't real?"

"It's real," Rennie said flatly.

"Pardon me," he said with exquisite politeness. "But after yesterday I find that hard to believe." He sat up, watching her.

"I told you—"

"Oh, spare me!" he snapped, making a sweeping gesture with his hand. "I'm not without experience, Rennie. You were way too angry to be brought round by a bit of lovemaking, to reach the pitch that we did just because I'm 'good at kissing.' That was me, the whole me, that you responded to, it was no impersonal animal mechanism. The sex was a trigger, but it came out of something much more complex. Something elemental, real. And we both know it."

Rennie looked away from him. She wished that he had not come to Sheerwind. Before, she had been convinced that she had reached calm waters after the storms and passions that had racked her life since meeting him. Now he had flung her into turmoil again. She was confused and angry and he was right when he said she wasn't indifferent. But if what she felt now was love, then it was a very peculiar kind of love. It was painful and violent and stark. It scared her, and she didn't want any part of it.

Grant said, "I promise I won't touch. Do you think you can handle being with me under those conditions? If you're really as indifferent as you say, it shouldn't be a problem."

His voice held a jeering note. Perhaps he knew that even now she'd not be able to resist a dare.

"All right," she snapped. She knew that whatever it cost him, Grant would always keep a promise.

"Good," he said, and unexpectedly got up. "I'll see about getting myself a bicycle."

She watched him plunge into the water, then gathered up her towel and returned to the house.

He got a bicycle from somewhere. It was new and shiny and looked rugged enough to cope with any terrain. Rennie climbed onto Janice's old ten-speed and led the way, determined to make him regret his challenge. She'd been cycling now for weeks, but she remembered the first couple of days of aching muscles and a sore seat. Grant probably hadn't ridden a bike since childhood.

She took him to the township first, to see the small museum and the little shops that sold souvenirs to the summer tourists. Then to one of the more popular beaches near Conneston, where families and holiday makers crowded the sand. She knew he'd have preferred somewhere quieter, but he didn't complain. The following day they toured the ring road that swept around the island, climbing sometimes around steep little hills, then sweeping down to the ocean's edge. She kept up a running commentary on every landmark, regurgitating all she had learned about Sheerwind from Ethan and from a history of the island written by his neighbour. Grant had asked for a tour guide, she thought, and a tour guide was what he was going to get.

"We have to stop here," she said, as they reached a headland looking down over a reef endlessly attacked by white-edged breakers. "It's the Sheerwind memorial."

"Oh, I must see that," Grant said solemnly as they left their bikes and walked along a narrow path to the cliff edge.

Rennie ignored the faint sarcasm, gazing at the ocean. A deep band of silver glittered on the horizon, and starpoints glistened off lazy waves as they entered the bay below.

Here stood the memorial to the first, involuntary settlers, survivors of a convict ship wrecked there in the nineteenth century.

"The island was named after it," she told him as he studied the plaque commemorating the wreck of the *Sheerwind*.

He nodded. "That much I know." They had seen some relics of the wreck in the museum the previous day.

"A convict, Tatty Connors—after a good deal of bloodshed—appropriated all the four women survivors for himself. One of the ship's crew was a black ex-slave—his descendants still live here. Before the wreck the island was

uninhabited, but since the nineteenth century all kinds of
people have settled here—Europeans and Pacific Islanders,
a few Chinese, and they all intermarried and picked up as-
pects of one another's culture.''

"You know a lot about the place for someone who's been
here only a short time," he said.

"I'm a fast learner." The phrase woke an echo in her
mind, and she saw the sudden smile in his eyes that meant
he'd remembered, too. Pushing that aside she asked innocently, "Am I boring you?"

The smile deepened. He knew perfectly well what she was
up to. "Not at all," he told her smoothly. "I'm fascinated
by all this esoteric knowledge you've stored up." He added,
"You could never bore me, Rennie."

She opened her mouth to say something tart, like, what
about when you thought I was infatuated with you? He'd
done his best then to make her feel a nuisance and a bore.
But she didn't want to open that subject again.

She remounted her bicycle, saying, "I'll show you Tatty's cottage."

"I can't wait," she heard him mutter as he followed. So
far he had shown no sign of tiring.

The ruined cottage was surrounded by weeds and regen-
erating bush. "It's haunted," Rennie said.

"Of course it would be," Grant answered tranquilly.

"An old drunk who slept the night here was found dead
in the morning." Rennie dredged her memory for several
other stories about the unexpected deaths of people who had
tried to remove stones from the cottage for building. "No
one touches it now," she finished.

"I'm not surprised."

Having exhausted her small store of knowledge about the
place she turned reluctantly back to the road. Grant was
much fitter than she'd expected.

"Where to next?" he enquired interestedly.

Surreptitiously Rennie eased aching shoulders. She
wouldn't have minded a swim to refresh herself and a long
laze on a quiet beach afterwards, but that would have been

admitting defeat. She forced herself to wax ecstatic about the view from The Camel, a double-humped hill that looked over almost the entire island, and he asked with every sign of enthusiasm, "Will we be able to go there today? Or aren't you up to it? I don't want to tire you, Rennie."

Of course she was up to it, she told him loftily.

They were both slightly sweaty by the time they made it to the top, but Grant still hadn't flagged. As they parked their bicycles against a handy tree Rennie began to wonder rather bitterly what it would take to tire him. The breeze on the lookout point was welcome. She pushed windblown hair out of her eyes and turned to walk the few yards to the best view, trying to breathe normally.

Grant stood close to her. "Sure you're all right?" he said, concern in his voice.

"Yes, of course." She kept her voice casual, her eyes on the sweep of green countryside with the town in the distance and the blue sea washing white-sand shores.

She was chagrined that when he suggested they head for home, taking it easy, she knew without doubt it was for her sake, not his. At dinner he told Ethan and Celeste that he'd seen most of the island, and with laughter in his eyes added, "Rennie was a superb guide. She's missed her vocation."

Grimly she stayed up until their hosts were ready for bed, and then thankfully followed them upstairs. But in spite of being dead tired, she was unable to sleep that night. The air was warm and heavy, and the perfume of night-scented flowers wafted in through the open window. An insect chirped intermittently nearby, a bird called once, clear and fluting, and the insistent sound of the waves on the shore came clearly from the beach.

The sound seemed to beckon her, and eventually she gave in to it. Pulling off her nightshirt, she shrugged a short robe over her naked body, took her small torch and, ignoring the ache in her calves, legacy of the long day's cycling, quietly went down the stairs and let herself out of the house.

When she reached the sand she switched off the torch and put it in her pocket. The moon came out from behind a smoky cloud, and lit the water with a pale glitter.

She scuffed along the sand for a little way, then was drawn irresistibly to the water's edge, standing with her feet sinking slightly into the wet softness as a ruffle of white curled about her ankles. The water was warm and caressing. On impulse she stripped off the robe and flung it onto the dry sand a few yards distant, then walked into the water until it reached her thighs before flinging herself down. Coolness folded around her; she stroked slowly forward, then turned on her back and floated, looking at the high round moon.

The water gradually warmed on her skin, and she kept afloat by the smallest movements, glancing at the shore to make sure she didn't lose her bearings.

Once she thought she saw a moving shadow on the sand, and her heart missed a beat. She turned quickly with a silvery splash, but could see nothing but the white sliver of sand and the dark trees beyond.

When she finally came ashore and pulled on the robe over her damp skin, she felt relaxed and clearheaded. Until she had almost reached the trees and the path, and saw the pale blur of a face a few yards further along, deep in the shadow of the trees, and the man standing there.

Chapter Twenty-One

Rennie gave a choked scream even as she turned and fled back along the sand, stumbling in its softness.

"Rennie!" A hand touched her shoulder, her robe slipped and she tore herself away, sobbing with panic, but tripped backwards over a piece of driftwood and went plunging onto the sand.

Before she could recover, he was on his knees beside her, gripping her arms as she tried to get up, to fight him. "Rennie, I'm sorry! I didn't mean to frighten you like this!"

Her breath caught, she went suddenly still. "Grant? Oh, Grant!"

She swayed forward into his arms, and he pulled her tightly to him, stroking her hair as she took deep, shuddering breaths, saying again, "I'm sorry, my darling. I didn't realise you wouldn't know me in the dark. It wasn't me you were running from this time, was it?"

Rennie shook her head. "I thought—Kevin. I know it's stupid but—" She was still shivering.

"Not stupid at all," he said. "It's all right, now. I won't hurt you."

"I know." Gradually the shaking stopped, and she lay quietly against him, unwilling to move.

"Did you come down here to get away from the nightmares?" he asked her.

Celeste must have told him about that. It didn't matter now. She said, "No. I couldn't sleep."

"Me, too. I was here when you came down, but you obviously wanted to be alone."

"You watched." She lifted her head from his shoulder.

He didn't answer for a moment. "I didn't know you were going to go for a nude swim. Once you were in, I—thought it safer if someone was about."

"You could have gone back to the house when you saw me come out."

A longer pause. "I couldn't bring myself to."

"The upright lawyer as Peeping Tom?" Her brave attempt at flippancy was marred by the tremor in her voice.

He said gruffly, "Are you angry?"

Rennie shook her head. He was embarrassed, more so than she, and she felt a strange welling of tenderness. "Not now." She reached up and touched his cheek.

"Rennie?" His voice was low. He moved so that he sat on the sand, holding her, and she leaned into him. "Rennie," he said on a different note.

She lifted her face to him, and he gave a long sigh and kissed her, easing her down on the sand. Rennie's arms went round his neck as he pressed closer to her. He kissed her more deeply and she responded with a passion that shook both of them.

His mouth wandered to her bare shoulder where the wrap had slipped. His hand slid it further down, baring her breast, too. He looked down at her, then into her eyes. "Rennie?" he said a third time. And now his voice, too, was unsteady.

She knew it was her last chance to say no. And knew that she didn't want to say it. She said his name instead, and fearlessly put her hands behind his head and drew it to her breast. And as she felt his mouth close over her, warm and moist and gentle, her breath left her throat in a rush of joy.

His hand brushed away the robe on the other side and made its own slow, erotic exploration, before his mouth returned to hers and she welcomed it with renewed passion.

When he half sat up to sweep off the wrap entirely, she opened the buttons of his shirt, running her palms over his chest, glorying in the sudden indrawing of his breath, and his hurried tugging at his belt.

He threw off his clothes and stretched out at her side, admiring her in the moonlight, one hand playing over her body, inducing drifts of pleasure that flowed from her lips, breasts, thighs, and eventually centred on one hot, spiralling core of need.

She bucked under his hand, and said, "Oh, please. Please, now!"

His shadow came over her, and his hand was under her head. "Not too fast, little virgin."

Slightly stung, even in the grip of her desire, she said, "How do you know I'm still a virgin?"

The hand in her hair convulsed, and she saw the stark passion on his face. "I'm about to find out," he said, as his legs parted hers, faintly harsh with sand. "So do I need to take this gently—or not?"

Staring into his eyes, she said rashly, "Take it how you like—but take it now!"

She stiffened with the shock of his first thrust, and saw his face change, and that he knew. She felt the way he stopped and held himself back and made it as easy as he could.

And then more than easy. As she felt him glide in deeper, and his mouth met hers again, excitement overriding the slight discomfort, she met him, matched him, closed herself about him and rode on wave after wave of golden light that splintered into shards of pleasure. And heard him murmur her own name over and over as he rode it with her.

It was dawn before they talked, sitting on the sand with Rennie's back against Grant's chest, their hands linked in her lap. Grant had put on his clothes and pulled Rennie's wrap about her because the air had cooled towards morning.

"Why did you deny that you still love me?" he asked her.

"I wanted it to be true. I accused you of being afraid to love me, being like Ellen, wanting to shut love out. Well, I know now how it feels." She stopped, dipped her head and then raised it, shaking back the damp mane of her hair. She said, looking out to the brightening skyline where it met the sea, "I suppose my life has been quite sheltered, privileged. Until last year I'd never been badly hurt by anyone—physically or emotionally. I always expected that people would like me and be kind to me."

"As you were to them," Grant put in quietly.

"I did try to be, mostly. That's how I was brought up. I guess I thought that within reason I could get anything I wanted, either by plain asking or with hard work. Perhaps I've been spoiled. To want something as much as I wanted ... your love, and have it denied, was almost unbelievable to me. And to have someone hate me and want to hurt me as Kevin did—that was an emotional shock, too. The world wasn't the friendly place I'd always taken for granted. It had another face, a face to be feared." She shivered again, and Grant's arm tightened on her. "It made me afraid of my love for you. Afraid of being hurt again."

His voice muffled in her hair, he said, "I never wanted to hurt you. I thought I'd die of the pain, myself, when I knew that I had."

She stirred. "And now? Why change your mind after sending me away, if it wasn't pity?"

He said, "There's only so much self-sacrifice a man can take. I've reached the end of mine."

"You said it was self-preservation, not self-sacrifice."

"In a way that was true. The other side of the coin. I couldn't stand the thought of seeing the laughter leave your eyes, seeing it replaced by hatred and resentment."

"You would never believe that I was different from Jean." Hurt made her voice husky. "You always had us mixed up in your mind."

"I know."

"I suppose it was inevitable, when you'd just lost her," Rennie acknowledged.

"I suppose it was. I loved you so much, your laughter, your love of life—the way you gave yourself, your love, to the children and then to me. It was all I could do to stop myself taking advantage of that generous, openhearted loving. But I had no right to take your lovely youth and your vitality and suck it dry, turn you into a bitter, unhappy woman. I was haunted by the thought that if I tied you to me, you'd die inside."

"I did that when you finally convinced me you didn't want me."

"I wanted you so that I ached for you, night and day. I was going crazy with wanting you."

A wave slipped up the sand, and slid back, leaving a glistening line of hissing bubbles behind in the moonlight. A faint breeze stirred Rennie's hair. She raised a hand and pushed it out of her eyes.

"Crazy enough to tell yourself that what you felt for me wasn't real and wouldn't last?"

"It wasn't my feelings I doubted." He bent and kissed her, his hand on her cheek. "Try to understand, Rennie. Jean's death and you coming into my life at the same time had me so screwed up I couldn't think straight. Being apart from you these past months had me on the rack, but in a way it was a necessary torture. I needed to make my peace with Jean's memory before I could truly believe that I could make you happy."

"Can you, now?"

"Yes. You're Rennie, and I have no grounds for making assumptions about you based on another woman's reactions. You're generous and capable and amazingly mature, and I still can't believe I'm lucky enough to have your love.

Lorna said that maturity hasn't much to do with chrono-
logical age. She was right.''

"Grant—what about Lorna?''

Grant stared down at their linked hands. "She'd been in
a long relationship with a man who never bothered to get a
divorce. He died about the time that Jean and I parted.
Lorna and I are good friends, that's all, and if I'd never met
you I suppose it might have been a reasonable basis for
marriage, eventually. She was . . . my protection.'' His voice
shook and he paused to steady it. "Because while you were
living in my house I needed a buffer to stop myself from seducing you, which would have been a despicable act, given
all the circumstances, and after you left there wasn't a day
when I didn't have to force myself not to call you with some
excuse for seeing you again. The day that bastard pushed
you through the window, Lorna was in my office. When I
realised it was *you* they were putting in the ambulance, I
practically shoved her out of my way to get to you. Later,
when I remembered her existence, I went back and apolo-
gised. She told me I'd better ask you to marry me. She
meant it,'' he added, answering her unspoken doubt. "She
said she'd dance at our wedding.''

Rennie was silent for a long time. He still held her hand.
She felt his fingers tighten on hers, felt the effort he made
to relax them. She could hear him breathing above the quiet
rhythm of the waves, feel the slight rise and fall of his chest.

"When you visited me in the hospital—''

"You seemed so distant that day. It was no time to be
forcing my attentions on you, though if you'd shown the
slightest sign of still wanting me, I'd have had a hard time
not to hold you—something you obviously weren't fit for.
You looked so bruised and sick.''

"It's a wonder you wanted me at all.''

He shook his head. "I'll always want you, Rennie, in
sickness and in health, bruised, scarred, scared—until death.
I thought I'd been served a kind of poetic justice. You'd
stopped wanting me, just when I finally gave in to the fact
that I couldn't stand to live my life without you. I thought

I'd give you some time, it was only fair to let you get over the accident in your own way, which obviously didn't include me, you'd made that abundantly clear. And then I was going to do my damnedest to make you love me again. Retreating here was a pretty strong message that you didn't want to be bothered by anyone, so I was trying to respect that, making myself wait until you came back. Then Celeste wrote that you'd called my name. I wanted so badly to gather you up and save you from any further hurt. I had to be here, if you needed me."

She looked up at him then. "When I left the hospital I kept thinking of Kevin and how he hated me. The look on his face when he said, 'I'll get you, you bitch!' And he was still out there. I was frightened, and ashamed of it. I couldn't bring myself to tell anyone about my stupid fear."

"Did I really scare you?" he asked, troubled. "That first day I arrived here?"

Rennie shook her head. "Not physically. You threatened my peace, though. I thought you came in arrogance. And pity."

"Everything somehow got into the wrong order. I hadn't meant to blurt out a proposal of marriage. But I never thought you'd react the way you did."

"You unsettled me. Here on Sheerwind I'd conquered the nightmares, the fear. Grown a shell and shut myself inside it, told myself no one could hurt me any more. Then you came, and I realised you still could. If I let you. The trouble is," she said, "in my shell I don't feel anything at all. That seemed okay for a while, but it's not much of a life, is it?"

Grant shook his head. "If you want to live, you have to accept you'll get hurt sometimes. I can stand that for myself. Even accept the pain of letting you go. But not seeing you hurting the same way."

She took a deep breath. "I think I'm ready to start living again. If I can rely on you to be there next time someone shoves me through a window."

"Next time," he promised, "I'll be there to stop him. Is this a yes to my proposal?"

"I think so. Yes." Mischievously she added, "What do you think I've been angling for ever since we met? And it wasn't," she added indignantly, "someone to relieve me of my virginity!"

He winced.

"Although," she said dreamily, "you've done that very nicely."

"I'm sorry about that crack. Even at the time I didn't believe it. And I didn't mean to seduce you last night, either. I shouldn't have taken advantage—"

She put a sandy finger to his lips. "Don't feel guilty. I could have stopped you. I didn't want to." Her mouth curved. "All those times I practically begged you to make love to me—"

He groaned. "Don't remind me. I never knew I had so much will power. You didn't make it easy for me, Rennie."

"Well, you can't back out now," she told him complacently. "You're such an honourable man." Her eyes were lit with tender laughter.

"No chance," he agreed. "And I won't let you back out, either. You're committed, now. I'm afraid," he said honestly, "that thought was in my mind last night, even as I tried to tell myself it was unfair to you. You drove me to desperate measures, Rennie."

"Not unfair. But, Grant," she added, meeting his eyes, hoping to make him understand, "I made an adult choice last night. I'm no child bride. I want you to be there for me, for the rest of my life. But I'll be there for you, too."

"I'll try to curb my protective instincts if they threaten your independence. Knowing you, I won't be allowed to get away with treating you like a child. Which in any case," he added, smiling, "is the last thing I want right now." He leaned forward and very carefully tipped her chin so that he could kiss her mouth.

Rennie responded, turning with an arm hooked about his neck, until he kissed her deeply, one hand behind her head, the other stroking her arm, her hip, her ribs, and coming to rest against her heart.

When he lifted his head, pushed her back again on the sand and kissed her cheek, her jawline, and her throat, she said, "The wedding will have to wait until after my surgery."

"No," he said. "Too long."

"I can't be a bride with this!" She touched her scarred cheek.

"Why not? I thought we agreed it wasn't important." His lips had reached the edge of the robe.

"It isn't," she gasped, "but—Grant, don't do that!"

He paused with his hand on the edge of the robe that he had just slipped off her shoulder. "Why not?"

"It's morning. Someone might see—" Ethan sometimes took a morning swim, and the Palmers were early walkers.

He pulled the robe back into place, and kissed her again. "Come swimming with me tonight?" he murmured. "In the dark. When there's no one to see."

"You have an ulterior motive!" she accused.

"Yes." He grinned. "I hope to talk you into an earlier wedding."

"I want to look beautiful on my wedding day."

"You will. You can't help it." He held up a hand. "All right, darling. If it's important to you, I'll wait until they've fixed your face. But tonight—we swim."

She nodded. "Did you know," she murmured, watching him with wide, teasing eyes, "that people here swim nude?"

"Is that a fact?" he mocked, and smiled into her eyes.

"Have you ever done that?"

"Not here," he said, glancing at the deserted beach. "And not with you."

"There's a first time for everything," Rennie said demurely.

He looked at her sternly. "You know, I believe I was right about you the first time we met."

"You thought I was a juvenile delinquent."

He laughed, playing with her hair, lifting a curling strand to his lips. "Something like that."

"Well..." she said, and gave him a look very similar to those she had been giving Ethan the night he had looked at her so disapprovingly. She looped her arms about his neck. "Aren't you lucky?"

* * * * *

THE DONOVAN LEGACY
from Nora Roberts

Meet the Donovans—Morgana, Sebastian and Anastasia.
They're an unusual threesome. Triple your fun with double
cousins, the only children of triplet sisters and triplet brothers.
Each one is unique. Each one is...special.

In September you will be *Captivated* by Morgana Donovan. In
Special Edition #768, horror-film writer Nash Kirkland doesn't
know what to do when he meets an actual witch!

Be *Entranced* in October by Sebastian Donovan in Special
Edition #774. Private investigator Mary Ellen Sutherland
doesn't believe in psychic phenomena. But she discovers
Sebastian has strange powers...over her.

In November's Special Edition #780, you'll be *Charmed* by
Anastasia Donovan, along with Boone Sawyer and his little
girl. Anastasia was a healer, but for her it was Boone's touch
that cast a spell.

Enjoy the magic of Nora Roberts. Don't miss *Captivated,
Entranced* or *Charmed.* Only from
Silhouette Special Edition....

Silhouette Special Edition®

Linda Lael Miller

Beyond the Threshold

Two stories linked by centuries, and by love....

There and Now

The story of Elisabeth McCartney, a woman looking for a love she can't find in the 1990s. Only with the mystery of her Aunt Verity's necklace can she discover her true love—Dr. Jonathan Fortner, a country doctor in Washington—in 1892....

There and Now, #754, available in July 1992.

Here and Then

Desperate to find her cousin, Elisabeth, Rue Claridge searched for her in this century . . . and the last. She found Elisabeth, all right. And also found U.S. Marshal Farley Haynes—a nineteenth-century man with a vision for the future....

Here and Then, #762, available in August 1992.

It's Opening Night in October— and you're invited! Take a look at romance with a brand-new twist, as the stars of tomorrow make their debut today! **It's LOVE: an age-old story— now, with *WORLD PREMIERE APPEARANCES* by:**

Patricia Thayer—Silhouette Romance #895
JUST MAGGIE—Meet the Texas rancher who wins this pretty teacher's heart...and lose your own heart, too!

Anne Marie Winston—Silhouette Desire #742
BEST KEPT SECRETS—Join old lovers reunited and see what secret wonders have been hiding...beneath the flames!

Sierra Rydell—Silhouette Special Edition #772
ON MIDDLE GROUND—Drift toward Twilight, Alaska, with this widowed mother and collide—heart first—into body heat enough to melt the frozen tundra!

Kate Carlton—Silhouette Intimate Moments #454
KIDNAPPED!—Dare to look on as a timid wallflower blossoms and falls in fearless love—with her gruff, mysterious kidnapper!

Don't miss the classics of tomorrow— *premiering* today—only from